ASSASSIN

THE ULTIMATE THRILLER

A NOVEL

HUGO N. GERSTL

Hugo N. Gerstl Collection

See below some of Pangæa Publishing Group's bestsellers by the same author:

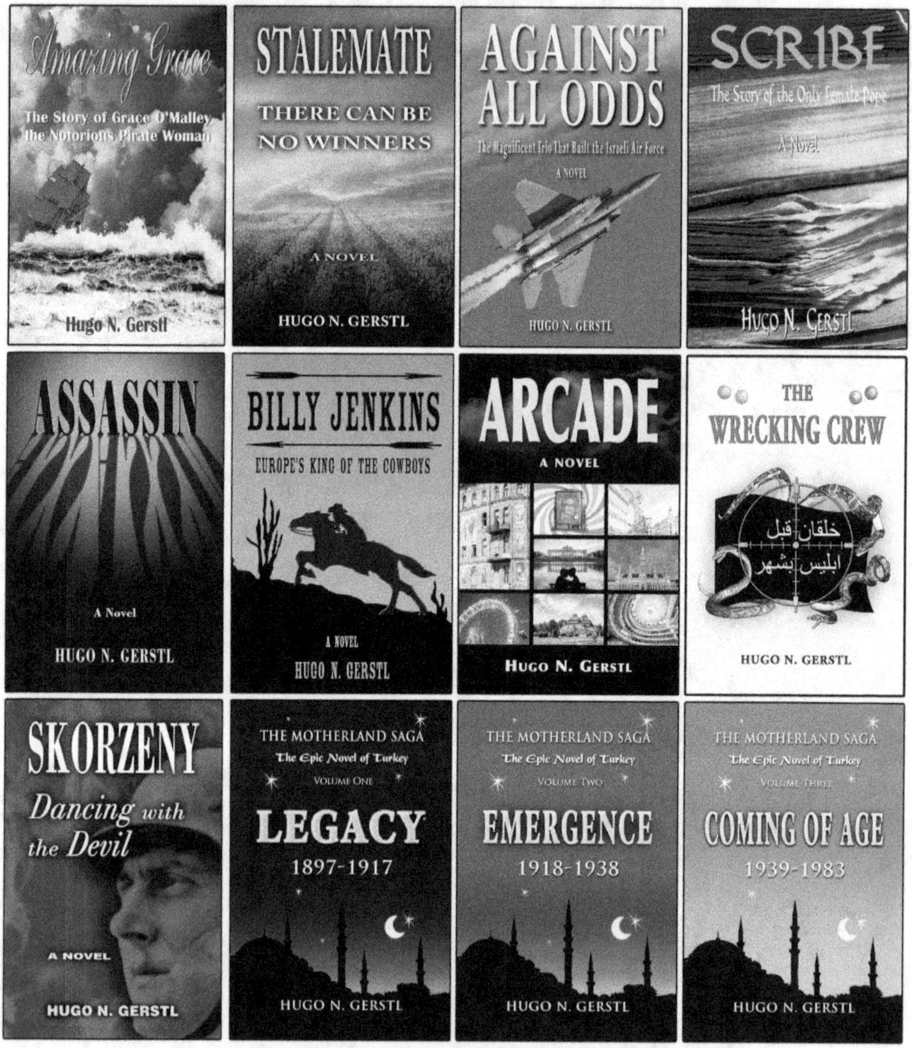

Do not miss them on your shelf!

For Hugo N. Gerstl's complete novels list and descriptions, go to www.HugoGerstl.com

PANGÆA

PANGÆA PUBLISHING GROUP
25579 Carmel Knolls Drive
Carmel, CA 93923
Email: info@pangaeapublishing.com

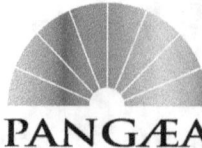

ASSASSIN

THE ULTIMATE THRILLER

A NOVEL

HUGO N. GERSTL

PANGÆA
PUBLISHING GROUP

ASSASSIN - The Ultimate Thriller

ISBN 978-1-950134-00-7
Pangæa Publishing Group
www.PangaeaPublishing.com

Cover design and typesetting by
DesignPeaks@gmail.com

For information contact:

PANGÆA PUBLISHING GROUP
25579 Carmel Knolls Drive
Carmel, CA 93923
Telephone: 831-624-3508/831-649-0668
Fax: 831-649-8007
Email: info@pangaeapublishing.com

To

Lisa & Richard

Zvi, Pnina & Dory Morik

Katie & Shlomo Roman

Colleen Miller,

Jake, Abrielle, Ryland

Oliver, Fineas, and Vivian

*

And, as always,

FOR MY LORRAINE

A FEW MONTHS AGO

Every society needs a pressure-release valve for the moral strictures it places on human life: Las Vegas, Mardi Gras, Rio de Janeiro's Carnival, and the German celebration of fasching are examples of the nod-nod, wink-wink laissez faire.

Before there was Dubai, the men of the Arab world relieved – and still relieve – the pressures and stresses of their conservative, closeted society by using an entire country as a "what goes on here stays here" venue: Lebanon, an uncommonly beautiful nation abutting the Eastern Mediterranean.

The crown jewel of the *glitterati* is the sophisticated and elegant *Casino du Liban*, 15 miles north of the capital. The Casino, which reopened in 1996 after a $50 million renovation, is one of the wonders of the modern world. Its main building occupies 377,000 square feet, has 500 slot machines, 65 gaming tables, two huge entertainment venues, a banquet facility, and five restaurants.

Its setting on a hill above the Mediterranean is gorgeous and the view from the top of the casino is breathtaking. There is, of course, a dress code at the Casino: suit and tie for men, formal dress for women.

At fifty-seven, Prince Hassan Ali Majid had one goal in life that had consumed him since early puberty – the sexual conquest of exceedingly beautiful women. He himself was the picture of a profoundly handsome and elegant Saudi Arabian sheikh: six feet tall with aquiline features, but without the hook-nose and stereotypical semitic mole-filled face. His hair, when not covered by a *kaffiyeh*, was silver, thick, and plentiful.

The prince made it a point to visit the *Casino du Liban* at least three times a year. He never brought any of his wives or children on these visits, but he invariably brought a small vial filled with tadalafil tablets.

Majid arrived at Beirut's Rafik Hariri Airport on MEA Flight 425 at 3:00 in the afternoon, after a short 2½ hour flight from Riyadh. His usual limousine met him at the airport and whisked him away to his suite at the LeRoyal Hotel. By five that day he was ensconced in the three-level spa overlooking the Mediterranean.

Returning to his suite, he donned an elegant tuxedo ensemble and was the epitome of Levantine-Middle Eastern charm as he strolled through the main casino enroute to the baccarat tables. A moment later, he stopped dead in his tracks and stared, slack-jawed. Fifteen feet ahead of him stood an apparition that struck him like a bludgeon.

Her Majesty, the raven-haired, sloe-eyed Queen Rania Al Abdullah of Jordan is said to be the most beautiful royal in the world, if not the most stunningly desirable *woman* in the world. Standing in front of him may not have been Queen Rania herself, but whoever it was looked enough like Jordan's Queen-consort to be her identical twin.

The woman approached him, smiling uncertainly, as if she felt ever tautening wires drawing them inexorably toward one another.

Unknown to Majid, Khadjieh Abi-Samra, thirty years of age, was neither a princess nor a courtesan. She was a graduate of Beirut's American University. Had the Prince known how deeply she had studied him before his arrival, he would have been amazed. She was quite high up in the organization with which she had aligned herself, and was well aware, not only of Majid's identity, but also of the wealth and influence he commanded. Her organization needed an infusion of both the money and the influence, and she was prepared to exert whatever effort she needed to achieve her goal.

"Excuse me, Mademoiselle," Majid said. "Have we not met someplace before?"

"I think not," Khadjieh replied demurely.

"We must have," he continued. "Once any man has seen you, that vision would be burned in his memory for the rest of his life."

Her smile widened. Khadjieh was by no means unaware of the bewitching influence she had on men. As her mother had told her on more than one occasion, "If Allah has blessed you with the gift of such extraordinary beauty, it would be spitting in His face if you did not take advantage of that beauty to advance your life."

"Thank you," she said simply. Her lack of guile worked an even more hypnotic spell upon the Prince.

"Might I treat you to tea, or, if it would not offend you, something stronger, Mademoiselle?"

"Perhaps," she said. "May I ask the identity of the gentleman who is inviting me to partake of such beneficence?"

As they entered the lounge area, Prince Majid did not know whether to act in an imperious manner to impress her, or to be humble. He decided to tread a middle ground. "My name is Hassan Ali Majid. I'm from Riyadh."

"I am Khadjieh Abi-Samra."

He looked vaguely disappointed. "Not Her Majesty Queen Rania? But of course you would not be she. You are far younger and, if I may say so, more desirable than the queen."

She laughed, a musical trill that jolted his insides. "You are rather a direct man, Monsieur Majid," she said.

"Mademoiselle Abi-Samra, if I were unmanly coy or less direct we would discuss small nothings and we would never progress beyond cocktail chatter. I would never be able to express to you how incredibly attractive you are to me, nor would I feel the smooth softness of your breasts or thighs, nor imagine myself pleasuring you beyond anything you and I have ever experienced."

Khadjieh blushed. "That sounds quite melodramatic," she said. "But then again, things do move a bit rapidly in Lebanon."

He nodded and let what he had said sink in. While they were in this state of silent anticipation, each measuring the other, Majid excused himself for a few moments. Once in the restroom, he swallowed a 20 mg. tadalafil tablet. It would take an hour to kick in, and just in case his most profound wish of that moment came true, he wanted to be ready. He returned to the table and ordered champagne for both of them. As they watched the lounge show, a trio of imported Mexican mariachi singers who sang soft, romantic ballads, she moved closer to him. She wore a scent of honey, cloves, and cinnamon.

Finally, he broke the silence. "May I ask what you are thinking, Mademoiselle?"

"If you must know, I am feeling a bit warm. Perhaps it's the champagne?"

A quarter hour later, they walked hand-in-hand to the limousine. Moments after, the limousine transported them to the LeRoyal.

~ ∫ ~

Their lovemaking had been even more intense than he'd anticipated. Khadjieh was a skillful lover, who had mastered every man's dreams. He'd climaxed three times in the span of two hours. Khadjieh was herself quite demonstrative when she came, which was as many times as he.

Afterward, as they lay stroking each other, happily exhausted, she urged him, as every woman can always entice any man, to tell her about himself. And, as every man reacts, so did Prince Majid. Although she looked wide-eyed at his every revelation, she was wise enough not to prod, but simply to let him talk.

At one point, she asked, "Isn't it a shame that the Arabs and the Iranians, who are Muslim brothers, have such a difficult time getting along with one another?"

"Ah, yes," he replied. "Such are the problems of the world, my beautiful Princess. As always, if people were left to their own devices, they would get along just fine. It's always the politicians, isn't it?"

"I suppose." She stifled a gentle yawn. "But what would you do if you were in charge of the world, my friend? The politicians have their own ends to gain and I think they too often posture to keep themselves in power."

"True," Majid replied. "But there should be an answer. The Muslims and the Maronite Christians got along for years in Lebanon until outside forces from everywhere else pushed them apart."

"I've never been that interested in politics or religion," she replied ambiguously. "As you said, if people were left to their own devices ... After the Hariri assassination..."

"Yes, of course," Majid replied. "Most times assassinations are dreadful and cowardly. Sometimes, though, they are necessary to cleanse a society and allow for a new beginning."

She turned her back to him and folded his right hand over her breast. "You sound as if you know something, Majid."

"Not really *know* exactly. Let's just say, hypothetically of course, that someone wanted to take out the Iranian leader for the good of the Middle East."

"Ahmadinejad? He's out of the picture now that his term of office expired."

"I was thinking more along the lines of the Grand Ayatollah Khamenei, the real power in the Islamic Republic."

"Are you serious?"

"I used the word 'hypothetically.' And now, my beautiful one, have we time for one more adventure, or would you rather we sleep for a while?"

"If you don't mind, Majid, you have exhausted even my capacities. Why don't we rest so we'll be stronger in the morning?"

Khadjieh pretended to sleep until she felt her lover remove his hand from her breast and turn over onto his other side. Another few minutes and she heard him snore quite soundly.

She crept out of bed, quietly took a cell phone from her purse, went into the bathroom, locked the door, and punched in a number in Beirut.

~ ∫ ~

The following morning, after one last round of passionate lovemaking, Khadjieh and Majid showered together, dressed, rode the elevator to the ground floor, and gave one another chaste pecks on the cheek as they departed, he to the limousine waiting outside the lobby, she to a destination unknown.

As the chauffeur held the limousine door open for him, Majid greeted the man who'd driven him to and from the LeRoyal for the past few years. "Brief trip this time?" the man asked, taking the overnighter and Majid's briefcase and tossing them into the boot.

"Yes, it was that, Charles," Majid replied diffidently. He entered the front passenger compartment. The chauffeur closed the door, went around to the driver's side, got in, and pulled smoothly into the Beirut Road.

Halfway to the airport, the limousine pulled into a roadside petrol stop. "I'm sorry," the chauffeur said. "Too much tea, no food, and I'm getting a bit older, if you know what I mean. I'll just be a moment."

As the chauffeur exited the car, Hassan Ali Majid laid his head back on the headrest and closed his eyes. It was close to 11:00 a.m. He heard the passenger door open, but in his semi-somnolent state he thought the rush of hot air intruding into what had been air conditioned comfort was momentary and ignored it. He hardly noticed the *thwock* of a hard object hitting his head before everything went black.

~ ∫ ~

Majid lay on a cot in a cell beneath an abandoned fortress barracks. The room's whitewashed walls, stained and musty, barely concealed the obscenities or prayers that had been scratched into them. It was hot and close, with an odor of carbolic acid, sweat, and urine. The Arabian Prince lay face up on an iron cot, the legs of which were embedded in a concrete floor. Apart from a thin, soiled mattress and a rolled-up blanket under his head, the cot contained no other linen. Two heavy leather straps secured his ankles, two more his thighs and wrists. A single strap pinned his chest down. He was still unconscious, breathing deeply and irregularly.

His face had been bathed clean of blood, the ear and scalp sutured. A patch of adhesive gauze spanned his broken nose. As the man in the white coat pried open Majid's mouth, he saw the stumps of two broken front teeth.

The doctor finished his examination, straightened up, and replaced his stethoscope in his bag. "What did you hit him with, an express train?" he asked, as he walked down the passage accompanied by the man who seemed to be in charge.

"It took four large men to do that," replied the other. "What's the damage?"

"Fracture of the right wrist, lacerated left ear and scalp, a broken nose, and two broken teeth. Multiple cuts and bruises, internal hemorrhaging, which could get worse and kill him. What worries me is the head. There's a concussion for sure. There seem to be no signs of a skull fracture, but the concussion could get worse if he's not left alone."

"We need to ask him certain questions," the man observed.

"If you start 'questioning' that man with your methods before he's recovered, he'll either die or become a raving lunatic."

The man in charge listened to the doctor's bitter prediction without moving a muscle. "How long?" he asked.

The doctor shrugged. "Impossible to say. He may regain consciousness tomorrow or not for days. Even then, he will not be medically fit for questioning for at least two weeks."

"There are certain drugs," murmured the man.

"Yes, there are. There's no way I'll prescribe them. You probably can get them, but not from me. Nothing he could tell you now would make the slightest sense. His mind is scrambled. It may clear, it may not, but it must happen in its own time. Mind-bending drugs would simply produce an idiot, no use to you or anyone else. You'll just have to wait." The doctor turned and walked out the door of the fortress.

But the doctor was wrong. Majid opened his eyes two days later. The same day he had his first and only session with the interrogators.

~ ∫ ~

The cellar was silent except for the sound of heavy, controlled breathing from the three men behind the table and the rasping rattle from the man strapped to the heavy oak chair in front of it. One could not tell how large the cellar was. There was only one pool of light in the whole place. It was a standard table lamp, but its bulb was of great brightness, adding to the stifling heat in the cellar. The bulb shone straight at the chair six feet away.

The torsos and shoulders of the three men behind the table were invisible to Majid. The only way he could have seen his questioners would have been to leave his chair and move to the side, so that the indirect glow from the light would pick out their silhouettes. That he could not do. Padded straps pinned his ankles firmly against the legs of the chair. From each of these legs, front and back, an L-shaped steel bracket was bolted into the floor. Majid's wrists were secured to the arms of the chair by padded straps. The padding of each strap was drenched with sweat.

The top of the table was almost bare. Its only decoration was a slit bordered in brass and marked along one side with figures. A narrow brass arm with a knob protruded from the slit. Next to slit, there was an on/off switch. Two wires fell beneath the table, one from the switch and the other from the current control, towards an electric transformer lying on the floor near the feet of the chief interrogator.

In a far corner of the cellar, behind the questioners, a man sat at a wooden table, face to the wall. A tiny glow of white came from the iPad, which was recording the proceedings and an equally small pinprick of green light issued from a digital recorder.

Apart from the breathing, the silence of the cellar was deafening. All three of the questioners were in shirtsleeves, rolled up high and damp with sweat. The odor was overpowering, a stench of sweat, metal, stale smoke, and human vomit. Even the vomit, pungent though it was, was overwhelmed by the unmistakable reek of fear and pain.

The man in the center spoke at last, his voice civilized, gentle, coaxing. "Listen, Prince Majid, you are going to tell us. Not now, perhaps, but eventually. You are a brave man and you gave your word to your associates. But even you cannot hold out much longer. You think your associates would forbid you if they were here? They would order you to tell us. They know about these things. They would tell us themselves, to spare you more discomfort. You yourself know, Prince, they always talk in the end. No one can go on and on and on. So why not now, my friend? Then back to bed and to blessed sleep, and no one will disturb you."

The man in the chair raised a battered face, glistening with sweat, into the light. His eyes were closed, whether by the great blue bruises or by the light, it didn't matter which. He looked at the table and the blackness in front of it. His mouth opened and he tried to speak. A small gobbet of puke emerged and dribbled down his chest to the pool of vomit in his lap. His head sagged back until the chin touched the chest again. He shook his head from side to side in answer.

The voice from behind the table began again. "You are a hard man, Prince Majid. We all recognize that. Even you can't go on. But we can, Prince Majid, we can. If we have to keep you alive and conscious for days, even weeks... There is no merciful oblivion like in the old days. Third degree is gone for good. Nowadays there are drugs... So why not talk? We understand, Prince. We know about the pain. But the little crabs, they just don't understand. They just go on and on … Electrodes, Prince Majid. Your own body tearing itself to shreds, you see? Now tell us, Prince Majid, what happened at the meeting in Santiago de Compostela?"

The Arab's head shook slowly from side to side. Little copper crabs gripped his nipples. Two larger crabs with serrated teeth held his testicles and penis in their relentless grip. The man nearest the slit in the table moved the toggle switch from the figure two to the figure four.

The little metal crabs fixed to the man in the chair appeared to come alive with a slight buzzing. The figure in the chair rose as if propelled by a fist. His legs and wrists bulged outwards against the straps until it seemed that even with the padding the leather must cut clean through the flesh and bone. His eyes, which were medically unable to see clearly through the puffed flesh around them, started outwards, bulging into vision and staring at the ceiling. His mouth was open as if in surprise. It was half a second before the demonic screams came out of his lungs. When they came, they went on without stop...

Prince Hassan Ali Majid broke at 5:05 in the afternoon and the operator turned the iPad recorder and the digital recorder on.

As he started to talk – or rather to ramble incoherently between whimpers and muted screams – the calm voice of his interrogator cut across the maunderings and kept Majid focused as best he could.

"Who is the Assassin, Majid? ... What did she look like? ... What do you mean sometimes it was a 'he?' ... What hotel was it? ... Who were the men with you? ... Whom did they represent? ... Whom did *you* represent? ... What bank? ... How much money? ... Who was the target? ... How much did she demand? ..."

Majid finally went silent after forty-five minutes. His last ramblings continued being recorded by the iPad and the digital recorder until they stopped. The voice behind the table continued more gently for another few minutes until it became clear that there were going to be no more answers. Then the man in the center gave an order to the others and the session was over.

The Hezbollah agent flew in a chartered flight from a small field in Eastern Lebanon to Tehran's Mehrabad, the old pre-revolution airport that had been largely replaced by Imam Khomeini International. Immediately upon landing, he was met by an agent of *Vezarat-e Etteláat va Amniyat-e Keshvar*, the Ministry of Intelligence and National Security of the Islamic Republic of Iran. The Iranian accepted the iPad and the digital recorder from the Lebanese, nodded peremptorily, slipped the visitor a small briefcase, and the two men separated. After refueling, the chartered aircraft took off and headed west from whence it had come.

~ ∫ ~

The brilliant sun that had warmed Tehran set as the day faded into a miasma of smog and haze. Myriad cars belched and hooted and crowded the wide roads and tunnels, their drivers jockeying for position to get home five minutes before their neighbor.

In a small office on the third floor of the VEVAK building, four men sat around a high-tech sound system. One man controlled the switches, continuously isolating and playing back ten-second passages. The man wore a set of noise-canceling headphones. He chain-smoked cigarettes, one after another. The blue smoke and the confined space made his eyes water, but he seemed oblivious to the discomfort. Every so often he would nod to the operator to hold on. Then he would dictate the last passage of speech.

Another man sat at a computer, typing the dictation. The question was always preceded by the letter Q, the answer by the letter A. The answers were disjointed and involved the use of several ellipses where the sense of what was being said broke down completely.

By midnight the men had finished.

Early next morning, ten copies were delivered to the governing board of the Ministry of Intelligence and National Security of the Islamic Republic of Iran.

~ ∫ ~

In Beirut a small, insignificant article in the morning newspaper four days later announced that the body of a man later identified as Prince Hassan Ali Majid of Riyadh, Saudi Arabia, had been found in a wadi just east of the Lebanese-Syrian border. He had apparently been robbed, then murdered and his body mutilated by an unknown band of assailants. Whether they were loyalists or rebels could not be determined.

Unknown to the man who'd typed the transcript in the VEVAK building, his computer had been secretly slaved to another computer in the same building some months earlier, and everything he typed appeared almost simultaneously on that computer. The regular operator of that computer, no friend of the current regime, transmitted what he found on his computer that morning to an opposition minister who, in turn, emailed it to a man in Ankara, Turkey.

SEPTEMBER 1968

"How frequently are they coming?"

"Every ten minutes, love – Oh, God! There's one now!" the woman said, trying to keep as calm as she could. The pains were not excruciating yet, but they were noticeable, and the duration between them was getting shorter. Eight minutes since the last contraction.

Her husband glanced at his wristwatch. Eleven-thirty.

When she'd telephoned him earlier in the evening and said the labor pains seemed to be starting, he'd become concerned. Their first child – children, actually. Doctor Edelstein had told them midway through her pregnancy that all signs pointed toward twins. Throughout the third trimester, the doctor had reassured them that everything pointed to a normal delivery and that the babies *in utero* seemed to be doing just fine.

"But it's – they're – our first," the husband, who was in his mid-twenties and had recently graduated law school had said.

"That's the way most couples start out," Doctor Edelstein had joked. "Besides," he said, pointing to the woman who was a good deal taller than his five-foot-two inch height, "all you have to do is lie on a gurney. I'm the one who'll have to climb on a stool to deliver you."

The father-to-be had suggested they dine at the Carlton Hotel – nothing to worry about, of course, but just in case … they'd only be minutes from Queen Victoria Maternity Hospital.

"But Hillbrow?"

"It gets a bit rowdy on the weekends," he replied, "but it's quiet as a morgue on Monday night."

After a delicious dinner, the wife noticed her pains were becoming sharper and more frequent.

"All right, Angel," her husband said. "Perhaps it's best we check into the hospital a little bit early? Not that I'm nervous, you know, it's just … and we're only a few minutes from the Queen Vic."

The husband strolled, and his wife waddled, out the door of Johannesburg's fanciest hotel toward the outdoor queue of assembled taxicabs.

As it turned out, they'd chosen a most unfortunate time to wander beyond the lobby. The moment they hit the street, the husband heard a crash of breaking glass and saw three black men running from a nearby storefront. Within seconds a Saracen police vehicle rounded the corner, sirens wailing, followed by a second patrol vehicle. Acting on animal instinct, the young father-to-be immediately pushed his wife toward the hotel lobby, but it was too late. The two of them were caught in the crossfire between the police and the robbers. She took a slug directly in the throat as he was trying desperately to shield her. The next shot slammed into his chest. As the red flowers started to blossom from their bodies, they never even knew they were dying.

~ ∫ ~

The paramedics arrived at the lobby of the Carlton within one-hundred-twenty seconds of the shootings. Two of them immediately surrounded the woman.

"Check her pulse, Mick!" the lead medic commanded.

"Fluttery. She's got a minute, maybe two."

"Get the forceps and a surgical knife right now. We're gonna' do a Caesarian right here in the lobby."

"Are you sure? There's blood and gore all over the place."

"Get the knife," he shouted. "I'll cut, you pull."

By a miracle of chance and hard, bloody work, the twins were delivered alive, and were immediately transferred to the Queen Victoria Hospital. Neither parent survived.

~ ∫ ~

"Telephone! Telephone!" shrieked Peter. It was 1:15 in the morning on Tuesday, September 3, 1968. Peter was an institution. Matron Reece's husband, had found him for sale cheap at one of the open air markets run by the natives on Louis Botha Road, in 1940. On impulse, he'd bought the parrot as a surprise gift for his wife's forty-eighth birthday.

The Reeces, who'd had no children of their own, actually had *several* children living with them at any given time since that night in 1936, when an abandoned baby in a basket had been left on their doorstep. Dorothy Reece had cared for it in her home in Mayfair. Word spread and the small woman found her residence to be a way station where she provided an abode for babies who had been abandoned as a result of death, alcohol abuse, drug abuse, and divorce until she could find suitable permanent homes for them. Peter the Parrot had been a permanent fixture of Cotlands Baby Sanctuary ever since he came to the Reece's home.

By 1963, Cotlands had become a source of national pride. South African Justice Minister B. J. Vorster himself dedicated the new Cotlands Building at 134 Stanton Street, Turffontein – one large enough to shelter 50 babies, 12 expectant mothers, and a staff of four sisters, 12 nurses and 13 assistants. The expanded facility had seven baby wards, all painted in different colors, kitchens, and two secluded gardens, one for the mothers and one for the nurses.

Last year Matron Reece, had passed away at 75, and Peter the Parrot, the "night watchman" and playmate of thousands of babies passing through Cotlands, was the sole survivor of the origins.

But beloved or not, when Peter screeched "Telephone! Telephone!" at 1:15 in the morning on Tuesday, September 3, 1968, the night attendant, Marius Coetzee, grumbled, "Bloody pain in the arse!" as he sleepily picked up the receiver.

"Cotlands, Coetzee here."

"*Meneer* Coetzee, Monica Broede, Queen Victoria Hospital on the line."

Coetzee came immediately awake. The Queen Victoria, one of the oldest and largest in the City, was situated between Kotze and Hancock Streets on the western edge of Hillbrow. Officially designated a 'whites only' area, it had become 'grey' after the Sharpeville Massacre. The much despised – and feared - Fort, the native men's prison, the women's prison, the city mortuary, and a slew of hot nightspots abutted the Hospital.

"Go ahead, *Mevrou.*"

"There's been an attack outside the Carlton ... Bantus and police ... Both parents killed. They were able to save the babies ... fraternal twins, a boy and a girl."

"Bloody hell, you say!" Coetzee swore. "I'm sorry, *Mevrou,* not your fault, of course."

"Bloody *kaff-*, I'm sorry, assailants, three of them, were taken out by the police. It's a mess, I'm afraid."

"The babies?"

"Beautiful little ones. White. D'you have room at Cotlands?"

"Five vacancies."

"Best I can make out, *Meneer,* the parents were Jewish. No immediate next of kin. Shame, really. Any chance you can come get them now?"

"At 1:20 in the morning?"

"I thought it best for their privacy – before it hits the papers and all ... and it could be a major blow to the Queen Victoria ... they like to keep this thing as quiet and anonymous as possible, you know."

"I understand *Mevrou*. I'll have a car there in less than an hour."

~ ∫ ~

The babies were indeed beautiful. They were at Cotlands for less than two months when the girl was adopted by an *Afrikaner* family headed by Pieter Terre'Blanche, who owned a farm in the Orange Free State, between Bloemfontein and the border with Botswana. Pieter's brother, Eugène, owned a farmstead close to a small asbestos mining town named Pomfret, which was just south of the frontier. Pieter and his wife promptly named their new daughter Morgan.

The baby boy was adopted by a Jewish family named Caen, who lived in the Kensington neighborhood of Johannesburg. The family, along with their son whom they'd named Ezra, emigrated to Israel in May 1976, barely a month before the Soweto Riots changed the face of South Africa forever.

THE PRESENT -
SOME MONTHS EARLIER

1

To have seen the five men sitting in the covered quayside restaurant across the street from their rooms at the Villa Dea in Ohrid, Macedonia, staring toward Albania across the lake, no one would have guessed that their combined net worth exceeded thirty billion dollars. They'd specifically chosen this place and wore jeans or khaki denim pants, cotton shirts, and scuffed sandals so they would not be recognized – not that such precautions were even necessary because hardly anyone in the world had the remotest idea what they looked like.

"Gentlemen," the acting chair said. "The world is a disaster heading toward destruction. Our project is the only thing that can save it. With the new 'agreement' between the latest incarnation of the Persian empire and the big powers, Iran is days away from becoming a nuclear power if they aren't one already. They've made it abundantly clear that they're desperate enough to mine the Strait of Hormuz, cutting off one-sixth of the world's oil supply, which could trigger the start of a nuclear holocaust. Our Israeli friends are not going to sit by and suffer a repeat performance of the first one."

"You'll pardon me, Howard," a younger man, in his mid-sixties, rejoined, "but what you propose still doesn't make sense to me. Each of us has substantial investment interests in the region. None of us wants a nuclear holocaust. But there's too much speculation and not enough thought here. You're telling us that you want the target dead because his country is a player in the nuclear arms race. But 'arms racers,' – and I include the kid in North Korea – haven't exploded a bomb in a war since 1945. Iran is a state actor. Its acquisition of a weapon will, more likely than not, create a *de facto* non-aggression treaty, just the way the balance of terror played out in the U.S.-Soviet cold war. If the target were a non-state terrorist, your proposal might seem more plausible, but the Osama bin Laden story has already been written."

"Ah, but you've put your finger on it, my friend," the Chairman rejoined calmly. "Let's not fool ourselves, our own interests in the region are, shall we say, more sacrosanct than the venom spewed forth by the more militant practitioners of the world's fastest-growing religious movement. I won't bother asking how much your oil investments are worth, but if they're anything like mine ..."

"John may have a point," the tall, red-haired man of fifty joined in. "Taking out Khamenei, who seems conservative when he's not spouting anti-American and anti-Israel rhetoric, and who's not manifestly unlikable – not to mention that he's twenty years my senior – might be a *de*-stabilizing influence that really could open a Pandora's box."

"True," the youngest of the group said, "but for the moment Iran *is* the destabilizing influence in the neighborhood. Not that I take their threats to 'nuke' Israel seriously, but they are the guys channeling weapons and chemicals to Hezbollah. Not to mention that the Ayatollah's pockets are deeper than even our own."

"What do you mean?" the red-haired man asked.

"Khamenei controls a business empire worth around $95 billion. *Setad* – its real name is *Setad Ejraiye Farmane Hazrate Emam* - Headquarters for Executing the Order of the Imam, one of the keys to his power, holds stakes in nearly every sector of Iranian industry: finance, oil, telecommunications, the production of birth-control pills, and even ostrich farming. Its name refers to an edict signed by the Ayatollah Ruhollah Khomeini, shortly before his death in 1989. It was intended to manage and sell properties abandoned in the chaotic years after the 1979 Islamic Revolution. According to one of its co-founders, Setad was created to help the poor and war veterans and was meant to exist for just two years. Didn't work out that way. Today, *Setad's* worth is made up of about $52 billion in real estate and $43 billion in corporate holdings – 40% bigger than Iran's total oil exports.

There was a whistle from one of the participants. "More than two-and-a-half times *our* combined net worth."

"I don't mean to switch gears, but why not take out Nasrallah and be done with?" the second of the group asked. "He's the guy who offed Hariri, he's backing Assad, and he's been Israel's biggest pain in the ass."

"If we get rid of Nasrallah, we'll more likely get another Mugniyah instead of another Fadlallah, so we'd be back to square one. Assad's already on the ropes, so we don't have to worry about him. Cut the snake's head off and the body dies. Without the backing of the current Iranian regime, Hezbollah withers and dies. And when that happens, we move in with normal, responsible, more … complacent … leadership."

"Gunboat diplomacy in the twenty-first century?" the fifth man mused.

"Stability insurance," the Chairman rejoined.

After more discussion, the Chairman called for a vote. "All in favor?" Five index fingers barely rose.

"Done. Have each of you reviewed the dossiers?"

Affirmative nods.

"Who wants to start?"

They looked at one another briefly. The youngest and newest member of the "club" said, "I don't think there's any real competition. The South African woman's light years ahead of the rest. She won't come cheap, of course."

"How cheap is *cheap?*" the next youngest man, in his mid-forties, asked.

"North of ten million, south of fifteen."

"And if she succeeds, how much is it worth to each of us?"

"Ten times that."

"All in favor?" the Chairman asked again.

Five index fingers rose again.

"Of course we can't be seen to be part of this. After all, our own privacy …"

"The people we entrust will not only have to be beyond reproach, but nobody can associate them with us. I trust each of you has such a surrogate in mind?"

~ ∫ ~

The meeting had been arranged to take place at 2:00 p.m. on the 27th in the conference room of Suite 116 of the *Parador Hotel* in Santiago de Compostela. The candidate arrived at 9:00 a.m. on the 25th, thirty-six hours ahead of the projected arrival of the five men who were to interview her.

She'd been contacted by means of an anonymous numbered drop box in the Mokhotlong post office in Lesotho. The message was automatically forwarded to an address in a farm community of less than a hundred souls somewhere between Bloemfontein and the Botswana frontier. She spent her first afternoon in the capital of Galicia, Spain, carefully inspecting, measuring, and observing every square meter of the *Parador*. She surreptitiously followed a maid as she made her rounds from room to room. The maid got off work at two that afternoon and rode the bus to a working class neighborhood fifteen minutes from the hotel. The candidate had boarded the bus at the same time as the housekeeper, then emerged just after the middle-aged woman had gotten off.

The maid stopped at a nearby butcher's shop to purchase soup bones for the evening meal. While she talked animatedly with the proprietor, the candidate brushed up against her and removed what she needed. By the time the woman turned around, the ring with her master key on it was gone. The maid only learned that the key had gone missing half an hour later. By that time the candidate had had an extra key made and returned to the *Parador*.

As she went from room to room, the candidate noted that each room had either one double or two single four-poster beds. The buildings consisted of vaulted ceilings, stone archways, and tapestries, set around a large courtyard. The hotel's two restaurants carried out the classic Spanish motif.

In Room 118, adjacent to the conference room where she was to meet her prospective employers, she found what she was looking for: an old-fashioned brass key holder with the name *Parador* inscribed on it. She dislodged the key from its holder and substituted the duplicate master key.

Next morning, a short, fashionably-dressed, swarthy man in his mid-fifties with a day's growth of dark beard, a stylishly short moustache and goatee, and coal-black hair cut to medium length, entered the *Parador's* lobby. The duty clerk thought the man looked slightly familiar, most likely from the Middle East – there were so many of them nowadays; maybe he was a Turk, maybe an Iranian. For all he knew, the fellow could be an Afghani terrorist. No matter, their money was as good as anyone else's.

The man spoke in a quiet, well-modulated, somewhat high-pitched voice. His Spanish was the impeccable unaccented Castilian of a highly-educated, cultured gentleman. "Buenos dias, Señor," he began politely. "I was wandering near the Cathedral earlier this morning, and found this," he said, extracting the key holder which bore the number 118 from his side pocket. "Perhaps one of your guests mislaid it?"

"Ah, it appears to be one of ours, indeed. I am much obliged, Sir,"

Pretending to look about as if seeing the quality of the lobby for the first time, the newcomer continued, "Have you by any chance a room available for the next two nights?"

The clerk looked through his register. "You are in luck, Sir," he replied after a few moments. "We have a lovely double room, number one hundred-eighteen. In fact, the room must have been readied with you in mind, since what you found in the street is the key to that very room."

The shorter man smiled, displaying even white teeth. "I trust you need a passport to show the authorities?"

"Please, Sir, if you would not mind."

The man handed the clerk a Lebanese passport in the name of Karim Mahhadi. The clerk glanced cursorily at the photograph, then back to the customer, and nodded. "Have you any luggage, Sir?"

"Only a small grip. I always find that it serves one best to travel light."

He handed the guest the same key the man had brought moments before. "Will there be anything more?"

"No, Señor," the man said. "You've been very kind."

After satisfying himself that the maids had cleaned, dusted, and left fresh toiletries and towels in the suite where he had been booked and the adjoining Conference Room, the small man used the duplicate master key he'd appropriated the day before to gain entry to the conference suite. A set of double doors connected the two suites. The locks were so well-oiled that they made hardly a whisper when unlocked.

The conference room, more than twice the size of his sleeping quarters, was the closest room to the end of the corridor. It contained a large rectangular oak table, four feet wide by eight feet long. Eight high-backed maroon-colored leather executive chairs surrounded the table, one at each end and three on each side. Beyond the table, there was a well-stocked bar adjacent to one wall. The windows were shaded by heavy floor-to-ceiling drapes which matched the chairs.

The man carefully inserted a microscopically small "button bug" under the oak conference table. He then checked the double doors between the conference room and his bedroom suite. Each door locked from inside its own room. With practiced attention to detail, the small man disabled the locking mechanism on the 116-side of the double doors, then injected graphite into the locking mechanism of each door to make it even quieter.

The representatives who were to interview the candidate met at 9:20 a.m. in the arrivals lounge of Lavacolla Airport. From there, a hired limousine whisked them to the *Parador*, where they arrived in time to avail themselves of the morning buffet.

Mehdi Karroubi, whose brother stood on equal footing with Mir Hossein Mousavi, the Chairman of his country's opposition Green Movement, had been selected by the billionaires as one of the "complacent" replacements for the current Iranian regime. His brother was presently under house arrest in Tehran.

Hsien Yun-Lo had been the private attaché to Hu Jintao, former General Secretary of the Chinese Communist Party, since 2002.

Hassan Ali Majid, a high-ranking Saudi prince, added a touch of mystique and dignity to the assembly.

Mustafa Karaca served as senior vice president of Alarko Holding, Turkey's largest company; and Count Marco Napolitano was a seasoned former senior Italian diplomat, now employed by different interests.

Each brought serious sophistication to the coming meeting. Each knew that this enterprise called for cooperation, security, and, above all, the ability to carry the secret of their mission to the grave if need be.

"Since we told the candidate that the meeting would start at 2:00 p.m., I suggest we congregate an hour earlier so we can appear at ease when she arrives," Napolitano commenced. "Each of you has, I assume, seen a series of recent digital photographs of the woman?"

"We have," the Chinese responded. "She'd disappear into the woodwork in any crowd," he said. There was general agreement that their principals could not have chosen a more anonymous-looking individual.

~ ʃ ~

The candidate sat patiently, rubbing her hands slowly along the upper legs of the man's trousers she'd worn for the meeting. As portrayed in most of the public photographs published by the media, the candidate wore an open-necked white shirt. The growth of "his" beard was thicker than the day before and the goatee was now a fringe.

At quarter to one, she stood to her five-foot-five inch height – actually an inch taller than the man she portrayed, stretched her arms high, and made certain that the band around her chest was sufficiently tight to mask any hint of curves. She prepared to greet her interrogators the moment they arrived in the conference room.

~ ∫ ~

At exactly one o'clock in the afternoon, the five men entered the conference room, relaxed and looking forward to what they hoped would be a businesslike negotiation rather than a confrontation.

At exactly one o'clock and ten seconds, Mehdi Karroubi, the Iranian, turned pale and felt a rush of bile in his stomach. He grabbed the top of the nearest executive chair to steady himself, but was unable to hide the tremor of his shaking hands. "My God!" he breathed weakly. "It cannot be. It simply cannot be!"

Hsien Yun-Lo sucked in his breath, then coughed to cover up what he felt in that instant. "There is no way," he said quietly, unsteadily.

"Gentlemen, welcome to our little conference. I regret that I do not seem to be the person with whom you thought you were meeting."

As each of them fought to regain his composure, they found themselves staring into the mocking dark-brown eyes of Mahmoud Ahmadinejad, who'd recently ended his term as President of *Jomhuri-ye Eslāmi-ye Irān*, the Islamic Republic of Iran.

2

Karroubi, the first to recover, addressed the other man in Farsi, which the others almost certainly did not understand. "Dare I ask how you learned of our meeting so quickly, Mr. President?"

"You may," the shorter man replied.

"Proceed, then."

"You ask my permission? After you and Mousavi and your accursed so-called 'Green Movement' called me an insane demagogue?"

"Mahmoud, you understand politics as well as I do. Today's insane demagogue may be tomorrow's political ally. If the Ayatollah – Peace be to him – were to fall into disfavor I wager you'd be the first in line to show how 'moderate' you always meant to be. You're as much a pragmatist as I am."

Count Napolitano asked Karroubi to summarize the conversation of the two men. The Iranian responded.

"An excellent translation, gentlemen," the former Iranian president stated in perfect English, with an accent somewhere between British and Australian.

The Saudi Prince raised his eyebrows. "I've never known you to speak English, Mr. President."

"Of course not," the small man snapped. "Certainly never in public and, as my wife Azam well knows, hardly ever in private. I prefer to let the stupid Americans and the slightly more sophisticated Brits think of me as a buffoon and say insulting things they think I'd never understand. But enough, gentlemen. Proceed with your meeting."

They all noted that the former Iranian president has used the words, "*Your* meeting."

Count Napolitano said, "If you know what the meeting is about, you know it cannot be held without the expected guest. You must realize the guest would be astute enough to observe the little item of your presence and is probably not within a thousand miles of this room."

"Or within five feet?" the former Iranian president said.

"Obviously not," the Chinese said. "Now you are toying with us, Mr. President. For all we know you may even have dispatched the expected guest."

The little man rotated his chair toward the credenza. Pushing a sliding door open, he took out a bottle and a tray with six small shot glasses. Turning back to the group, he smiled. "Glenlivet 21, anyone?"

The shock on each face was palpable.

"I beg your pardon?" This from Mustafa Karaca, the Turk.

"Gentlemen, we're not within the confines of the Muslim world," the man said. "We are, all of us, of some sophistication, are we not?"

While the forehead of each man still glistened with a thin sheen of perspiration, Count Napolitano was the first to sense something amiss. "You'll pardon me, Mr. President," he said, "but if I may ask this without risking my life, who exactly *are* you?"

"Don't your own eyes answer that question?"

"My eyes tell me one thing, Signor, but your mannerisms deliver an entirely different message." Napolitano picked up a shot glass from the table and tossed it toward the other man's lap. Involuntarily, the president spread his legs and the glass dropped neatly and without breaking onto the thickly carpeted floor.

Count Napolitano smiled. "So now we know you are not a man at all," he said.

"How dare you!" the other exclaimed.

"I did indeed dare," Napolitano continued smoothly. "That's a trick so old I learned it from my mother."

"What do you mean?" the Chinese man asked.

"Quite simple," Napolitano responded. "Let me show you." He picked up another glass and tossed it toward the Turk. Without thinking, that man cupped his hands at his crotch and simultaneously smacked his legs together, nearly smashing the glass. "You see," Napolitano continued, "when an object is thrown toward a man's lap, he instinctively shuts his legs together to catch what is thrown, or, equally instinctively, to protect his male parts from harm, he cups his hands near them. A woman, on the other hand, who is used to wearing dresses and such, *spreads* her legs to catch that object in the folds of her clothing."

"So," Karroubi mused, "the guest we expected may not be a thousand miles away after all?"

"That is for our guest to answer," Count Napolitano said.

"Gentlemen," the small man said, "If you will excuse me for a few moments, I need to relieve myself." He picked up the small grip he'd set down by the side of his chair. "I don't suspect any of you will look inside, but you understand that I'd feel more comfortable if I had my belongings with me." He lifted his grip and walked into the adjacent bathroom.

Less than five minutes later the bathroom door opened and out stepped a reasonably, but not ravishingly, attractive woman in her late thirties or early forties. "I trust you're more at ease with me in this configuration, Count Napolitano?" Facing the rest she said, "Gentlemen, it's time we started talking."

~ ∫ ~

"Your name is?"

"For your purposes, Agrippina will do, Mr. Karroubi. I trust my name did not appear on any of the dossiers you gentlemen read?"

"The elder or the younger?" Napolitano asked, smiling knowingly at her use of the names of two of the most powerful women in Rome during the first century A.D.

"Whichever one you wish, Signor."

"But surely it would not hurt you to reveal to us ..." the prince interjected.

"As a matter of fact, gentlemen, it would. Think for a moment. I'm in a rather specialized field of endeavor. Those of us in such a club do not make details about ourselves readily available."

"But how do we know your *bona fides*?" continued the Saudi prince. How do we know you've done what you claim to have done?"

"You don't, and I claim nothing," the woman said. "As regards absolute proof, there is none. If there were, it would be a bad sign. It would mean I'd be listed somewhere as an undesirable. As I'm sure you've learned from your investigation of my dossier and your own observation of me, there is nothing against me but rumor. If the intelligence services of any country, or even a network like Interpol, were to list me, they could put no more than a question mark. That does not merit filing me with Interpol, or even the chances that one agency would tip me off to another. Indeed, my very anonymity will protect you as much as it protects me. As you probably noted before inviting me here, there is only one downside to your retaining my services."

The Turk lit a small, artfully carved meerschaum pipe and gazed at the woman for a long moment. "That is …?"

The woman looked fixedly at Karaca. "I don't come cheap."

"That is not an insurmountable problem."

"I am aware that your principals are quite well-heeled." The woman placed her hands in her lap and waited patiently for any of her interrogators to speak next.

Count Napolitano looked at the woman. His face was blank. In his day, he'd learned the art of betraying nothing, but he was troubled by the woman in front of him. He had seen many pairs of eyes in his time – shadowy, veiled, frightened, arrogant. The eyes of the woman facing him were wide open and looked back at him with frank candor, with not a hint of a mask. They were, Napolitano concluded, quite lovely eyes, even though the color was nothing more than an ordinary brown. It took Napolitano a few seconds to realize what made him uncomfortable. The woman's eyes had no expression at all. Whatever was going on behind those eyes, absolutely nothing came through. Napolitano felt a chill of unease. He did not like the unpredictable, the uncontrollable. He realized that unless he had even a remote inkling of what the woman was thinking, he was at a decided disadvantage.

"So we won't know your name and that is final?" he asked.

"As I said, but for the name Agrippina, that much is as final as the fact that my price is what it is. Again, I tell you it is for your own good as much as mine."

"Very well, Madame Agrippina," said Karroubi. "Agreed. Would you permit us to introduce ourselves?"

"That will not be necessary, Mr. Karroubi. As you have read your principals' dossiers on me, I have acquainted myself with each of you in advance of this meeting. What I know of each need not concern you. Let us be frank, we both have 'unusual' occupations. We are hunters rather than prey. The difference between us is that I am free to move anywhere I want in the world and I will not be noticed, or, if I am noticed, I'll be forgotten in a few moments. On the other hand, each of you is bound to certain – interests – men who are wealthy, powerful, influential, and, above all, do not *want* to be known. If anyone has any animus against your principals, you, not they, are in the direct line of fire."

Napolitano started to raise his hand then thought the better of it and put it back down on the arm of his chair.

"The difference between us, Count Napolitano," she said, directly fixing him with a neutral stare, "is that you operate from loyalty or even a sense of idealism, whereas I operate for money. But when it comes to practical details, we are all professionals at our jobs. Therefore, we need not waste time with pleasantries and posturing. Rest assured I am well aware of every inquiry you made about me.

"You could have been seeking revenge against me or you may have wished to employ me. I concluded by your invitation it was the latter, at which point I became interested. No matter how wealthy he is, a lawyer always wants a large new client; the brain surgeon lusts after an operation which will further cement his reputation; and a businessman would not be a businessman if he was not constantly seeking additional customers. You want me to take down the Ayatollah Khamenei?" She glanced around the table. "I thought as much."

There was silence around the table for several moments. Prince Majid and Mehdi Karroubi followed one another into the bathroom. Mustafa Karaca remained impassive, puffing at his pipe. Hsien Yun-Lo and Marco Napolitano left the suite to walk along the corridor. The candidate was the only one who sat absolutely still, as though in a state of suspended animation.

When they returned, Napolitano took up the conversation. "The Middle East is unstable …"

"Count Napolitano, the Middle East has been unstable for the last two thousand years. Tell me something I don't know. I'm not a politician and I'm not a moralist. Your principals have their own reasons for hiring me and I really don't care what they are."

"We are considering engaging the services of a professional to do the job. As such a professional, I must ask you preliminarily, is it possible?"

There was a flicker of interest, but nothing more, in the woman's dark eyes.

"Count, there is no human being in the world who is immune to an assassin's bullet. Of course it is possible to kill him. The problem is that the chances of escape would not be very high. A fanatic prepared to die in the attempt is always the most certain method of eliminating a target. As you are undoubtedly aware, there is no shortage of such fanatics in the Muslim world. Half of the Palestinians believe that *Jihad Warriors* will ascend to the highest levels of heaven immediately and they will have four-hundred-year-long orgasms with forty beautiful virgins." She laughed without humor. "Obviously, those heroic young men never stopped to consider that an inexperienced virgin makes the worst possible lover."

"I am sure we can find patriotic Iranians prepared even now ..." Karaca started.

"Perhaps, Mustafa Bey," she said, using the Turkish honorific. "But a professional does not act out of emotional motivation. Therefore, such a professional will be calmer and less likely to make elementary mistakes. Not being idealistic, a professional is not likely to have second thoughts at the last moment about who else might get hurt by whatever method is employed. Being a professional, an assassin has calculated the risks to the ultimate contingency. So such an expert's chances of success are better than anyone else's. But a professional will never commence his operation until he or she has formulated a plan that will enable him not only to complete the mission, but to escape unharmed after the job is done."

There was silence around the table for some thirty seconds before Prince Majid said, "Do you believe you could assassinate the Grand Ayatollah and escape?"

The candidate parted the window curtains ever so slightly to see if there was anyone in the corridor before turning back to face the five men. "In principle, yes. In theory, it is always possible with enough time and planning. But in this case it would be extremely difficult, particularly since, in our modern, drone-inhabited world, such attempts have become commonplace and counterterrorist organizations have become ever more vigilant."

She continued, "The Grand Ayatollah survived a notoriously botched attempt more than thirty years ago, but it cost him the use of his right arm. There have been other attempts through the years, none of which were publicized. Although he wields supreme power in the Islamic Republic, he is, in that respect, not that much different from any other powerful leader, man or woman.

"All of such people have bodyguards, but over a series of years – and particularly in the situation which presently exists, with the Grand Ayatollah well into his seventies and not expected to live forever – the checks become formal, the routines more or less mechanical. The single bullet that takes out the target must be completely unexpected and must breed instant panic. Under cover of this panic, the assassin escapes. In the case of Iran's Supreme Leader, however, his age notwithstanding, the level of watchfulness is constant. If the bullet reaches the target, many would not panic, but would go for the assassin. Make no mistake, gentlemen, it could be done, but it would be one of the hardest jobs in the world. And the past failures would only make my job harder."

"In the event we decide to hire a professional to do the job ..." Karaca started.

"You have no option but to employ a professional," the woman rejoined.

"You yourself concede there are many suicide warriors who would love nothing better than to perish as martyrs."

"True," the woman responded. "And we can go round and round on this subject for the next several hours and get absolutely nowhere. You gentlemen did not call me here to chat in general terms about the history of political assassination, nor because you have a shortage of candidates for the job. You called me here because you know as well as I that if the job is to be done properly, an outsider needs to do it. The only questions that remain are who and for how much. Now, gentlemen, you have examined the merchandise and it is up to you to make a decision. I trust you have your principals' authority to do so?"

"We do," Napolitano replied. "Will you assassinate the Grand Ayatollah Khamenei?"

The woman's eyes came back to him. Eyes that were absolutely blank.

"Yes, but it will cost you ten million dollars U.S. plus five hundred thousand for expenses. All of the costs out front. Half of the fee in advance, the other half when the job is completed."

"So high," the Arab mused.

"Indeed," the woman responded. "Whoever is hired to do the job will, in the highest likelihood, never work again. The chances of remaining not only free but undiscovered are very slim. One must make enough from this one job both to be able to live well for the rest of one's life, and also to ensure that there is protection against those who would certainly seek revenge."

"There are, of course, other professionals." This from Karroubi.

"Obviously," said the woman, "and I'm certain you could get cheaper estimates," she continued without emotion. "Then again, they might take your fifty percent out front and vanish, or make a million excuses why it could not be done. When you employ the best, you pay for the best."

Silence pervaded the room.

"Please understand," the woman said, "I do not need the job. After my most recent assignment, I have more than enough to live well for several years. But the idea of having enough to retire permanently, not to mention the challenge, is appealing. Therefore, I am prepared to take the necessary risks for that price." She half rose from her chair, her grip in her left hand.

"Please be seated, Signora," Napolitano said. "We will meet your price."

"Very good," said the South African. "But there are also certain conditions."

"Such as?"

"The reason you need an outsider in the first place is because the world of security is a leaky sieve. How many people in your organization know of your plan to hire any outsider at all, let alone me?"

"Our principals plus us. So far as we are aware, no one else," Napolitano said.

"I am disturbed by your candor in using the term '*So far as we are aware.*' Please understand, all records of all meetings, files, and dossiers must be destroyed. There must be nothing available to anyone but you and your employers."

"What if any of us are captured?" Hsien Yun-Lo asked. "Although we all obviously take every step to protect our security, as you yourself pointed out, no one is immune. If sufficiently tortured …"

"Why should such a thing happen?" This from Prince Majid. "I doubt any of us would deliberately put himself in harm's way."

"But it happens," the Assassin said calmly. "While I shall feel free at my sole discretion to call off this assignment and to retain my advance fee if any of you are captured, or if I learn that information has been passed on which would, in my opinion, make this job more difficult, I reserve all my rights to do whatever I feel to be in my best interests – and I shall have the final decision on what that will be. *D'accord?*"

"Agreed," said Karaca, striking the nearest ashtray and removing the burnt tobacco from his pipe before tamping in a fresh plug. "What else?"

"I shall disappear. The planning and the operation will be entirely mine. I have full authority and full autonomy to carry out this assignment as and when I choose to do so, with no interference -

absolutely none - from anyone. I shall divulge the details to no one, not to you and not to your principals. You may hear nothing from me again. I may find a way to advise you of when I am prepared to make my move, but this, too, will be entirely at my discretion."

"*Siamo d'accordo,*" Napolitano said. "Anything more?"

"Yes. Although you will have an indirect way of contacting me, there may be a time in an extreme emergency where I will need a means to contact one or all of you."

"Done," replied Karaca. He handed her a small piece of paper. "Here is an encrypted email address. It is simple enough I trust you can remember it. Simple, yes, but, without your individual password you will never be able to access is. Have you a password you prefer?"

"Yes. I was expecting such a security system. My password will be RED ANGEL, all upper case letters with a space between the two words. Rest assured, I will only use it in the most exceptional of circumstances."

"Very well. That code will be programmed in so it contacts all of us, but *only* us."

"Good. Your principals know how to contact me indirectly, the same way they did three weeks ago. Here is the name and account number of my bank in the Cook Islands," she said, handing him a discreet, handwritten business card. "When they tell me that five million, five hundred thousand dollars have been deposited, or when I am fully ready, whichever is later, I will make my move. I will not be hurried, nor will I be subject to interference of any kind."

"Madame," Karaca said, "Please consider that our principals have resources in a position to offer you a great deal of assistance ..."

The woman considered this for a moment. "I will give it careful thought. You are undoubtedly aware of how your principals contacted me. Now you have given me the means of contacting you if need be. At my discretion, I may send one of you a more direct address. If I decide to send you such an address, in addition to what we have discussed, you will mail to that address a single telephone number where I can ring anywhere in the world at any time. I will not reveal my own whereabouts to anyone, but may simply ring that number for the latest information about the Grand Ayatollah's security. Whoever is on the line when I call is not to know where I am calling from or what I am doing. You will simply tell that person that I am employed by you and need the information I request."

"Are there no other ways? Simpler ways?" Karroubi asked.

"Simpler, yes. Quicker, yes. But my security might be compromised. I prefer to receive communication the old fashioned way, thank you."

"How about identity papers?" asked Hsien Yun-Lo.

"I will acquire my own."

"Suppose something should go wrong?" the Chinese man persisted.

"We've already discussed that. Nothing will go wrong unless it comes from your side. I will operate without contacting, or being known to, your principals."

The Arab prince looked shrewdly at the candidate. "Pardon me for seeming so rude, Madame, but what is to prevent you from taking the first five million and disappearing?"

"I told you, Prince Majid, I wish to retire. I am well aware that your principals have unlimited funds. I do not need an army of specialists or even a single sniper of my own kind hunting me down. I would have to spend more protecting myself than the money I had made. It would soon be gone and, most likely, so would I."

"And what," the prince asked, "is to prevent us waiting until the job is done and then refusing to pay you the balance?"

"If that were to happen, I would feel compelled to do what I had to do to ensure the honesty of my employers. I trust my meaning is clear. However, I don't think that will occur, do you?"

Count Napolitano rose. "Gentlemen, if that is all I don't think we need detain our guest any longer. There is, however, one last point. I fully understand you wish to remain anonymous, but you should have a code name, don't you think?"

"Agrippina will do," the woman said. "But if I decide later on that I should have a different name, I will transmit it to you in the same manner as I transmit the request for the telephone number."

Napolitano escorted the woman to the door and opened it. He smiled and held out his hand to the Assassin. "We will be in touch in the agreed manner. In the meantime, you may begin planning – in general terms, of course – so as not to waste too much time. *Ciao Signora* – and good hunting."

"That," the woman remarked, "depends on your good faith. Gentlemen," she concluded. "Might I suggest you remove the button mike I placed under the table last night?"

And she was gone.

3

Looking at the clock on the nightstand, Ezra saw it was 1:30 in the morning. He got up, went to the bathroom, voided himself, then went out through the living room to the kitchen. He knew the steps by heart, so the lack of light did not disturb him.

He opened the fridge and found a glass in the abutting cabinet, which he filled from a bottle of Pellegrino water, closed the refrigerator door, and shuffled back to the living room, where he seated himself in the reclining armchair, the one luxury in this otherwise spartan room.

He switched on the table lamp and took the scrapbook Galit had made ten years earlier as a gift on his thirty-fifth birthday. Ezra Caen was not one to boast about his achievements. He was a very private man. But during the past few months he would often find himself opening this book of memorabilia to remind himself that once upon a time his life might have had some small measure of worth to others.

The first page contained a picture of Galit, Meir, and him at the beach in Ashqelon, in happier times. Turning to the second page of the book, he came upon a front page story which had been published in the Jerusalem Post fourteen years ago. The page, now yellowed with age, showed a picture of a much younger Ezra cradling a small child.

~ ∫ ~

He'd received the radio call five minutes earlier. Older model sedan, dirt-smudged plates, three unidentified males between eighteen and twenty. Suspicious. The car approached the area across the street from the *Egged* bus terminal where a school bus waited at the front.

School kids, half Israeli, half Palestinian going on an outing to the International Peace Park. Trying to show that both sides could live together in peace. Couldn't be a more perfect setup for a suicide bomber.

A car pulled to a stop in a dirt lot five hundred feet ahead of him. Ezra pulled his unmarked car over.

Looking toward the bus, he saw a dozen kids, eight or nine years old. Neatly dressed, backpacks … hard to tell who was Jewish and who was Muslim. The way it should be. As they packed into the bright yellow vehicle they were oblivious to anyone else in the area except the four chaperones.

As Ezra turned his head toward the direction of the parking lot, he saw one of the scruffy young men reach into the back of the car and extract what looked like an Egged driver's jacket and billed cap. He put the jacket on over his tee-shirt and buttoned it. Then he placed the cap on his head at a jaunty angle. A man in the front passenger seat handed him a lunch pail. To Ezra, who'd experienced this sort of thing in the past, the scene looked very much amiss.

The chaperones herded their charges into the back seats of the large bus. The gleeful sounds of shouting and kids engaged in horseplay spilled into the street. Moments later, the man who'd been in the car and who'd donned driver's attire, crossed the street, lunch pail in hand, walking diagonally toward the bus.

"Subject moving toward the vehicle. Doesn't look like a real driver to me," Ezra radioed to an unknown recipient.

"Stay close. I've called the Egged people to be on the alert and make sure the back door's unlocked until they depart. And Ezra …"

"Yes?"

"Be careful, you hear."

Ezra and the driver approached the front door of the bus coming from different points on a triangle. The driver, who paid no attention to anything outside the line of sight to where he was heading, did not see Ezra Caen, a mere twenty feet away.

Ezra noticed the man's right arm seemed to have a slight palsy and his forehead bore a light sheen of perspiration. His face was expressionless. The man mounted the stairwell of the bus. He turned toward the rear and raised his right hand over his head. He bent his elbow and reached back, preparing to toss the box.

It seemed to Ezra that everything took place in slow motion. He drew his weapon, took careful aim following the trajectory of the man's arm, aimed, and slowly exerted pressure on the trigger.

Blam-**BLAM!** The single shot was deafening. Perhaps one-hundredth of a second went by before there was an even louder ka-**BOOM!!!** as the "lunch box" detonated. Less than two seconds later, the entire front end of the bus exploded into flames.

Screaming everywhere! Panic! Without a thought, Ezra ran around to the back door of the bus, yanked it open and commanded in a loud, but calm, voice, in Hebrew and in Arabic, "Out! Out! Out! Now! Right now! Jump! Don't be afraid! Run as fast as you can, as far away as you can!"

Of the dozen children in the back of the bus, he pulled more than half of them out himself. By that time, Egged personnel had come near enough get the remaining children and their chaperones out of the burning inferno. All except one, a small Palestinian girl who'd been trampled by the others and who was sitting on the floor, holding her arm, and moaning.

Without a second thought, Ezra climbed into the bus, grabbed the child in his arms, and, not even thinking of his own safety, tossed the child to a waiting chaperone. There was the shock of an explosion immediately behind him and the next thing he knew Ezra's rear end was scraping the concrete ten feet away from the fatally mauled bus as flames licked at its innards.

The headline in the next day's Jerusalem Post got it almost right. The banner screamed, **"HERO DISARMS SUICIDE BOMBER! SAVES TWELVE CHILDREN ON SCHOOL BUS!"** What was deliberately inaccurate was the description of him as "an off-duty policeman," which his real employer had insisted be printed.

There were other stories about Ezra from time to time in various other newspapers, but he found that story particularly meaningful. He recalled taking a stuffed teddy bear to the little girl when she was in hospital.

Galit reminded him later that he'd never given a teddy bear to his own son.

~ ∫ ~

To see Ezra Caen on the street would have been to have forgotten him a moment later. He was an unprepossessing man, at five-and-a-half feet, shorter than average, and of slight build with a small potbelly. His once dark hair was now wispy and thin, with the bald crown prevalent in males his age and older. If one had looked closely, the observer would have been surprised to note that but for the difference in sex, Caen looked remarkably like a woman who, at that moment, was leaving Santiago de Compostela, Spain for Johannesburg, South Africa.

Never a natty dresser, there always seemed to be a stain of some sort on Ezra Caen's rumpled shirts, and his bifocals were neither stylish nor flattering. In short, he was everyman – not as everyman liked to picture himself, but like everyman truly was.

~ ∫ ~

For the fiftieth time – or maybe the hundredth – in the past half-year, Ezra revisited the miserable existence he'd endured for such a long time. He felt more at peace now than at any time since Galit had left.

When Galit departed, he was not exactly heartbroken. For the past several years they'd never even used the word "love." Truth to tell, they hadn't even *liked* one another. But at least when she had been in the apartment there was *someone* there. She'd cooked to a greater or lesser degree, and she'd kept the place passably clean. After Galit left, Ezra had nothing except emptiness to come home to. Even her occasional biting remarks were more tolerable than the mindless drivel and the banal garbage that passed for entertainment on the small television set. And since Meir's death in a mine explosion on the Gaza border two years ago, there was no one else to talk to, unless he counted the deaf old couple who lived in the next apartment.

During the initial period after Galit moved out, Ezra'd had nothing to do but work the longest hours possible, come home late in the evening, heat food from a can, and collapse onto the bed without even removing his clothes or folding back the bedding. The day after Galit left, he'd tried resorting to alcohol to help dull the void in his life and to get to sleep faster each night. That had worked for about a week.

Early in the second week, he experienced the most excruciating pain he'd ever known. It started in his chest and spread down to his gut, where it had become truly vicious. Initially, Ezra thought he was having an onset of stomach cancer or a heart attack.

Neither was true. It turned out that Ezra Caen was incapable of becoming a full-fledged alcoholic, not because he didn't want to, but because of a quirk of bad – or good – fortune induced by natural causes beyond his control. Prior to Galit's departure, Ezra had hardly ever drunk a drop of alcohol, save the obligatory cup of wine at *Shabbat* and *Pesach* and the occasional toast at a life event. He'd never felt the need for alcohol. Indeed, he'd never liked the taste of the stuff.

Fearing the worst, Ezra had gone to see an internist at Hadassah Hospital. He was admitted immediately, since he'd made many connections during his career. The doctor ran a battery of tests and thankfully ruled out both a heart attack and, even worse, cancer. Then the wise older man, who'd migrated from the Soviet Union many years before asked Ezra, "Permit me to intrude on your privacy by asking if you've recently increased your consumption of alcoholic beverages?"

"Why do you ask? Do you think I could have cirrhosis?"

"Not even close. When did you start seriously drinking?"

'Two weeks ago, when my wife and I separated."

"May I ask whether your ancestors came from Eastern Europe?"

"I haven't the faintest idea, Doctor. I was born in South Africa, but never knew my real parents. I was told they died in some kind of an accident and I was adopted very shortly after my birth."

"A lot of Eastern European Jews emigrated to South Africa in the mid-30s: Litvaks, Poles, Ukrainians. Were your parents Jewish?" the doctor inquired, frowning and staring at a light on his phone, which had started blinking.

"I don't know," Ezra said, rubbing his two thumbs and forefingers together. "Why?"

The doctor picked up a thick magazine with a plain white cover. "Some recent clinical research studies have shown that many men of Eastern European Jewish stock experience the same symptoms you've been experiencing after drinking alcohol."

"What causes that, Doctor?"

"In plain language, it seems Ashkenazic Jews have an enzyme that actively fights alcoholism in the most natural way possible: it makes it so uncomfortable that you'll think twice before consuming alcohol. That's probably why there are so few Jewish alcoholics."

"So nature's given me a lifetime ban from alcohol?"

"Pretty much so, Mr. Caen. That's not to say you can't have the occasional glass of wine. That's not enough alcohol to stir up your insides. But if you want to drink more than that, it's entirely up to you – and you can live with the consequences."

"I accept what you say. But how do you suggest I deal with -- ?"

"The separation? I don't have any simple answers. I could send you to a counselor or a psychiatrist, but the end result would be the same: the only one who can solve the problem is you – and the only way you can start to solve the problem is to face it directly. Make no mistake, Mister Caen, for the first several weeks you'll live through twenty-four hours a day of sheer, unmitigated hell."

"Several weeks?"

"Maybe more, maybe less. Eventually you'll have twenty-three hours and fifty-nine minutes a day of hell, and one minute a day of relative peace. Then the hours of hell will start to decrease and you'll find that somehow life goes on, even yours. In any event, here's a prescription for a very mild sedative to help you sleep for the next few nights. It's non-renewable because I don't want to encourage you to be stupid enough to start relying on drugs instead of alcohol. Good luck, Mister Caen."

With that, he shook Ezra's hand and sent him on his way.

Ezra Caen stopped drinking alcohol "cold turkey" that night. It had now been five-and-a-half months since he'd last touched a drop of alcohol. He used half of the sedatives, threw the rest away, and started to dig out from under the wreckage of his life.

~ ∫ ~

Ezra was forty-five. He could retire from his present line of work in two years. But work had been his life for as long as he could remember. His one consolation was that his superiors – and as he had ascended the ladder in his chosen field they became fewer as *he* had become more and more the superior – acknowledged that there was no one better, more astute, or more successful in his field than he.

Twenty-five years ago, when he was in the IDF, he'd fallen head-over-heels in lust with Galit, when they were doing their military tours of duty at the same base. Galit had just celebrated her nineteenth birthday. By almost every objective measure, she was one of the ten most desirable women he'd ever seen in his life. The face of an angel framed in blonde straight hair. Not tall – 5'3" at most – her body was slender everywhere except for her high, thrusting breasts. And a walk that could drive any man insane with desire.

With danger facing them twenty-four hours a day, and with those moments of danger yielding to hours of boredom, it was only natural that the two of them drifted from frankly appreciative stares, to holding hands and talking under the clear, star-filled skies, far from Jerusalem and Tel Aviv. From there, it was a simple leap to touching one another, caressing ... and more. Like most young people everywhere, they were immune to any consequences. They lived for the passion of the moment, and it was overwhelming beyond anything they'd ever known.

Two months after their first time together, Galit discovered she was pregnant. Ezra had no idea what to do – an abortion was unthinkable, - and while Ezra's commander had concluded that the young soldier was as brilliant and naturally talented a detective as anyone he'd ever met in his life, being a cop was not designed to lead to the wealth and lifestyle Galit believed she deserved. She knew, as exceedingly beautiful women often do, that much of her future depended on an accident of birth that had made her a consummate object of desire. Now that accident had been compromised by another.

Two more months went by. Galit was torn between the motherly instinct of nurturing what was growing inside her and the stark realization that if she kept the child, it meant her own childhood's end – the end of a carefree life and *freedom* – freedom from a child *and* freedom from a man who, although she found him attractive if a bit simple in bed, promised a life in purgatory.

Ezra was not certain of his own feelings. It was one thing to feel that intense few seconds of the strongest pleasure one human being can give to – or take from – another. It was yet another to have one's life circumscribed by events before one was ready to accept responsibility for the unexpected – and largely unwanted – occasion of *another* life coming onto the scene. One that ate and shat and demanded attention twenty-four hours a day. He'd heard from a couple of his buddies who'd been in similar straits that the unbridled sex on demand came to a screeching halt with the arrival of the so-called "bundle of joy."

In the end, though neither of them truly wanted or was prepared for it, they did the "honorable" thing. Their parents scraped their hard-earned *shekels* together and somehow managed to give them a wedding party with over a hundred guests. By that time, Galit was five months along and, although still attractive, it was hard to hide that she was thickening.

Their military obligations came to an end a month short of their son's arrival and they now faced the specter of finding and furnishing a tiny, threadbare apartment in *Bet Hatikvah*, which, as Ezra remarked sourly for the two years they struggled in this ugly backwater town, was "a pimple on the arsehole of the Negev Desert."

Life was anything but easy for the young Caens. Ezra floated from job to job as a cashier in a general store, a construction worker, a gardener (how does one "garden" sand?), and even as a bartender-cum-bouncer at the town's only nightclub. Galit kept the weight she'd put on carrying little Meir. The demands of the baby, coupled with the remoteness of the place, the absolute lack of anything to do, and the ever-threatening shortage of money, weighed heavily on their necks and contributed to breaking the back of their marriage early on.

Still, the young couple struggled valiantly to keep up the pretense that they were in love with one another, even though their definition of "love" was an amorphous one.

Three years later, it seemed that fortune finally smiled on them. Ezra's former military commander had become involved in *Sayeret Matkal*, the IDF special forces, known throughout the IDF simply as "the unit." *Sayeret Matkal* served as a field intelligence-gathering unit and conducted deep reconnaissance behind enemy lines to obtain strategic intelligence. The unit also shouldered the tasks of counterterrorism and hostage rescue beyond Israel's borders. The commander had predicted great things for Ezra early on, and had followed with regret his protégé's declining life trajectory. When his former mentor offered young Caen a career-starting position in the unit, Ezra couldn't say yes fast enough.

Although life changed materially and geographically for the Caens – the *Bet Hatikvah* slum-dwelling was replaced by a modern, air-conditioned, brightly-furnished apartment in *Petah Tiqva*, a suburb of Tel Aviv, courtesy of *Sayeret Matkal*, Ezra was home considerably less than he had been when they'd lived in the desert. The financial rewards were greater, but Ezra Caen had traded one marriage for another – he was "at the office" or even out of country more often than he was home.

When Meir reached his fifth birthday and enrolled in kindergarten, Galit found herself with time on her hands. She attended a local gym four days a week. After a month she obtained a job there as a fitness trainer. The weight she'd put on melted away. Within half a year, she was down to her pre-pregnancy weight and, with the application of emollients and makeup, she displayed the eye-stopping beauty and desirability that had earlier captivated more than one man.

It seemed almost foreordained that Galit would drift into an affair with one of her co-workers. Ezra was furious that his wife had strayed from the marriage bed and threatened immediate divorce, not to mention the dire consequences he would bring to her paramour. But in the end he did not carry through on either of his threats, first because he feared being alone, paying spousal support and child support, and second because when he reflected on what she had said – since he was hardly ever home anyway, either as a husband or as a father, what did he expect? – he found her reasoning to be unassailable.

While the trust between them seemed irretrievably ruptured, nothing else really changed. Ezra buried himself deeper in his work to the extent that he hardly ever saw his son, let alone his wife; and Galit drifted from one sad affair to another without ever attaining the love she so much needed. Matters went on like that for several years – two lonely people with no exit from the hell each had created for the other, and a child who was left to his own devices. On his eighteenth birthday, Meir joined the Israel Defense Forces, looking for the caring parents he'd never had. Meir had grown up to be just like them.

The tragedy of Meir's death in one of hundreds of daily border tragedies severed the last ties that Galit and Ezra had to one another, and their marriage had spiraled down into each blaming the other. Perhaps it was just as well that Galit had had the courage to call it over. By then, still in her early forties, her youthful looks had faded. She'd put on an extra thirty pounds and had become a hard-looking, bleached blonde woman who looked ten years older than her true age.

~ ∫ ~

Ezra Caen did not consider himself a particularly bad man, nor, as things had turned out, could he claim to have led a worthwhile life in the things that mattered. He just happened to suffer from the same disease as everyone else: he happened to be human.

4

In another era, the Assassin's preparation would have been far different. She would have gone to the Johannesburg Public Library or the library at the University of the Witwatersrand to commence her research. But today the iPad, the iPhone, and the Samsung Galaxy S-something were fast making the Personal Computer as much of a dinosaur as "snail mail" and the fax machine. Researching every paper written on what she needed to know was needlessly complicated.

During her first evening back at the remote farm outside Bloemfontein, she typed in her password – 9268@job.za – and entered Google's search engine. For the next several hours, she accessed many subjects and pulled up an average of ninety entries for each. Wikipedia contained the best general introduction, but it never ceased to amaze the Assassin how much she could learn through blogs, both credited and anonymous.

Back in the day, one would have sought out denizens of the darker underbellies of Brussels, Amsterdam, and Berlin. Deals were made in clandestine surroundings – false storefronts, dead-end alleys – with cloak-and-dagger arrangements more akin to fog-shrouded nights in a Nineteenth Century London graveyard than the hurry-up world of Twenty-first Century Piccadilly Circus, Times Square, or the Champs Elysée.

Today, with eBay, Craigslist, and their myriad copycat competitors, one could purchase anything anonymously, either directly or through an intermediary. All you needed was a PayPal account or, better yet, a prepaid PayPal card, which offered further layers of protection from disclosing one's true identity. Bloggers arrogantly provided detailed instructions on how to build any sort of weapon up to and including submachine guns, assault weapons, and rocket launchers. And if the purchase exceeded a certain amount, the seller even provided free shipping anywhere in the world.

"Agrippina" recalled that day when she was thirteen and had first read the by-then ten-year-old novel, *The Day of the Jackal*. Although that book still held a thrill for her, the details of that novel seemed so much a part of another time – so romantically naïve, so *quaint.*

After reading more than a hundred comprehensive references about her target, whose every word was paramount in the Islamic Republic of Iran, the Assassin scoured every speech or edict the Great Man had delivered in the last thirty years – each of which had found its way onto the internet – for the next two weeks. By so doing, she constructed a most detailed and accurate picture of Iran's current emissary to God, from his earliest days to the present.

The Grand Ayatollah Khamenei didn't miss a chance to call the United States "the great Satan" and to condemn the Zionist state as "the little Satan."

The Assassin thought for a fleeting moment that there was something that did not quite ring true about the consistently passionate vituperation against the Jewish state. For one thing, the extraordinarily secret oil pipeline, which ran from Iran through Saudi Arabia to Israel even in the darkest days of the wars in the Middle East, and which had provided Israel with its critical oil supplies during the days of the long-discredited Shah Mohammad Reza Pahlavi, had never, to her knowledge, been shut down.

The Assassin recalled auditing a psychology class at Stellenbosch University where the professor said that the opposite of love is not hate; the closest emotions between two people are love and hate; the opposite of love or hate is *indifference.* By all rights, if the enmity between the Islamic Republic and the Zionist State was so overwhelming, why was there such passion on both sides?

The Assassin read voraciously, planned meticulously, and possessed the capacity to store in her mind an enormous amount of factual information on the off chance that she might later have a use for it. In that respect, she was very much like the computers she used to assist her in her research, with one exception. Lawyers call it the ability to think on one's feet – the ability to make tactical maneuvers which change as instantly as circumstances change.

But now she needed to work out answers to the three most critical questions that confronted her: *when, where, and how should the hit take place?*

~ ∫ ~

The answer to *when* came three nights later as she lay in her bed watching a trashy "reality show" from the States. Khamenei spoke only at special gatherings, such as an occasional Friday Prayer or at commemoration ceremonies of one sort or another. The Leader met with foreign dignitaries, almost exclusively Muslim, but limited any televised and public words to generalities, such as Iran's support for the country or entity whose emissary he was meeting, Iran's peaceful Islamic nature, and Iran's eagerness to expand trade and contacts with the friendly country in question. He pointedly did not meet with representatives of Western powers and did not travel overseas. If anyone wished to see him, that person must be willing to travel to Iran.

Ultimately, she concluded that there was a single eleven day period each year when, notwithstanding illness, bad weather, or even international catastrophe, totally irrespective of any considerations of personal danger, Grand Ayatollah *Sayyid* Ali Khamenei, the Supreme Ruler of Iran, would stand up publicly and show himself in venues throughout the Islamic Republic. From that moment forward the Assassin's preparations moved out of the research stage and into a program of practical planning.

Next, she considered alternative places for the deed to take place. Iran was huge – nearly one-third larger than South Africa. Tehran, occupied the central-Northwest portion of the country. Four hundred fifty-two miles to the northwest, nearly on the Azerbaijani border, the summer resort town of Tabriz, 5,000 feet above sea level, sat at the confluence of the Quru and Aji Rivers. Mashhad, the Supreme Leader's birthplace, was situated more than a thousand miles away, 560 miles east of Tehran, on the Turkmenistan frontier, at an elevation 2,000 feet lower than Tabriz. As a result, Mashhad enjoyed cool winters, pleasant springs, mild summers, and beautiful autumns.

Either of those border cities promised a quick escape route out of Iran if things went wrong. On the other hand, the holiest of Iranian cities, Qom, less than ninety-two miles south of Tehran, would place her even closer to the center of the country. She could become simply another anonymous face in the crowd if she dressed like a man, or she could obey the rules of *hijab* and wear a dark *chador* which would make her even less conspicuous as she made her way to the nearest accessible frontier.

While Tehran was an option, it was more the center of politics than a religious seat. Khamenei would be much more at ease, and thus less suspecting, among his own people, the clerics, in someplace other than the capital. That narrowed the consideration to Mashhad, Tabriz, and Qom.

Ultimately the Assassin decided she would have to explore each of the three cities to determine the most propitious place to carry out her assignment. During the time before her window of opportunity, she would do as she had done on other assignments. She would immerse herself in the land of the ancient Shahs: eat, sleep, dress, and even *smell* like an Iranian. Before the appointed day and hour, she would *become* Iranian. And then, like time, the greatest thief of all, she would quietly slip the bonds of that accursed nation seconds after she had done the deed.

There was no great hurry to accomplish this. There were four months to go.

OCTOBER - NOVEMBER

5

On Tuesday, October 3, the Assassin received word from her bank in the Cook Islands that $5,500,000 U.S. had been deposited to her account.

"Agrippina" was a chameleon, able to change her identity in a matter of moments, from man to woman, old to young, spry to deathly ill, and back again. At five-foot-five inches, she was tall enough to pass for either a fairly short man or a moderately, but not excessively, tall woman. Without a wig, she wore her hair in a short unisex style, which allowed for instantaneous changes, and since its natural color was a medium brown it would pass unnoticed almost anywhere. If the natural shape, length, or color of her hair needed alteration, she could change it in an instant by the simplest of wigs, making it still easier to fit in anywhere at any time and to be forgotten a moment later. She could appear plain, but with a touch of carefully applied makeup and appropriate supporting undergarments, she could remake herself into a siren if need be. The Assassin's ability to make any change she needed within five minutes could be the difference between success and failure, between life and death, in her profession.

In the latter part of the twentieth century such ability to change was by no means unheard-of, but it had been slower, cumbersome, and infinitely more difficult. Back then, being what she was entailed purchasing or stealing numerous passports, posing for hundreds of grainy photographs to get the right ones, then hoping that the border patrolmen would not look *too* closely to see if the face in the photograph matched closely enough to escape detection.

She thought about this idly as she flipped through her iPad pictures. Every face was different, but every one was clearly hers. No more grainy ambiguity. These were sharp, full-color portraits, whether head-on or side-profile. Any frontier agent on duty would swear that the photo on the passport in question was that of the bearer.

Nowadays, many governments used radio frequency identification (RFID) enabled passports. E-passports contained microscopic RFID chips, which utilized basic access control (BAC) to allow the extraction of personal information without the bearer actually handing over the document. Extended Access Control protected other information, such as fingerprint data. Even with the requirement of an encrypted key to use, passport hackers found ways to read stored information remotely.

Several, but by no means all, paper passports contained embedded microelectronic chips to ensure that the holder of the passport was the person he or she claimed to be. Thus, the archaic "maybe it is, maybe it isn't" had gone the way of the manual typewriter. Nowadays surveillance was left to electronic interpreters which might not be able to think tactically like humans, but which were nearly impossible to fool when it came to information. On the other hand, many fingerprint scanners were so easy to fool that a reasonably intelligent nine-year-old could do it.

Unquestionably, it was *possible* to gain entry and exit into a country, no matter how sophisticated, unless it was a country the size of Monaco. In the United States, there were miles-long "holes" in borders. One could tunnel underground, arrive by small boat coming into an unwatched bay at midnight, or even drop in from a low-altitude aircraft. If one were traveling in an EU country, the borders were not patrolled at all.

The value of a passport lay in having security once in the country, being able to check into a hotel, except those that were less than reputable, and being able to exchange money. Once in-country, the banker, hotelier, or local petty government official simply did not have the time, the patience, or the expensive equipment necessary to closely check each passport. Given sufficient nerve and ingenuity, the game had not changed much. Only a few of the rules had changed. Not an insurmountable problem.

One of the easiest ways to get into and out of a country anonymously was to use a legitimate passport issued by an "off" country – one that, while not entirely unknown, was not a major player on the world stage, and then convert in-country to a more readily identifiable means of identification. The "off" country should, of course, be on reasonably friendly terms with the host country. Traveling to Iran on an American, British, Canadian, Senegalese, or Gambian passport was plain stupid. On the other hand, coming into Iran from South Africa, Zimbabwe, Turkey, Ecuador, Mexico, or Belarus made much more sense.

The Assassin had often used an old, well-worn British trick to successfully obtain several South African passports, and now she set out to do so again.

On October 7, she motored through the small villages of the flat, boundless plain of *Vrystaat* Province, the former Orange Free State, an Afrikaner redoubt. She had grown up in the area and knew it well.

Her first stop was Petrusburg, a farming town of 558 souls halfway between the provincial capital of Bloemfontein and the diamond mines of Kimberley. 92% of Petrusburg was still never-say-die white and spoke only Afrikaans. The Old Church was situated between the town's two main streets, Pretorius and Ossewa.

The graveyard of the *Nederduitse Gereformeerde Kerk* proved invaluable. The Assassin found a stone to suit her purpose, that of a young boy, Petrus Jooste, who had died of an unidentified illness at the age of four in August 1972. Had he lived, he would have been very close to the Assassin's age.

The elderly vicar was most courteous and helpful when the visitor presented herself at the parsonage and advised him that she was an amateur genealogist attempting to trace the family tree of a family called Jooste. She had been advised that this particular line of Joostes, not related to A.J.C. Jooste, after whom the local high school was named, had settled on the outskirts of Petrusburg in years past. She wondered, respectfully, if the parish records might be able to assist in her research.

The vicar was the heart of kindness, and on their way over to the Kerk, a compliment on the simple beauty of the Dutch Reform-style building and a contribution to the donations box for the restoration fund, only served to make the vicar even kinder. The records showed that both Jooste parents had died during the past five years, and, alas, their only child, Petrus, had been buried in this very churchyard over forty years before. The Assassin flipped through the pages of the parish register of births, marriages, and deaths for the year 1968. The records for the month of August with the name of Jooste, written in bold hand, caught her eye: Petrus Augustus Jooste, born August 17, 1968 in the *Nederduitse Gereformeerde Kerk*, parish of Emmaus, Transgariep Administrative Division, *Oranje Vrystaat*.

She noted the details, thanked the vicar for his courtesy, and left.

Some hours later, she repeated the same procedure at the *Gereformeerde Kerke in Suid-Afrika*, in the slightly larger metropolis of DeWetsdorp, another Afrikaner stronghold. This time the gravestone she selected was that of Hannelore Christiaana deWet, born October 13, 1968, died in childbirth December 10, 1993.

The Assassin then made two trips to the Central Registry of Births, Marriages, and Deaths in Bloemfontein. The first time she presented as a man, where a helpful young assistant clerk accepted the Assassin's business card showing "him" to be a partner in a firm of Solicitors in Pretoria and his explanation that he was trying to locate the whereabouts of the grandchildren of one of the firm's clients, who had recently died and left a trust of which his grandchildren were the residuary beneficiaries. One of these grandchildren was Petrus Augustus Jooste, born August 17, 1968 in the *Nederduitse Gereformeerde Kerk*, parish of Emmaus, Transgariep Administrative Division, *Vrystaat* province.

The clerk was as kind and forthcoming as the vicar had been. A search of the records showed that the child in question had been registered precisely in accordance with the information the Assassin had provided, but had died on August 28, 1972 of an undisclosed illness. Proffering several South African Rand notes, the Assassin purchased certified copies of both the birth and death certificates.

The following day, the Assassin returned to the Registry, this time as a woman. After ensuring that the first clerk was otherwise engaged, she enlisted the assistance of an older female clerk, this time on the pretext that she was a paralegal for a firm of solicitors in George seeking information on one Hannelore Christiaana deWet, born October 13,

1968 in DeWetsdorp. After receiving the sad news of Mevrou deWet's passing, the Assassin purchased certified copies of the deceased's birth and death certificates.

In Pretoria, the Assassin also made two trips, one as a woman and the other as a man, to the Passport Office where she duly filled out the necessary *BI-73*, *BI-9* and *BI-529* forms, submitted her fingerprints, both with the same putty-carved "replacements," the requisite photographs, and birth certificates (she had conveniently disposed of the death certificates) for Hannelore Christiaana deWet and Petrus Jooste. She filled in the application forms, making sure to state exactly the right age, date of birth, sex, height, color of hair, and color of eyes. Under the designation "Profession,' the Assassin put down "Farmer" for Mevrou deWert and "Educator" for Meneer Jooste. She filled in the full names of the parents of each of these applicants, and provided certified copies of the birth certificates. Since those certificates had been authenticated by the Central Registry of Births, Marriages, and Deaths in Bloemfontein, they were duly accepted for filing. She then made two trips to the Department of Drivers Licences, where she demonstrated her driving skills and quickly qualified for a pair of South African Drivers' Licences.

The following week, the Assassin applied for Visas for each of the persons named in the new passports to visit the Islamic Republic of Iran for up to 90 days, commencing October 16.

During the next two weeks, the Assassin flew to Harare where, using the same process she had used in South Africa, with a substantial under-the-table payment in South African Rand, which, in cash-strapped Zimbabwe, were far more acceptable than Zimbabwean dollars, for immediate service, she obtained a man's and woman's Zimbabwean passport, visas, and driving licences; to Windhoek, where, by greasing the palms of an older passport officer with additional Namibian dollars, she obtained two Namibian passports in different names the same day she applied; and to Moroni, where, with the help of several thousand Comorian francs, she picked up two passports from the independent, if universally suspect, nation of Comoros.

~ ∫ ~

The Assassin next considered *how* the Ayatollah should be removed. She dismissed the idea of an explosive. It would be cumbersome, and unless she wanted to be near enough to it to be maimed or killed herself, she would have no control over it once it left her possession. Plastique explosives installed under vehicles had been derailed by increasingly sophisticated detection devices.

The injection of poison into the human body, whether by way of food or syringe, had severe limitations. Undoubtedly the Supreme Leader of Iran not only had bodyguards who surrounded him every minute of his life, but everything he ate was pre-tasted and analyzed. The idea of injection was riddled with risks. The Assassin would have to be in such close proximity to the target that the chances of successful delivery and subsequent escape were minimal.

The clear method of choice was the oldest: from the beginning of the human conflict, the only sure way one human being could kill another was to use a projectile to make a hole in the victim's body that was large enough or deep enough that the life fluids would drain out and the target would die before the drainage could be stopped. A single, clean shot from a distance: was the only way the Assassin could be in total control, the only way that she, and only she, would be planner and executioner, the one ultimately responsible for the deed.

The Assassin had no intention of purchasing a "one-off" from an illicit small arms dealer, reputable or not, in Brussels, The Hague, or

South Africa. Regardless of how clean the deal was, there would be at least one more person implicated, at least one other person whose mouth might not be controlled. While the weapon itself would probably be perfectly suited for the task, the Assassin would have to learn everything there was to know about that particular piece in a very brief window of time, by no means a foolproof task.

No matter. For the past decade she'd come to know and love her duplicate weapons of choice. They had served her well and had never let her down. In each weapon, the chamber and the breech were no larger than 3 inches in diameter, which meant they could not be repeaters, since a gas chamber would be larger than that, nor did they contain a bulky spring mechanism. They were bolt-action rifles with incredibly slim working parts.

Neither weapon had a bolt with a handle that stuck out sideways like a Mauser 7.92 x 55 mm or a Lee Enfield 303. The bolts slid straight back towards the shoulder, gripped between forefinger and thumb for the fitting of the bullet into the breech. There were no trigger guards. The triggers themselves were detachable so they could be fitted just before firing. The entire mechanism could pass into a tubular compartment for storage and carrying, and the compartment which carried it would neither attract attention nor look remotely like a weapon.

The guns were not of a heavy caliber and the barrel of each was precisely 14 inches in length. The rifles were accurate to a distance of 150 yards, 1½ times the length of a football field. The downside was that there would be almost no chance of a second shot, since it would take several seconds to extract the spent cartridge and reload a fresh one, close the breech, and take aim again. The only possibility was if the Assassin used a silencer on the first shot, that shot was a complete miss, and it was not noticed by anyone nearby. Even if she got a first hit through the target's head she would need the silencer to affect her own escape. She would need several minutes of time before anyone nearby had even a rough idea of where the bullet had come from.

The Assassin would use an explosive bullet, mercury rather than glycerine, since mercury was much cleaner. All the woodwork of the handgrip beneath the barrels of each of the rifles had been removed, as had the entire stock, further reducing the weight and bulk of the weapon. For firing, the rifle had a frame stock akin to a Sten gun. Each of the three sections unscrewed into three separate rods. When used, the weapon would be attached to a tripod to steady its aim.

Finally, the Assassin's rifles each had a completely effective silencer and a dependable telescopic sight which, like the rifles themselves, were removable for storage and carrying. The killer was familiar with every component of her rifles. She'd taken them into and out of hot spots in many countries. They had never failed her.

Now, with the *when* and *how* in place, it was time to explore the alternative venues concerning *where.*

6

Wednesday, October 16 was a brilliant spring day in Johannesburg. The Assassin, who had assumed a male identity, boarded Qatar Airways Flight 585 at 1:45 p.m., an hour before takeoff, for the eight hour flight from OR Tambo Airport in Kempton Park to Doha International Airport. "He" watched a movie for a while, then took a long nap. The Boeing 777 arrived in Doha just before 11:30 that night.

The Assassin had a 1½ hour layover in Qatar, during which "he" purchased the print edition of yesterday's Tehran *Times*, the English-language Iranian newspaper, skimmed it while sipping a cup of hot, sweet tea, then discarded it just before he boarded Flight 484 to Imam Khomeini Airport, thirty miles from the center of Tehran. He arrived at IKA at 3:35 in the morning. The Assassin had calculated the taxi fare from the airport to central Tehran at 350,000 Rials – USD $29.00 – and had booked a room at the Escan, a three-star hotel between Somayeh and Engelhab Avenues, rather than the far more ostentatious

Espinas. Since it was much easier to enter and exit Iran as a man, the Assassin had booked the hotel reservation in the name of Rudolph Hostetler, petrochemical buyer, resident of Swakopmund, Erongo Province, Namibia.

"Agrippina" declared 12,285,000 rials, a thousand U.S. dollars, when he arrived at the capital. If necessary, he would exchange South African Rand for rials in one of the numerous offices on Ferdosi Street.

During "Meneer Hostetler's" first day in Tehran, he slept until mid-afternoon, then took the elevator down to the gift shop and purchased a detailed city map of Tehran and a larger-scale one of the Islamic Republic. Returning to his room, he studied the maps in great detail and concluded that the only spot near Tehran where the target would appear with absolute certainty was the place he'd investigate the following day.

~ ∫ ~

Sunday, October 19, was not a holy day for Tehran's Islamic population. Meneer Hostetler hired a taxicab, which took him south of the capital, just off the Qom road, to the Behesht-e Zahra cemetery.

His destination seemed to be very much a work in progress. He'd read the night before that the government has budgeted USD $2 billion for the erection of a complex that would cover five thousand acres and include not just the centerpiece, the Imam Khomeini Mausoleum, but also a university, a seminary, and a hundred shops. According to the brochures, when completed it would be the largest Muslim shrine anywhere in the world. Today, he found nothing to indicate when it might ultimately be finished.

The taxi driver stopped at the inner edge of a huge car park, which, he told Hostetler, could accommodate 20,000 vehicles. But today the park was nearly empty. The Assassin felt this was what it would look like had he turned up at Johannesburg's Sandton City Shopping Centre after a complete evacuation. As Hostetler exited the vehicle, he saw a few other vehicles and a smattering of strange little tents. When he asked about these structures, the driver explained that Tehranis regularly made a pilgrimage to see the mausoleum and to spend the night in a tent in the car park.

Hostetler approached the men's entrance, removed his shoes, and handed them to the attendant on duty. Passing through the curtain, he was given a pat-down search. Since the Assassin had bound her chest with a tight band, as she'd done many times before when enduring such a search, she had no worry about anyone discovering her true sex.

Hostetler, who carried only a backpack containing his lunch, a notebook, three pens, and what looked like a long, narrow camera lens, passed through the x-ray machine with no trouble. Then he was sent on his way with a smile and a welcome.

When he arrived at the enormous main building, it seemed as empty as the parking lot. He observed a huge mass of concrete, metal pillars, and uncountable glass chandeliers. For all the encomiums he'd found in the slick brochures, the centerpiece of Iranian Islam resembled nothing more nor less than a tidied-up building site.

Proceeding to the glass-sided room that held the tombs of the late Ayatollah Khomeini and his second son, Ahmad, who'd died in 1995, Hostetler noticed several women praying and pushing money and letters through openings in the walls and windows. He mentally calculated the distances between the vast spaces, trying to determine if there would be any place within the structure from which he could line up a good shot and, more important, escape after the deed was done. As he looked up, he observed stained glass windows decorated with seventy-two tulips and four towers, each of which was 91 meters high, reflecting the age at which Khomeini had died.

Leaving the main building, he wandered about the complex. There were plenty of half-constructed spaces where the Assassin could hide and get off the single shot that would dispatch his target, but the area, which was now ghostly in its vast emptiness, would be packed elbow-to-elbow during the Days of Awe on which he would strike.

After a few more hours calculating angles and distances, in between nursing several cups of hot tea and sweet pastries, the killer concluded this place would be far too risky.

The following morning, Meneer Hostetler checked out of the Escan Hotel. During the next ten days, he traveled to three different cities. On the tenth day, the Assassin found the most conducive place for the assassination to take place.

~ ∫ ~

When the Assassin returned to the huge, ungainly capital, he took a cab to *Terminal-e-jonoob*, the Southern bus terminal, where he anonymously rented a left-luggage locker to store a large duffel bag he'd purchased in the Bazaar. The bag contained a tripod, a small telescope, and some hardware that may have been just about anything, but, in fact consisted of a fourteen-inch gun barrel, a silencer, which looked like a large gray sausage, and fittings. Upon entering the Islamic Republic, these items had been packed partly into the Assassin's checked luggage and partly inside a carry-on bag, to avoid any hint of their true purpose. Now, almost everything she needed was in one place, in-country, and it would not excite any interest when she next returned to Iran bringing the rest of what she needed for her task.

Returning to Imam Khomeini Airport, Meneer Hostetler checked through customs, was cleared immediately, and boarded his return flight to South Africa.

7

The meeting of the executive board of the Ministry of Intelligence and National Security of the Islamic Republic of Iran convened promptly at 11:00 a.m. the following morning. Ten men sat around an oval conference table. Heyder Moslehi, sixty-four and a survivor of numerous changes in government, chaired the meeting.

There was a soft knock. Moslehi rose, went to the door, opened it, and embraced a man his own age, who had a pleasant, open face. Immediately, the assembly stood as one and applauded as the man, Hassan Rouhani, the newly-elected President of Iran, entered, found an empty chair, and sat. "I trust I am not intruding?" he said.

"Anything but, Mister President. We feel most honored," Moslehi responded. "Are you certain you won't accept the chairman's chair?"

"Sixteen years was quite enough, thank you." Rouhani had occupied Moslehi's position from 1989 to 2005, when he became Iran's chief nuclear arms negotiator with the West. Unlike his predecessor, Mahmoud Ahmadinejad, Hassan Rouhani was known as a moderate, who was intent on healing the breach between the Islamic Republic and the West, if it could be done within the limited parameters of his power. The executive board was equally aware that even if Rouhani had captured one hundred percent of the popular vote in the election instead of fifty-one percent, the sole and exclusive power – the *real* authority in Iran, rested entirely in the hands of the Supreme Leader, the Grand Ayatollah Khamenei, and that while Rouhani was much more palatable than his outspoken predecessor, in the grand scheme of things it made little difference.

"Gentlemen," Moslehi began, after they'd all reseated themselves. "I trust you have all read the transcribed record of the interrogation?"

There were affirmative nods around the table, even from President Rouhani. "Rahman," he said, turning to a uniformed man five years younger. "You've been the chief of the Supreme Leader's body guard for … ?"

"A decade-and-a-half, Mister Chairman."

"How many attempts have there been on his life?"

"Nine that we know of. None successful, Praise Allah."

"All from within the country?"

"Yes, Excellency."

"Does what you read concern you?"

"Of course, Excellency. For many reasons. First, even the Arab did not know whether the threat came from a male or female. Especially dangerous in a nation like ours where women have taken to being more … conservative."

"Hiding under a *chador* you mean," said Yousef Abbasi, at thirty-five the youngest man in the group. He made no pretense of buying into what he believed to be the hypocritical quasi-mores of the fundamentalists who currently ran the country. Still, he had not been purged because he was fiercely loyal to his country, right or wrong, and because he had cemented relations with the opposition, which a large number of Iranians believed would be waiting to come back to power when the present government fell.

"True," the Chairman said. "Such a person would not only be able to shift sexual identities, but also affect different ages, and other characteristics. Although we have no indication one way or the other from the mangled garbage our Hezbollah friends got, we can assume that the risk comes from a foreigner."

"The worst possible scenario. The question is how do we deal with such a threat, is that what I'm hearing Mister Chairman?"

"Indeed. Saeed, you're head of recruitment. What resources do we have within our service?"

"Fifty agents, well-trained by Iranian standards."

"And by international standards?"

"You mean like DGSE, SIS ... ?"

"Or better."

"What do you mean, 'or better' Mister Chairman?" The question came from seventy-year-old Ghasem Habib, the oldest member, a legendary retired veteran of SAVAK and now a consultant to the Islamic government. He knew the answer, as did the rest of them.

There was silence around the table.

Saeed Paria, like Habib, knew exactly what the chairman meant. "None," he said.

"Gentlemen," President Rouhani said quietly. "We are all beating about the bush and we all know exactly what is being said. You want me to say it? All right, I'll say it. As good as our service is and as proud as we are, there is only one counterintelligence service capable of dealing with this threat: an agency of a state we don't even pretend to mention by name because it doesn't exist."

No one displayed shock or anger. Rouhani was, first and foremost, a professional. He knew that no matter what the country, the ideology, or the nature of one's political friends or enemies of the moment, people in their circle had a tight-knit community filled with respect even for the worst of "enemies," since law enforcement officers throughout the world considered themselves the "good guys," united against the "bad guys."

"How would we even approach them?" This from Omid Ghormani, in appearance a nondescript, middle aged political hack, in reality the service's most astute spymaster.

"What alternative do we have? We admit, if only around this table, that we might not be able to handle this thing alone," the chairman remarked. At that moment there was a soft rap on the door. "Come in," Moslehi called out.

Two women, silent as ghosts, their heads covered respectfully, approached the table and set eleven silver tea sets and small chinaware plates around the table. They left the room, but returned a few moments later wheeling in a cart bearing three plates of pastries and five filled teapots. After they had left, the men continued their conversation.

"For all we know their government might be behind the plan," Habib remarked.

"Possible," Moslehi replied. "The last Jew living in the Third Reich?"

"I am quite familiar with the story," President Rouhani said. He was not only a politician, cleric, lawyer, and academic, but was also fluent in English, German, French, Russian and Arabic, along with his native Persian. "Although Hitler publicly proclaimed that he wanted a *Judenfrei* world, that's the very *last* thing he wanted. As long as he had Jews as scapegoats, he could hold onto his power and control by directing anger and hatred away from the shortfalls of his own government. Mister Chairman, I concur. Iran needs the Zionist archenemy and Israel needs the Iranian nuclear threat, not because there is any possibility of mutually assured destruction by either state, but because every political leader in every nation in the world needs a target beyond his borders. I think we can agree that it is *not* in Israel's best interests, under any circumstance, that the Imam be taken out."

"What about the fringe groups?" Abbasi asked.

"There will always be fringe groups, my young friend," Habib remarked. "Have you any idea what percentage of a country has successfully motivated revolutions in the last hundred years? The answer may surprise you, Yousef. *One percent.*"

"I don't believe that," Abbasi retorted. "The Iranian Revolution that overthrew the Shah was …"

"Ten percent of the population," Habib said. "Ten times the average."

"Can that be correct, Mister Chairman?" Abbasi asked.

"It can and it is," Moslehi responded. "I have no doubt that minority movements within Israel are ready to engage us in a war of devastation, but the majority will never allow that to happen. They're too busy raising the hackles of the Palestinians in their own backyard."

"Ah, yes, our revered Palestinian freedom fighters," the President remarked. "Have you ever noticed how many troops the Arab world, or even we Persians for that matter, have sent to aid our Palestinian brethren in their time of need?" There were knowing looks around the table. "Exactly none," he continued. "We condemn the Israelis and we ship arms to the downtrodden Palestinians, but not one Iranian or Arab has ever spilled a single drop of his own blood to destroy the Israelis for the good of the Palestinians and the world."

"Gentlemen," Moslehi said, "are we agreed on *what* we need to do?" Affirmative nods without a voice of dissent. "The motion is carried on a white ballot," the Chairman continued. "Now the questions are *how* do we make contact, and *where*?"

"One thing I can answer," Abbasi said. The *when* must be as soon as possible because the planned act may very well be imminent."

~ ∫ ~

Iran and Israel refuse to acknowledge the legitimate existence of one another. Egypt and Turkey have diplomatic relation with both of them. Saudi Arabia and Israel share secret, back-channel relations.

Until the accession to power of Recep Tayyip Erdoğan's Islamist government in 2002, Israel and Turkey shared a strategic alliance. The military establishments of both nations still cooperate to a major degree and secularist Turks despise the freeze in Israeli-Turkish relations which occurred after the *Mavi Marmara* incident. Likewise, the Jewish State enjoyed cordial relations with its giant neighbor Egypt until the overthrow of Hosni Mubarak on February 11, 2011, and appeared to be returning to a *modus vivendi* after the military ouster of Mubarak's successor, Mohammed Morsi, in the summer of 2013.

No one denies that Turkey is a stabilizing influence in the neighborhood. Like a wise older brother, Turkey seeks to mediate differences rather than exacerbate them. The Turks are neither Arabs, which Westerners seem to think they are, nor are they Persians. They are Ottomans, originally from the steppes of Central Asia, *nonpareil* warriors, and the present day custodians of the crossroads of history.

~ ∫ ~

The ancient, dusty steppe town of Ankara only rose to prominence in the 1920s when Kemal Atatürk made the place, hundreds of miles from nowhere, the capital of the new Turkish Republic. No one would ever claim that Ankara is a beautiful city, or even a charming one. Four-and-a-half million people call it home, but the only real industry of Ankara is *being a capital.* As far as Turks are concerned, "The City" means Istanbul.

Ankara sits in a bowl on a steppe 3,100 feet above sea level. Atatürk Bulvari, the city's main thoroughfare, climbs steadily south as it carries most of Ankara's vehicular traffic, passing posh hotels and the American embassy, enroute to the sparsely-forested top of the ridge. Çankaya, Ankara's wealthiest district, spreads over the upper edges of the city. The Pink House, the Prime Minister's residence, is situated in Çankaya, as is Ataküle Tower, which, until the early 1980s, had been the site of the American Air Force Officers' Club.

At the top of Atatürk Bulvari, the main road proceeds east from the Pink House, winding, snakelike, down the hill to the city proper. On its way, it passes through the residential section of Gazi Osman Paşa.

Number 5 Içaçan Sokak occupies the northeast corner of the intersection of Içaçan and Kader Streets. It is a solidly-built structure, three stories high from street level, four stories high if one includes the basement, which houses a neighborhood pizza parlor.

November 10 was a typical late fall day in the Turkish capital: gray, cold, with not even a slight breeze rustling the scrub-trees. In summer, the view from 5/4 Içaçan Sokak, the topmost apartment, is glorious. The entire city lies at one's feet. But on October 15 of each year, the government declares that the heat be turned on throughput the city, and since Ankara's heat is generated by soft coal, the result is a smudgy agglomeration of soot, so that no one can see farther than halfway down into the bowl.

The five men gathered in apartment 4 at 10:00 that morning. The Turk who hosted the meeting provided hors d'oeuvres and glasses of bottled spring water. The largest room in the apartment, the living room, contained a three-piece sectional couch, a glass-topped coffee table, and two lounging chairs facing the sofa. Heyder Moslehi and Yousef Abbasi comprised the Persian delegation. The *Mossad* and *Shin Bet* were each represented by their deputy directors. The Turk sat in the adjacent dining room, within earshot, but otherwise not participating in the meeting.

"Gentlemen," Moslehi began, "I cannot tell you how much I personally appreciate your meeting with us. It goes without saying that this transcends political hyperbole."

The Mossad chief nodded deferentially. Heyder Moslehi was a known quantity through the intelligence community: a calm, rational, and honorable man, who would have risen high in any service in the world.

"You must know how difficult it is for one sovereign nation to admit to another, and a sworn enemy at that, that while we consider ourselves insurmountable in many fields, this is one area where we frankly need your help."

"I understand, Minister Moslehi," the Mossad man said. "No explanations are necessary. We are of the same fraternity. Let's get down to business."

"You Israelis are the most direct people in the world," Abassi said. "No one ever accused you of being the most diplomatic." He smiled to show he was trying to add levity to a dead-serious situation.

"True," the Shin Bet representative said. "We are the best in the world at winning every war and losing every opportunity for peace."

"Gentlemen," Moslehi continued, "You've seen the transcribed 'confession,' such as it is?"

"We have," the Mossad man replied. "Not much to go on. A target. No date, time, place, or circumstance. An expensive professional killer that might be a man or a woman, young or old, with no name and a numbered bank account in the Cook Islands. Five sponsors. We have no idea who they are or what reasons they have in common. This is not only looking for a needle in the proverbial haystack, it is looking for a gold-colored needle in a haystack on a dark night when there are five hundred silver needles in that same haystack. Your people do not present us with an easy task."

"It is a bit of a challenge," Abassi said.

"Who's your best man – or woman?" the Shin Bet representative asked.

"On the ground or in the sky?" Moslehi responded. A field agent was the one on the ground, his supervisor was the one in the sky.

"Both. We'll need access to each of them."

"Omid Ghormani."

"A good man," the Shin Bet agent said. "And on the ground?"

"Manucher Tabrizi."

"Never heard of him," the Mossad agent said.

"That's the best kind, isn't it?" Moslehi replied. "Like the Assassin, he'd never be picked out of a crowd. Do you have anyone specific in mind for this job, gentlemen?"

The Israelis looked at one another. The younger of the two, the Shin Bet man, nodded. "It's not Mike Harari."

"I didn't think so," Abassi said, cracking a genuine smile. "He'd be eighty-eight years old. A bit long in the tooth."

"Our man's a combination of Tabrizi and Ghormani," the Mossad man replied, "but if I might add with typical Israeli arrogance, he's better than both of them put together. Perhaps it's best that I don't say anything more about him except that to look at him on the street you'd never suspect how good he is."

"How will we know him?" Abassi asked.

"You won't until you meet him. He's very expensive though."

"We wouldn't have expected otherwise," Moslehi said. "Nor would we have expected your agencies to do this out of love for the Iranian leadership. How much?"

"We'll continue to pay his regular salary out of our own funds," the Mossad chief replied. "You'd have to provide him with a small apartment and reimburse us for his living expenses, unless you provide them yourself. The largest expense would be his one apparent addiction."

"Which is?"

"I've never seen anyone drink so much Pellegrino water. I would wager he goes through two cases a week."

The laughter among the four of them was the relieved camaraderie of men who had just been given a reprieve from the worst of their fears. The ice was now broken and the Turk brought them a quart bottle of *rakı*, the fabled Turkish firewater, and a pitcher of water to pour into each man's draught.

During the next two hours, the four men, now bonding as a team, listened to an iPad account of the confession, read the transcribed notes that had been rendered by the technician in Tehran, and engaged in questions, suggestions, theories, and brainstorming. At the end of that time, they signaled to their host that they were ready to depart in separate conveyances to Esenboğa Airport, 17 miles northeast of the city.

Moslehi spoke for the assembly when he thanked the Turk for the superlative assistance of his government in arranging the meeting.

He thanked the man himself for providing the perfect venue for the meeting and for being the perfect host.

"Are you part of the Foreign Service, a Law Enforcement official?"

"Nothing so impressive, I'm afraid." The middle-aged Turk grinned. "I'm just an ordinary businessman whose pleasure it has been to help you."

"Not that it's my business, and you certainly don't have to answer if you don't want, but I would like to commend you to your Prime Minister and President by name."

"I have no problem with that, and I appreciate your kind words," the Turk replied. "My name is Mustafa Karaca."

~ ∫ ~

By that evening, all five of the Assassin's employers had received a recording of the entire meeting.

~ ∫ ~

While Ezra Caen's personal life had, at least in his own mind, been a disaster, his professional career, which was not generally known outside of higher-ups within the international intelligence community, had been a series of successes. He was known to his Israeli compatriots as ולהבטל (V'havtel) and by his French collegaues as le bûcheur – the Plodder. The nickname masked his steady series of counterterrorist coups, both inside the Israeli services and beyond.

Ezra Caen lacked the imposing bulk of the traditional image of the authority of the law. He did not have the facile smoothness that exemplified so many of the new breed of young detectives who could bully and browbeat a witness into tears. But these shortcomings, if in fact they were shortcomings, did not bother him in the least. Ezra knew that most crime in any society is either carried out against, or witnessed by, the little people: the shopkeeper, the janitor, the hairdresser, the postman, or the store clerk. He could make these people talk to him.

That was partly because of his size. He was slightly more than five-feet-five inches tall. In many ways he resembled the cartoonist's image of a henpecked husband, which he had been until Galit's departure. His dress was dowdy and his manner was as rumpled as the clothes he wore. When he requested information from a witness, it was so different from the attitude exhibited by most of the younger detectives that witnesses unconsciously warmed toward Ezra as a refuge from the rough handling they'd received from others.

But there was something more. He had been the top cop in numerous unheard-of agencies for more than twenty years. Behind his mildness and seeming simplicity he possessed a combination of a shrewd brain and a dogged refusal to be cowed, intimidated, or ruffled by anyone when he was carrying out a job. He had been threatened by some of the most vicious criminals, including gang bosses, in more than one country, who had thought from the rapid blinking with which Ezra Caen greeted such approaches that the little detective had duly and seriously taken note of their warnings. Only later, from a prison cell, had they had the leisure to realize that they had underestimated the soft brown eyes and the look which bordered on sympathy mixed with fear.

Despite the oft-deserved reputation of the various intelligence agencies as being in sharp competition with one another, the Israelis, like virtually every other intelligence service operating on the same side of international politics, realized the value of "you scratch my back, I'll scratch yours." Starting in the late-1990s, numerous of these agencies in several countries dispatched the best and brightest minds they had to offer to other services in different countries, often for extended periods of time. *The Plodder* was regularly detached to such agencies throughout the United States and Europe.

Although Ezra Caen's two most heralded public successes were his being instrumental in the 2002 Alliance Base Operation in conjunction with the American CIA and the DGSE, which resulted in the arrest of Christian Ganczarski, a German-born citizen of Polish ancestry who had converted to Islam and become a top al Qaeda leader, and the 2004 liberation of two French journalists, Georges Malbrunot and Christian Chesnot, who had been held hostage for 124 days in Iraq, his greatest source of personal satisfaction, aside from the time he had rescued twelve children from a burning school bus, was something that had never been publicized and had never appeared in so much as a single newspaper, magazine, or television program. Between 2005 and 2012, he had prevented more than eight terrorist attacks in different countries, some friendly to Israel, others not.

Ezra Caen was neither particularly concerned nor surprised when he received a summons to attend a joint meeting of the heads of the *Mossad, Sayeret Matkal, Aman, Shabak,* and *Shin Bet.* He had done nothing to merit severe criticism and he knew that from time to time the joint intelligence and action services worked together if a case was particularly sensitive or important. He was more curious than anything else.

At twelve noon on November 13, Caen entered the room in which the meeting was to take place. When he arrived, the five chiefs were already seated.

"Good afternoon, Ezra," the man who'd initially recruited him, now the head of Mossad, said, without preamble. "We have a rather unique assignment for you, one that will take all of your years of cunning and initiative and one that is more sensitive than any case you've ever had. Our internal agents have already packed your bags and they're waiting at Ben Gurion Airport." The clock on the wall showed 12:05 p.m. "Turkish Airlines Flight 787 departs for Istanbul at 3:45 and arrives at 6:00. Turkish 878 departs at 1:10 a.m. tomorrow morning. You'll arrive at your destination three-and-a-half hours later."

Ezra glanced down at the ticket that the Chief had just handed him. His face was expressionless. "How long will I be there?"

"Until the job is done."

"Can you brief me on what this assignment is all about?"

"I can," his superior said. And he did.

8

"Sister Mary Salvatore" felt strangely unnerved as the man behind her waited until she took her seat in 6A, nodded deferentially to her, and walked past her to his seat, somewhere toward the rear of the aircraft. The flight from Atatürk International to IKA was less than half full, so each passenger could stretch out and sleep until the plane landed.

The Assassin could not understand why the man had so affected her or why she had felt a sudden chill. He was neither tall nor short. For a fleeting moment, she thought that if he were a woman, he'd look very much like her, except that his hair was wispy and thin, with a balding crown. His eyeglasses were neither stylish nor flattering, and there was a thrown-together look about his attire. A moment later, she forgot all about the fellow, lay back, and had already fallen into a light sleep by the time the A-320 took off.

As they deplaned at 4:00 a.m., the Assassin noticed that the man she had seen earlier was greeted by a man of similar age. While she stood in line to have her passport stamped, the man flashed a card case to the customs official who waved both men through without checking any documents.

"Sister Mary Salvatore?" the passport agent asked, looking at her documents, at her face, then back to the documents. "You are from Zimbabwe? But I thought everyone left there was black."

"I served as a nun at the Sisters of Mercy Orphanage outside Harare. It was burned to the ground last month and the authorities advised that it might be best for me to leave the country for awhile."

"But why the Islamic Republic of Iran, Sister?"

"There are fifteen thousand Roman Catholics here and my Mother Superior told me they would put me to good use." She withdrew a letter from her handbag. "I'm sure Cardinal Tauran advised members of the government that I was coming."

The customs official glanced briefly at the letter, which was written in a language he did not understand, looked once more at her photograph and compared it with the face in front of him. No question it was the same person. Her head was covered, like virtually all female nuns of a Roman Catholic Order, which was nothing abnormal. "Of what Order are you, Sister?" he asked.

"Dominican."

"Thank you. We try to accommodate all religions, Sister. You may pass. Have a pleasant stay in the Islamic Republic."

The nun proceeded to baggage claim, where she picked up two medium-sized soft-sided pieces of luggage, placed them in a nearby four-wheeled cart, and passed through the secondary inspection point, stating she had nothing to declare. She wheeled the cart to a waiting taxi queue, hailed a cab, and left the airport.

She had made reservations at the Firouzeh Hotel. The single room cost a modest 300,000 rials, $24 USD, a night. While it was simple, it was clean, had a private shower, and was centrally located on Dolat Abbadi Alley, off hotel-lined Amir Kabir Street, four blocks from Imam Khomeini Square.

Sister Mary Salvatore, who'd enjoyed a restful two nights in Istanbul and a three-hour nap on the plane, had no need of further sleep, and took five minutes to freshen up, after which she unpacked her suitcases. She extracted a nylon bag, which took up virtually no space, which she had rolled up and stuffed into the bottom of one of her cases. She filled the bag with the remainder of her weapon, twenty rounds of ammunition, and two explosive bullets.

Shortly afterward, "Meneer Hostetler" emerged, wearing a casual outfit, took the elevator down to the small lobby, and asked the desk clerk on duty where he could hire a car. The functionary directed him to an inexpensive rental agency nearby. Hostetler, who had used an X-acto knife to neatly cut out the page bearing his exit stamp from Iran when he had departed two weeks before, showed his passport, his Namibian driving license, and his current International Driving Permit to the rental agent. The cheapest available car was a four-year-old Samand.

"Do you drive a manual transmission, Sir?" the agent asked.

"Of course. Is the car that gray sedan out front?"

"It is."

"Quite a few dents."

"That happens in Tehran. Have you driven in our city before?"

"I have," the Assassin said. "Tehran's traffic is a good reason to purchase Collision Damage Waiver insurance. Aside from the way it looks, is the car mechanically sound?"

"Of course. How long will you need it?"

"Five days."

"If you rent it for a week or more you get unlimited mileage. Would you care to rent a GPS system as well?"

"Yes, please."

Within ten minutes, the agent filled out the paperwork, the Assassin signed the contract, and "he" drove to a public parking structure near the *Terminal-e-jonoob*, where he had stored the duffel back containing the tripod, scope, gun barrel, silencer, and fittings. Removing the duffel bag, he returned to the parking garage from whence he'd come.

Driving in Tehran was hectic, to be sure, but the Assassin was half an hour behind the heaviest morning traffic, as he took the belt road to Highway 7, the Qom Highway. Meneer Hostetler stopped at Shahr-e-Rey, a southern suburb, where he purchased a string shopping bag, a two-tube package of heavy duty glue, a hammer, some spikes, a small loaf of bread, two apples, a few slices of cold meat, and two Persian melons. The Assassin stuffed these into the trunk of the car. At a nearby petrol station, "Hostetler" filled the Samand with gasoline and checked the tires, as well as the oil and water levels.

The Assassin continued south on Highway 7 for several miles until she'd reached a side road halfway between Tehran and Qom. She turned off the main road and headed east, into the semi-desert of the *Dasht-e-Kavir*. A smaller side road climbed into the hills. The killer had not seen so much as a village since she'd turned off the main road.

Once in the hills, she came to a small grove of scrub oak trees, sufficient for her purpose. The late November day was not hot and there was only a mild breeze. The Assassin brought the Samand to a stop next to a clump of undergrowth, turned off the ignition, and waited in the shade of the grove, listening to the ticking of the engine block as it cooled. From somewhere in the distance, she heard the distant cooing of a pigeon.

Shortly afterward, she climbed out, unlocked the trunk, laid the duffel bag and the larger nylon bag on the car's hood, and unwrapped the component parts of the rifle, fitting them together piece by piece. She slipped the silencer into one trouser pocket and the telescopic sight into the other. She tipped the twenty shells from the box into one breast pocket, and the two explosive shells, wrapped in tissue paper, into the other.

When the rest of the rifle was assembled, the Assassin returned to the trunk. She took out the two Persian melons, the string bag, the hammer, and the spikes. She placed one of the melons on the ground near the left rear wheel of the car and carried the remaining melon, the string bag, the hammer, and the spikes to the tallest nearby oak.

Putting the melon into the string bag and placing both on the ground in front of the tree, she hammered one of the spikes into the trunk of the tree, six feet above the ground, and hung the handles of the string bag containing the melon over the hilt. When suspended, the melon looked like similar to a detached human head. At a hundred and fifty yards, it would serve its purpose.

Looking out from the tree, she fanned her sight from left to right until she found a trail that edged upward for what she estimated was a hundred fifty yards, to a level plateau. Perfect. Carrying the remaining spike and the hammer, she paced out a hundred and fifty paces – about a third of a way onto the flatland – and hammered the spike into the ground. She returned to the rifle, which was lying on the car's hood.

It was easy to install the silencer, which she swiveled around the barrel until it was tight. The telescopic sight fit snugly along the top of the barrel. After she had returned to the plateau, she slipped back the bolt and inserted the first cartridge into the breech. Squinting down the sight, she searched the far end of the clearing for the hanging target. When she found it, she was slightly surprised to find how large and clear it looked. To all appearances, had it been the head of her target, it would have seemed no more than thirty yards away. She could make out the lines of the shopping bag's strings.

The Assassin altered her stance slightly, leaned against a nearby rocky outcrop to steady her aim, and squinted again. The two crossed wires inside the telescopic sight did not appear to be quite centered, so she reached out with her right hand and toyed with the two adjusting screws until the cross in the sight appeared to be correctly in line. She took careful aim at the center of the melon and fired.

The recoil was not great. The restrained '*phut*' of the silencer could not have carried fifteen yards. Carrying the gun under her arm, she walked back toward the oak and examined the melon. Near the lower left-hand edge, the bullet had traced a path across the skin of the fruit, snapping part of the string of the shopping bag, and had buried itself in the tree. She walked back up the rise to the level ground and fired a second time, leaving the setting of the telescopic sight exactly where it had been before.

The result was the same, with less than half an inch of difference. She tried three more shots without moving the screws of the telescopic sight. She was convinced that her aim was true, but the sight was firing low and slightly to the left. She adjusted the screws.

The next shot went high and to the right. To make quite sure, she again walked down to the tree and examined the hole made by the bullet. It had penetrated the upper right corner of the melon. She tried four more shots with the sight still adjusted to this new position. The bullets all went in the same area. Finally, she moved the sight back by a whisker.

The ninth shot went clean through what would have been the forehead, had the melon been a human head. Exactly where she had aimed it. She walked down to the target a third time. She took a piece of porous desert rock and marked the existing areas touched by the bullets – the small cluster to the left and down, the second cluster in the upper right quadrant, and the neat hole through the center of the dummy's forehead.

From then on, she plugged, in succession, where each eye would have been, the imaginary bridge of the nose, the upper lip, and the chin. She turned the target into a sideways, profile position and used the last six shots through what she perceived to be the temple, ear, neck, cheek, jaw, and skull. They were all on-target.

Satisfied with the gun, she noted the positioning of the screws that adjusted the telescopic sight. Taking the two tubes of glue from her pocket, she squirted a drop of liquid from each tube over the heads of both grub screws and the surface adjacent to them. Once again, she returned to the car. For the next half hour she tore off pieces of the broad-grained bread and alternated eating a chunk of bread, a bite of apple, another chunk of bread, and a slice of meat. Walking behind a tree farther in, she unbelted and dropped her pants, squatted, and relieved herself.

By the time she returned to the rifle, the cement had set and hardened. The sights were set for her eyesight with that particular weapon at a hundred fifty yards with dead-aim accuracy.

She walked back to the top of the rise, carrying the gun. Once on the level plateau, she took one of the explosive bullets out of her other breast pocket, unwrapped it, and slid it into the breech of the rifle. She took particularly careful aim at the center of the melon and fired.

As the last plume of blue smoke curled away from the end of the silencer, the Assassin carried her rifle back down to the car, laid it on the hood, and walked toward the oak tree. The string bag sagged, hanging limp and almost empty against the scarred trunk of the tree.

The melon that had absorbed twenty lead slugs without coming to pieces had disintegrated. Parts of it lay scattered on the ground in front of the tree. Pips and juice dribbled down the bark. The remaining fragments lay broken in the lower end of the string bag.

The Assassin removed the bag and tossed it into the underbrush. The target it had once contained was nothing more than meaningless pulp. The Assassin hammered the spike deeper into the tree trunk until, from a distance of five feet or more, it looked like a gnarled bump on the tree.

Walking back to the car, she disassembled the rifle, which, by his time, was completely cool to the touch. She spent the better part of an hour carefully cleaning every part of the weapon and oiling the moving parts with light oil she had stored in the duffel bag, after which she meticulously rewrapped each constituent piece in the bubble wrap in which it had previously been protected. She placed some pieces in the nylon bag and others, along with the oil and the rags with which she had cleaned the rifle, in the duffel bag.

"Agrippina" walked over to the remaining Persian melon, hacked it open with the claw end of the hammer, and ate most of the delicious fruit, after which she wiped off the hammer with the sleeve of her shirt, placed it in the duffel bag, zipped up the two bags, placed them in the trunk of the Samand, and drove back toward Tehran.

She arrived in the city shortly before 4:00 p.m., just ahead of the homebound rush, parked the car in a structure near the southern bus station, stored the two bags in the left luggage locker, and drove to a car park near the Firouzeh Hotel. Since "Meneer Hostetler" had not returned the keys to the front desk earlier that morning, there was no need to retrieve them from the duty clerk. Hostetler and the clerk exchanged nods. The guest took the elevator to the third floor, exited, and entered "Sister Mary Salvatore's" compact single room.

The Assassin showered, lay down on the narrow bed, and slept until nine that evening, when, dressed in her nun's habit, she took the elevator down to the lobby and enjoyed a Persian meal of *chelaw kebab* in a restaurant on nearby Amir Kabir Street.

~ ∫ ~

The Minister of Intelligence and National Security sat at his desk that morning and stared out the window into the courtyard beneath the grandiose Ministry Headquarters. To his right, at the far end of Amir Kabir Street, he beheld the onslaught of cars and trucks circling Imam Khomeini Square. Farther afield, his eyes were drawn to the modern showpiece Milad Tower, the fourth tallest tower in the world.

Heyder Moslehi had undergone a shaky and dispiriting last few years. It was much easier before Ahmadinejad had been elected president back in 2005. Moslehi had served as the Ayatollah Khamenei's representative to the *Basij*, Iran's volunteer militia. When Ahmadinejad was elected in 2009, he'd appointed Moslehi as his own adviser for clerical affairs.

Two years later, at Ahmadinejad's "request," he had resigned from his position. Relations between the Minister and the former president had turned frosty since then. The chill thickened when the Supreme Leader had reinstated Moslehi to his position, but the newly reinstated Minister's political troubles were far from over. Ahmadinejad refused to hold cabinet meetings in protest of Moslehi's presence. After April 2011, cabinet meetings were held without Ahmadinejad. The vice president of Iran chaired the meetings, and parliament endorsed Moslehi as Minister of Intelligence. He was optimistic that things would change for the better under newly-elected President Rouhani.

This morning his mind was not concentrating on past history. Rather, he was concerned with how best to approach his mentor and sponsor, the Grand Ayatollah Khamenei, with the intelligence he had received. One thing for certain: he could never – nor would he ever – so much as suggest to the Supreme Leader that his Ministry had engaged an Israeli agent to assist in the pursuit of the putative Assassin.

His thoughts strayed momentarily to the massive traffic jam around Khomeini Square. Angry, hell-bent motorists hooted and honked and shouted epithets at the cars or trucks immediately preceding them in the chaotic mess. Heyder Moslehi, Minister of Intelligence and National Security of the Islamic Republic of Iran envied them the simplicity of their concerns. He would have been nonplussed had he known, or even suspected, that the Assassin was, at that very moment, driving a nondescript Samand in the middle of the traffic jam, headed south toward Qom.

"Well, what do you think?" Moslehi asked, turning to face Rahman Almotahari, Chief of the Supreme Leader's bodyguard and one of the foremost experts in Iran on all questions of security, particularly as they related to the protection of a single life against assassination. That was why he held his job, and that's why nine known plots to kill the Supreme Ruler of the Islamic Republic of Iran had failed.

"Ghormani, Tabrizi, and the Israeli are right," he said, his voice flat, unemotional, and final. He might just as well have been giving a judgment on the result of a soccer match. "If what the Israeli says is true, the plot is exceptionally dangerous. The entire filing system of all the security agencies of Iran, the whole network of agents and infiltrators presently maintained by our intelligence ministry, are all reduced to nothing in the face of a foreigner, an outsider, working completely alone, without contacts or friends. And a professional to boot. As Mister Caen put it, it is the most dangerous single concept one can imagine."

Moslehi toyed with his *kufiya,* his head covering, and spun slowly toward the window behind him. After surviving numerous political and clerical wars, he was not easily ruffled, but he was deeply disturbed this morning. Throughout his many years as a devoted follower of Ali Khamenei, he had built up the reputation as a tough man, a survivor, and those talents had brought him to the Minister's chair.

In the middle period between the Khomeini revolution and the first decade of the twenty-first century, Moslehi had learned infighting the hard way. Until the present perceived plot, the Minister had felt that the most recent internal struggle was waning, with the exception, of course, of the showpiece public statements made by the Americans and their running-dogs, the British and the Israelis. Despite these statements, trade still trumped war every time.

Now he knew that the troubles were not over yet. A group of powerful men he did not know had devised a plan that could rip the entire fabric of the Islamic Republic to shreds by organizing the death of a single man. Some countries have institutions stable enough to survive the death of a president or even a Supreme Leader such as the Grand Ayatollah. But Heyder Moslehi was astute enough to have no illusions that the death of Ayatollah Ali Khamenei could only foreshadow a civil war.

"Well," he finally said, still looking at the huge tower in the distance, "we must tell him."

The Security Chief did not answer. One of the advantages of his position was that you did your job and left the hard decisions to those who were paid to make them. He did not intend to volunteer to do the telling. The Minister turned back to face him.

"Very well, Rahman. I shall seek an interview this afternoon and inform the Supreme Leader." Moslehi's voice was crisp and decisive: a thing had to be done. "I trust I don't need to ask you to maintain complete silence on this matter until I have had time to explain our position to the Leader and he has decided how he wishes to handle this affair."

The Security Chief rose, bowed slightly to the Minister, and left. Alone again, the Minister of Intelligence and Security looked down at the manila folder enclosing the report and read it through for the hundredth time. He had no doubt that the assessments of his "man in the sky," the Ministry's "man on the ground," and the Israeli who "didn't exist" were right. Almotahari's confirmation left him no room for doubt. The danger was there, it was serious, it could not be avoided, and the Supreme Leader had to know.

~ ∫ ~

The appointment was fixed for four that afternoon, as soon as the Leader had finished his post-meal prayers and awakened from his mid-afternoon nap. For a moment, it crossed the Minister's mind to tell the appointments secretary that what he had in the manila folder was more important than a nap, but he stifled that idea as quickly as it had emerged. One did not cross the soft-voiced civil servant who had the ear of the Supreme Leader at all times, and a private filing system of intimate information about which more was feared than was known.

~ ∫ ~

The man guarding the inner sanctum rapped briefly on the double doors, opened one of them, and stood in the entrance. "The Minister of Intelligence and National Security, my Imam," he announced.

There was a muffled response from inside. The guard stepped back, smiled at the Minister, and Heyder Moslehi went past him into the Grand Ayatollah Ali Khamenei's private study.

The furnishings in the room were surprisingly bare of adornment except for a series of exquisite hand-woven carpets. To the right were three tall, elegant windows. One of them was open. Minister Moslehi could hear a dove cooing and the sound of a water fountain in the garden below. Somewhere beneath the trees, quiet men lurked, carrying automatics with which they could shoot the bill off the dove at twenty-five paces, leaving the rest of the bird's face untouched.

Nothing in the room was gaudy, nothing was remotely less than in the best of taste. There was nothing that did not amplify the pride of the Persian Empire. The Supreme Leader of the Islamic Republic of Iran rose and held out his right hand to the Minister. The Minister bent his head, kissed the Leader's ring, and raised his head.

"Welcome, Heyder, My Son," the Ayatollah spoke, his voice a soft, raspy half-whisper, the result of an early failed – but nearly successful – attempt on his life.

"My respects, my Imam. May Allah the all-merciful grant you long life and peace."

"I am told, My Dear Mister Minister, that you wished to see me on a matter of some urgency. What have you to say to me?"

Heyder Moslehi breathed in deeply once and began. He explained briefly and directly what had brought him here, aware that the Grand Ayatollah did not appreciate long-winded oratory except his own.

While he talked, the man sitting opposite him stiffened perceptibly.

The Minister finished his message, which had lasted a little more than one minute, by mentioning Ghormani's, Tabrizi's, and Almotahari's comments – pointedly avoiding any mention of the "non-existent" Israeli agent. He concluded his remarks by saying, "I have the committee report in this folder."

Without a word, the Leader's hand reached out across his desk. Moslehi slipped the report out of his briefcase and handed it to the Supreme Leader.

Grand Ayatollah Ali *Sayyid* Khamenei took out his reading glasses, put them on, opened the manila folder, and started to read. The dove in the garden had stopped cooing. Heyder Moslehi stared out at the trees, then at the Ayatollah's brass reading lamp. The Ayatollah was a quick reader. He finished the report in less than five minutes, put it back in the folder, closed it, and handed it back to his Minister.

"Well, My Dear Son, what do you want me to do?"

Moslehi took a deep, uncertain breath. He began to speak about the steps he thought should be taken, stating, "In my judgment, My Imam, these actions will be necessary if we are to avoid this menace." When he attempted to further emphasize the gravity of the situation by using the words, "For the good of the Islamic Republic …" the Supreme Leader peremptorily cut him off.

"My Dear Mister Minister, the good of the Islamic Republic requires that the Supreme Leader is not seen to be cowering before the menace of a miserable hireling, and a *foreign* hireling at that."

The Minister of Intelligence and National Security of the Islamic Republic of Iran had lost. The Ayatollah did not lose his temper as the Minister had feared he might. He spoke directly and precisely, as one who has no intention that his wishes should be unclear in any way. "As the Supreme Leader of our Islamic Republic, indeed, as the very *symbol* of the Islamic Republic, I cannot, and I *must* not, dignify the threat of one who is not worthy of passing beneath my feet like a serpent."

Two minutes later Minister Heyder Moslehi left the Supreme Leader's presence. He nodded soberly at the guard, walked out through the door, and down the balconied stairway to the vestibule.

The guard thought, "There goes a man with one hell of a problem if ever I saw one. I wonder what the Imam said to him?" But being the chief of guards, his face retained the immobile calm of the leader he had served for the past decade.

9

"And that, my friends, was exactly what the Ayatollah said. He was absolutely immovable on that point." The Minister looked beaten, downtrodden. "We are not yet absolutely certain that the conclusions reached by our experts are necessarily true. They are based on the ramblings of a Saudi Prince who was tortured and then murdered. We are still conducting inquiries in far corners of the globe. Our operatives, and," he said, nodding to Ezra Caen, "our 'nonexistent' friends, are hoping to have at least some answers sooner rather than later. But I suppose one must agree that to launch a nationwide hunt for a foreigner who could be a male or a female, young or old, physically whole or a cripple, at this point in time, would hardly be realistic.

"Beyond that, our Supreme Leader has ordered that there is to be no publicity, no nationwide search, no indication to anyone outside our small circle that anything – I repeat *anything* – is amiss. The Supreme Leader feels that if the matter were somehow to become known to the media, every nation who is out to destroy our way of life would gloat. Any extra security precautions would be interpreted both here and abroad as the Supreme Leader of the Islamic Republic of Iran cowering and hiding from a single man, or, worse, a single woman, and a foreigner at that. This he will not tolerate. He made it abundantly clear that if the details, or even the general impression of what is going on, becomes public knowledge, heads will roll. I have never seen the Supreme Leader so adamant."

"But the public appearances must be curtailed. There must be no public appearances until the Assassin is caught," protested Youssef Abassi.

"He will cancel nothing," Moslehi sighed. "There will be no changes, not by an hour, nor by a minute. Our entire operation must be handled in complete and utter secrecy."

"If we are not allowed to act, what can we do?" Ghormani asked.

"I did not say we are not allowed to act," Moslehi said. "I said we are not allowed to act *publicly*. The whole thing must be done in secret. That leaves us only one alternative. The identity of the Assassin must be learned by a secret inquiry. He or she must be traced to wherever he or she is, in Iran or abroad, and the Assassin must be destroyed without hesitation. That, gentlemen, is the only course left open to us."

The Minister of Intelligence and Security looked around the table. There were eight men in the room, including himself, Manucher Tabrizi, and Ezra Caen. The Minister sat at the head of the table. To his immediate right were Rahman Almotahari, Chief of the Supreme Leader's bodyguard, Yousef Abbasi, Saeed Paria, head of recruitment for the agency, and the legendary Ghasem Habib. To his left, Omid Ghormani, the spymaster, Manucher Tabrizi, and the Israeli, Ezra Caen.

"So that is where we stand, gentlemen," the Minister continued. "You have all read the report, yes? And now you have heard from me the considerable limitations which the Supreme Leader has imposed on our efforts to avert this threat to his person. I stress again, there must be absolute secrecy in the conduct of the investigation and in any subsequent action to be taken. Needless to say, you are all sworn to total silence and you will not discuss the matter with anyone outside this room, unless and until that person has been made privy to this secret.

"I have called you all here because whatever we are to do, the resources of each of your departments must sooner or later be called upon. Each of you should have no doubts as to the priority this matter demands. On all occasions, this affair will require your immediate and personal attention. There will be no delegation of authority to anyone else."

The Minister paused. Down both sides of the table some heads nodded soberly. Others kept their eyes fixed on the speaker. "Gentlemen, I suggest we have all heard what we need to hear at this meeting. What you do from this point on is done at your own discretion. I suggest we meet every three days, first thing in the morning." He noticed Paria's open mouth. "Yes, Saeed," the Minister said, "it is that important, it is that urgent, and it takes priority over anything – I repeat *anything* – else."

~ ∫ ~

"Well, Ezra," Manucher Tabrizi commenced, "hell of an assignment, wouldn't you say?" They were seated at a kebab house in the affluent northern quarter of Tehran. During the two days since Tabrizi had picked Ezra up at the airport, they'd developed a genuine personal liking for one another. But for an accident of birth that had placed them in two different countries in two contrasting – but not *so* contrasting – cultures, each acknowledged they would have become the closest of friends.

"Just great," Caen said sardonically. "Our masters are demanding the impossible. There's been no crime – yet. No clues, no witnesses that we know of. Not even a name, and we really don't even know if we're dealing with a man or a woman. So far I've only been able to ascertain the smallest shred of evidence. Five men met at the Parador hotel in Santiago de Compostela, Spain, early last September. I brought a couple of pages of the transcript with me." He took out the writing and scanned down to a brief passage.

"Q. Who is the Assassin, Majid?

"A. South Afric …

"Q. What did she look like?

"A. Can't describe. Not tall, not short...

"Q. What do you mean sometimes it was a 'he?'

"A. First a he, then …

"Q. What hotel was it?

"A. Don't know … near big church …

"Q. Who were the men with you?

"A. Napoli … Count … don't know.

"Q. Whom did they represent? … Do you hear me? … Whom did they represent?

"A. (Garbled)

"Q. Whom did *you* represent?

{No response)

"Q. What bank?

"A. Pac ... Pacific ...

"Q. How much money?

(No response)

"Q. Who was the target?

"A. Iran ... leader ...

"Q. How much did she demand?

"A. Ten ..."

Ezra Caen knew he was a good cop. He had always been a good cop, slow, precise, methodical. Just occasionally he had shown a flash of inspiration that had made him a remarkable detective. But he had never lost sight of the fact that in police work ninety-nine percent of the effort is routine ... dull drudgery ... inquiry, more inquiry, checking, double checking ... unspectacular labor, thankless slogging. Gathering tiny particles which, of themselves, were meaningless. Then building a web of parts until they became a whole, until the whole became a net, and the net finally surrounded the criminal with a case that would not just make headlines, but would stand up in court.

Ezra Caen had never sought publicity. He had never given the sort of press conferences on which some of his colleagues had built their reputations. *V'havtel, le bûcheur*, the Plodder. And yet he had gone steadily up the ladder, solving his cases, seeing his criminals convicted. When a vacancy had occurred in his present position four years ago, even the others in line for the job conceded that Caen was the right choice. He had never sought his position by climbing on – or over – the backs of others. He had never knowingly stabbed any of his colleagues in the back.

Manucher Tabrizi had enjoyed a similar career trajectory in the service of Iran: unspectacular, not showy, the cop on the beat. The one who would be forgotten five minutes after being met. In that very narrow regard, he was very much like the Assassin he had been detailed to hunt.

"Even though there was some ambiguity there and although the Assassin seems able to shift sex and shape at will, her most natural guise is that of a woman," he said.

"There's no need to speculate that if she demanded a very high price, she was very much a professional."

Manucher lit up a Bahman cigarette and offered the packet to Caen. The Israeli declined, but ordered a small bottle Pellegrino water as the waiter passed by.

"Nasty habit," Tabrizi muttered,

"Cigarettes?"

"No, that sparkling water you always drink."

" Hey, I'd make a great Muslim."

"So she's a professional," Tabrizi continued. "That means she's probably known to her colleagues and competitors. And being South African …"

"We don't know that for sure, Manucher."

" 'South Afric-' Majid said. Can you think of anything close to that except South African?"

"Not really."

"So that narrows the field still more. A South African woman professional Assassin – a very high-priced South African woman professional Assassin who shifts shapes. Israel's got some expertise in that field – Mike Harari…"

"Yeah, right. The guy's almost ninety years old."

"But he's one of the granddaddies of them all. And if you think a professional opts out of the game just because he's old …"

"Let's say I *could* get to Harari. Most likely this Assassin's more than fifty years his junior – two generations back. Bob Denard's dead, Kony's got his own kettle of fish to fry… "

"Mad Mike?"

"If he's even alive, Hoare's eight years older than Harari. That'd make him a hundred-fifteen or so."

The two men laughed.

"Do your people have any connection with the South African good guys?" Manucher asked.

"Not too much with the new service," Caen replied. "But I understand they're cozying up to the guys who replaced Pahlavi, so you'd probably have better luck with them than I would."

"But you were born in South Africa."

"True, but I'm white."

"And Jewish. I thought your people were always the liberals – Helen Suzman, Gideon Slovo …"

"Yeah, and today they can't tell one white from another," Ezra said. There was no hint of bitterness in his voice. He was just stating a fact of life. "You know and I know that we can sit here and talk about who we know and what we know and it's not going to get us very far. Manucher, it's been a long day for me. Now that you've planted some seeds and I've planted some seeds, both of us can use some quiet time and neither of us will probably get much sleep if you're anything like me."

"I get the message." Tabrizi smiled and hugged his comrade.

The two men parted and Ezra Caen went back to the comfortable, but totally pedestrian, apartment with which the Iranian government had provided him.

So it was that on the same evening Sister Mary Salvatore awoke from her nap, dressed in her nun's habit, took the elevator down to the lobby, and enjoyed a Persian meal of *chelaw kebab* in a restaurant on nearby Amir Kabir Street, Ezra Caen began his manhunt in earnest.

~ ∫ ~

"Indeed Sister, we can always use help," the priest who was apparently in charge said. "While we received no advance word from your Mother Superior, that's not surprising. Communications between Zimbabwe and the outside world have been strained for years."

The nun smiled. 'I wouldn't exactly call this the 'outside world,' Father."

"That's for sure, Sister. We're spread out pretty thin around here. Cardinal Touran's letter said you'd be traveling throughout the country and into some of the other 'Stans.'"

"Wherever I'm needed, Father."

"You understand we won't be able to give you support in the smaller enclaves. There'll be times you'll be on your own for weeks at a time."

"I'm no stranger to that, Father. I didn't sign up to be the belle of the ball."

"May I ask what you do in your spare time? For entertainment, I mean."

"Spare time, Father? I haven't much thought about it. Harare's certainly not New York, nor even Johannesburg." She removed a missal from a capacious pocket within her cassock. "This helps me devote my life to Jesus."

"Of course. Any thought of where you'll go from here?"

"I thought I'd get an overview of the spiritual centers first: Qom, Mashhad, Isfahan."

He took a card from his own cassock. "This is a number where you can reach me any time, day or night. If you follow me into the business office, I'll get you a cell phone you can use anywhere in-country."

"Thank you, Father. That's very kind of you." As she reached out to take the card, she accidentally dropped the missal she'd been carrying. As he bent down to pick it up, the priest noticed the writing on the cover: *Heidelberg Kategismus, Nederduitse Gereformeerde Kerk, Kaapstad, Suid Afrika.*

The priest said nothing, but he had traveled extensively and was conversant enough with European Church theology to know that the book was one of the touchstones of the largest and most well-established Dutch Reformed Church of South Africa – a distinctly and militantly Lutheran *Protestant* Sect.

~ ∫ ~

"Jean-Claude, I need a favor – a big one."

"Of course, Ezra. It goes without saying. Not official, I trust."

"Absolutely unofficial. I need to use DGSE facilities to make a few phone calls."

One of the Ezra's closest professional friends, Jean-Claude DeNault, associate director of France's Security Intelligence Service, was astute enough to recognize that his Israeli colleague had not said anything else for a reason. The trace on the call said it was coming from Iran, but, of course, that was impossible unless Ezra Caen had somehow defected – and that would be absolutely unthinkable for a man of Ezra's integrity.

"Let me know the flight and the date and I'll make arrangements to transport you direct from Charles DeGaulle to *La piscine*."

The *Direction Générale de la Sécurité Extérieure* is France's external intelligence agency. Its headquarters are located at 141 Boulevard

Mortier, one kilometer northeast of the Père Lachaise Cemetery in Paris. The building is often referred to as *La piscine* – the swimming pool – because of the nearby Piscine des Tourelles of the French Swimming Federation.

Within two days, Ezra was ensconced in a private office which his French colleague had set aside for him. He had three telephone lines, all encrypted to avoid detection. Jean-Claude had asked no questions of the Israeli, knowing that Caen would speak only when he had something he wanted to share with the DGSE agent.

"I will ask though, *cher ami*, why you had to come all the way to Paris to do your business."

"No doubt you figured out where my initial call came from?"

"Of course."

"Although I cannot tell even you much more at this moment, I can tell you that this is an operation where the intelligence agencies of my country and its sworn 'nonexistent' enemy are working together."

The Deputy Director's eyebrows lifted.

"You are surprised?"

"Ezra, very little surprises me anymore. I assume this 'shotgun marriage' is not for publication anywhere ...?"

"Correct."

"... and that the stakes are very high indeed ..."

"Correct."

"... and the powers that be have ensured that international heads will roll if the veil of secrecy is pierced in any way?"

"Right on all counts, Jean-Claude."

"So why Paris?"

"Because any telephone call, cell phone or landline, regardless of where in Iran it originated, would be intercepted by the 39th Air Base Wing at Incirlik, Turkey."

"Ah yes," the Deputy Director said, puffing at his pipe. Ezra Caen had never seen the man without a pipe close to hand. "Those famous people who brought you the U2 incident a hundred or so years ago. But you've got some of the most sophisticated equipment in your own country. Why not simply fly back there, do what you have to do, and then return to the latest incarnation of the Persian Empire?"

"We're not any more immune from snooping by our American friends than the 'bad guys.' Not only are the Americans just as eager to find out what's going on in Tel Aviv as in Tehran, but Israelis themselves are so damned nosy that if someone passes gas in Tel Aviv, you can smell it on the Golan Heights within a couple of hours."

DeNault chuckled and blew out a breath of sweet smoke. "And France is less susceptible to espionage?"

"No, but the Middle East gets more headlines than French politics nowadays."

"Was my Department one that you intended to call?"

"Of course, but as long as you'll be the first one I speak to, is there a more private venue where we could meet?"

~ ∫ ~

The café was far removed from tourist Paris, three blocks from the terminus of the newest Metro line, generally inhabited by working-class men who couldn't care less about the goings-on beyond the few-block radius where they lived and worked. DeNault and Ezra Caen sat in a back corner of the room, where they would not be noticed by anyone looking in from the street.

"Jean-Claude, commencing tomorrow morning I will make five completely unofficial calls to people I know or people whom I know have heard of me. People I'm told can be trusted to keep matters confidential. Each call will be timed to take place either early in the morning or at the end of the workday, to intelligence agencies in Washington, London, Brussels, Berlin, and Moscow."

"Not to your own people?"

"They already know what's going on. That will be my next round of investigation."

"And Iran?"

"Do you know of Manucher Tabrizi?"

"Yes. He trained with DGSE. An excellent man, as good in his own way as you, This must be of critical importance if they've put the two of you in harness together."

"I'll deliver the same message to each of them as I'll give you now."

"I'm listening, my friend."

"You know I cannot yet put this request for your help on the level of an official inquiry between our two police forces. For the moment, I am not sure if even the intent to commit a crime has been formulated or put into the preparation stage. It's a question of a tip-off, purely routine for the moment. We are looking for a woman – at least we think it is a woman, but it could as easily be a man, and we suspect that this person is easily able to shift sexual identities as the situation requires. We know extremely little about this person ... not even a name or an accurate description."

The Deputy Director remained silent, puffing his pipe, alert.

A middle-aged waiter came by. He wore a soiled apron and was obviously at the end of his shift. He looked at the two men, but said nothing.

"*Café Americain, s'il vous plait.*"

"The same," Ezra remarked.

After the man had brought two cups of Nescafe to the table, Ezra continued. "Whoever this person is or may be, she or he must have one qualification that marks her – and I will assume at this point the person is a 'she' – out. She would have to be one of the world's top professional contract-for-hire Assassins – not a gangland hit person, but a political Assassin with several successful kills to her credit. Not an Iranian. A foreigner. And the only lead we have is the possibility, and it is only based on the word of a Saudi prince who was 'interrogated' in a most brutal manner before he was mutilated and killed, that she is South African. We would be interested to know if you have anybody like that in your files, even if she or he has never operated in your own country. Or anybody that even springs to mind."

"*Mon cher ami*, would it not stand to reason that your first inquiry would be to the South Africans?"

"I have other ideas as far as they are concerned."

~∫~

Caen's conversations with the intelligence services took place over the next week. Ezra had no illusions that the homicide departments of the major police forces of the world in which he functioned would fail to understand what he was hinting at but could not say. There was only one target in Iran that could interest a world class political killer.

Without exception, the reply was the same. "Yes, of course. We'll go through all the files for you. I'll try and get back to you before the day is out. Oh, and Ezra, good luck."

When he put down the encrypted telephone for the last time, Ezra wondered how long it would be before the Foreign Ministers, and even Prime Ministers or Presidents of the countries he'd called, not to mention Israel and Iran, would be aware of what was going on. Probably not long. Even a policeman had to report to the politicians something of that size. He was fairly certain the Ministers would keep quiet about it. There was, after all, a strong bond over and above political differences between men and women of power the world over. They were all members of the same club: the potentates. They stuck together against common enemies, and what could be more frightening to any of them than the threat of a political Assassin? He was aware all the same that if the inquiry did become public knowledge and reached the media, or, worse, the internet, it would be blasted across he world and his career could be finished.

10

Ezra Caen had no illusions about the South Africans. Since the assumption of power by the ANC, the entire face of that country had changed, and not simply from white to black. No one knew who could be trusted. The NIA, the South African National Intelligence Agency, had only been formed in 1994, following the first multiracial elections. It had taken over from the NIS, the extremely well-respected National Intelligence Service under the old regime. Several former NIS operatives had been recruited by the Israelis, the United States, and other advanced intelligence agencies throughout Europe. The new NIA was notoriously underfunded and, because it was not a high priority service and pay was relatively poor, it was notoriously corrupt, reflecting the growing pains of the young country.

Ezra decided not to enlist the *official* intelligence agency of the Republic of South Africa. Instead, he searched a compartment in his old-fashioned wallet on which he had handwritten a single first name and a telephone number. If there was anyone he could trust in that far-off land, coincidentally the country of his birth, it would be that man.

~ ∫ ~

Heinrikus Pretorius VI – "Henk" – former head of the NIS, had been "retired," that is to say pushed out, when the new government took over in 1994. But he had remained in South Africa and founded a small, discreet private detective agency, which had done very well indeed. There would always be those who relished professionalism and could afford to pay for the best, particularly when they viewed the "official" intelligence service as sadly lacking.

After he'd received the call from Paris, Pretorius put down the telephone with a thoughtful frown. A friend in need, particularly an old and close friend in need, who'd done Henk a lot of favors, was a friend indeed.

~ ∫ ~

"There's no doubt in my mind what kind of inquiry Ezra's making, nor of his motives for making it," Pretorius said to his old friend, Yvette Van Ruys, who was still on the government payroll, and a perfect mole to search out the NIA's records and the old NIS files down in the cellar. "The Israelis and the Iranians – an unlikely marriage if ever there was one – got some kind of a tip-off that a top-class Assassin was on the loose, and it affects them both. It doesn't take too much gray matter to figure out who'd be the only possible target in Iran for that kind of killer. Yvette, I'm asking if you would, as a personal favor to me, check every existing record of known living professional Assassins in this country. Not run-of-the-mill gangland thugs who either have or are known to be capable of knocking off somebody in a feud with the underworld. Political killers, men or women, capable of assassinating a well-guarded politician or statesman for money."

Within two hours, Yvette Van Ruys called Henk Pretorius from a secure phone outside NIA. "Apparently there's no one in Criminal Records who fits the description, unless you count Colonel Hoare."

"Mad Mike? He's got to be as old as Methuselah."

"Ninety-three. Last I heard, the old guy still had all his marbles," Yvette said.

"Can you get hold of him?"

"Probably. He might be someone Ezra'd be interested in talking to. As for the rest of your request, I found eighteen known contract-hire killers from the underworld. Ten in jail, of which six are black – not likely they'd be able to sneak into the Islamic Republic even if they were on the loose. Of the eight on the outside, they all work for the big gangs, either here or in Pretoria or Cape Town. None of them would be appropriate for a job against a big-name country leader."

"So it's a dead end?"

"Not necessarily, Henk. Have you thought of calling Rhys Davis, who's still with External Security?"

"Good idea, Yvette. He'd have his hands in a lot of international cookie jars."

Shortly thereafter, Pretorius emailed a brief message to Ezra Caen at DGSE. "Following your inquiry of this date fullest research of criminal records reveals no candidate known to us. Request was passed on to a contact at Special Branch. Should we try to contact Methuselah?"

In Paris, Caen received the email. He knew exactly who Pretorius meant. He sent back a two word reply. "Yes, please."

~ ∫ ~

Deputy Superintendent Rhys Davis of External Security emerged from the Commissioner's Office just before five in the afternoon feeling perfectly miserable. Not only had his summer cold lodged in his chest and become the worst kind of bronchitis, which had left him sleepless the night before, but there'd been a cock-up in the cordon protecting the Russian trade minister and even though he'd had nothing to do with it, he'd been the closest one whom the Commissioner could blame.

After Pretorius' call, Davis felt still worse. There are few things that any policeman, regardless of the branch, likes less than the specter of a political assassination. But in the inquiry he had just received from Henk Pretorius, he'd not even been given a name or anything else of value to go on.

Although the short list of known suspects would be extremely short, it still presented Davis and his department with hours of checking files, records for political troublemaking, convictions, and, unlike the criminal branch, mere suspicions. All of these would have to be checked. There was only one ray of light in what Pretorius had told him: the killer would be a professional operator and not one of the numberless bee-in-the-bonnet types that made External Security's life a misery when there was a hint of a possible assassination attempt but nothing else to go on.

Davis summoned two detective inspectors whom he knew to be presently engaged in low-priority research work, told them to drop whatever they were doing, and report to his office. His briefing to them was shorter than Henk Pretorius's had been to him. He told them what they were looking for but not why. The suspicions of the Iranians and the Israelis that such a person might be out to kill the Grand Ayatollah Khamenei need have nothing to do with the search through the archives and records of South African External Security. The three of them cleared the desks of outstanding paperwork and settled down.

~ ∫ ~

"Nothing."

The second of the two young detective inspectors in Rhys Davis's office closed the last of the folders he'd been directed to read and looked across at his superior. His colleague had also finished and his conclusion had been the same. Davis himself had finished five minutes before and had walked over to the window, standing with his back to the room and staring at the traffic flowing past in the night. His throat was raw from cigarettes, which he knew he should not have been smoking with bronchitis, but he found it hard to shake the habit, particularly when he was under pressure.

The incessant calls he had made through the late afternoon and into the early evening checking on characters that turned up in the records and files had uniformly proved negative. Either the man, or, in two cases, the woman, was fully accounted for, or simply not of the professional class to undertake a mission like killing the Supreme Leader of Iran.

"That's it, then," he said firmly, turning back from the window. "We've done all we can, and there just isn't anybody who could possibly fit the guidelines laid down in Pretorius's request."

"Could it be that there's a South African who does this kind of work, but who's not in our files?" suggested one of the inspectors.

"They're all in our files," growled Davis. It did not amuse him to think that as interesting a subject as a professional assassin existed in his jurisdiction without being on file *somewhere*, and his temper was not improved by his bronchitis, which was now coupled with a sharp headache.

"But Sir," the other inspector persisted, "a political killer is an extremely rare species. There probably isn't such a thing in this country. It's not quite what South Africans do, is it?"

Davis glowered back. He did not appreciate having his authority challenged.

"All right, boys, Pack up the files and take them back to registry. I'll reply that a thorough search has revealed no such character known to us. That's all we can do."

The two younger men had gathered up all the material and headed for the door. One of them turned back with a thoughtful frown.

"Super, there's one thing that occurred to me while I was checking. If there is such a person, and he or she has got South African nationality, it seems that person probably wouldn't operate here anyway. Even someone like that has to have a base somewhere, sort of a place to come back to. Chances are such a person would be a respectable citizen in his or her own country."

"What are you getting at, Inspector?"

"Something like a Jekyll and Hyde character. I mean, if there really is a professional killer of the kind we've been trying to track, and he or she is big enough for somebody to pull the kind of weight necessary to start an investigation like this, with a man of your rank leading it, the person in question must be big. And if he or she is that, such a person must have a few jobs behind him or her. Otherwise, he wouldn't be anything, would he?"

"Go on," said Davis, watching him carefully.

"Well, I just thought that a man or woman like that would probably operate only outside his or her own country, so that such a person wouldn't normally come to the attention of the internal security forces. Perhaps one of the services might have got wind of him once ..."

Davis considered the idea, then slowly shook his head. "Forget it, go on home. I'll write the report. And just forget we ever made the inquiry."

But when the inspectors had gone, the idea remained in Davis's mind. He could sit down and write the report now. Completely negative. Drew a blank. There could be no comebacks on the basis of the records search he had just made. But supposing there was something behind Pretorius's inquiry? Henk Pretorius was an honorable man. More important, he was a balanced, seasoned law enforcement professional. Suppose there was more to the story than a mere rumor? Chances were heavily odds-on there was no killer, and if there were, then he or she came from one of those nations with long histories of political assassinations. But what if Pretorius's suspicions were accurate? Henk had dropped the name Ezra Caen. Rhys Davis did not know Caen personally, but his reputation had preceded him. What if the killer turned out to be South African, even by birth alone?

Davis was intensely proud of his department's record. They had never lost a visiting foreign dignitary. There had never been even a whiff of scandal. Deputy Superintendent Rhys Davis had three years to go before retirement and the cottage on False Bay in the Western Cape Province. Better be safe. Check everything.

Davis lifted the telephone on his desk and asked for a number …

~ ∫ ~

"How many countries have you served in as cultural attaché, Barry?"

"More than I care to count."

The two men had met for a drink in a quiet pub halfway between Johannesburg and Pretoria at eight-thirty that evening.

"I surmise this meeting has nothing to do with the local football game in some rum little pimple-on-the-arse of an even less significant country."

"I've got a bit of a problem and hoped you might be able to help."

"Well ... if I can," said the diplomat.

Davis explained the situation to his friend and recited the blanks drawn by Special Ops and External Security. "It occurred to me that if there ever was such a person, and a South African at that, he or she might be the kind who'd never get his or her hands dirty inside this country. Might just stick to operations abroad. If he or she had ever left a trail, maybe they'd come to the attention of the Service,"

"Service?" asked the diplomat, Barry Diehl, quietly.

"Come on, Barry. We have to know a lot of things from time to time." Davis's voice was barely above a murmur. "We had to turn over a lot of files during the Zuma investigation. A lot of Foreign Office people got a peek at what they were really up to. Yours was one, see. You were in Zuma's section at the time he came under suspicion. So I know what department you work with."

"I see," said Diehl.

"Now look, I may be Rhys Davis down at Ex-Security, but I'm also a superintendent of criminal investigations. You can't all be anonymous from everyone, now, can you?"

Diehl stared into his glass.

"Is this an official inquiry for information?"

"No, I can't make it that. The initial request was from Ezra Caen ..."

"The Israeli?"

"Yes. One of your coreligionists. He made a request on the quiet to Henk Pretorius. Sometimes things have to be done that way. Very delicate, all this. Mustn't get out to the media or anywhere else if you get my drift. Chances are there's nothing here in South Africa that might help Caen in any way. I just thought I'd cover all the angles, and you were the last."

"This assassin is supposed to be after Khamenei?"

"Seems to be by the sound of the inquiry. But the Israelis and the Iranians are playing it very cagey. They don't want any publicity."

"Obviously. But why not contact us directly?"

"The request has been put through on the old boy network. From Caen to Pretorius direct."

Diehl nursed his drink a while longer.

"What are you thinking?" Davis asked.

"Do you remember the Hariri incident?"

"Of course. The Lebanese Prime Minister was killed by a car bomb outside Beirut in '05."

"Struck a very sore nerve in our section," Diehl continued. "The old regime had cozied up to the Israelis all along and we were just starting to make inroads into the Arab Middle East. A lot of people got moved around. Had to be done. One of the men who had to be removed very fast was our top resident in Lebanon. He was rotated back to Pretoria for a few months while things were cooling down. The accepted version of the story was that unknown persons, presumed to be Hezbollah in concert with Syrian intelligence services, had planted the bomb.

"I worked in the same office with the fellow who'd been rotated back. One day he happened to mention a rumor that Hariri was dead even before the bomb went off. The rumor was, of all things, that

Hariri had been killed by a single shot from a marksman with a rifle. A shot from a hundred-fifty yards away while the car was accelerating. Went through the little triangular window on the rear passenger side. According to my informant, the limousine had been in the shop two days before because the window had been broken, and they hadn't yet replaced the armored glass in that one little window."

"Interesting story," Davis commented.

"The odd thing was, rumor had it that the shooter was a South African woman."

There was a long pause as the two men considered what Attaché Diehl had said. Finally Davis broke the silence. "This … woman … in the rumor. Did she have a name?"

"I don't remember. It was just talk in the office at the time. We had an awful lot on our plate then, and a Prime Minister in a faraway little country wasn't the most important thing at the time."

"This colleague who talked to you, do you know if he wrote a report?"

"Must have," Diehl replied. "Standard Operating Procedure. But it was just a rumor, understand? Just a rumor. Nothing to go on. We go on facts, solid information, not wild-arse hearsay."

"I understand. But it must have been filed somewhere?"

"I suppose so," the attaché said. "Very low priority, only a bar rumor. Pretoria abounds in rumors."

"But you could just have a look back at the files, couldn't you? See if the woman had a name or anything else about her?"

"I suppose there'd be no harm in me looking. Chasing down a several-year-old rumor might get me sent to Tara," Diehl said, mentioning the old white-regime mental institution in Johannesburg. "But it wouldn't get me canned or demoted. You get on home. I'll call you if I find anything that might help."

They walked back to the rear of the pub, deposited the glasses, and made for the street door.

"I'd be grateful," Davis said as they shook hands. "Probably nothing to it. But just on the off-chance. ..."

DECEMBER

11

Pomfret is less than five kilometers from the border with Botswana. It is difficult to find a more remote town in South Africa. To get there one must pass Eugène Terre'Blanche's old farm in Ventersdorp and drive thirty kilometers down a white dirt road, too insignificant for a road map. At the end of the road to seemingly nowhere, you stumble across an old red Coca-Cola sign, with "Welcome to the Republic of Pomfret" sprayed on it in black ink. The older Pomfret children remember being trained to shoot guns in Namibia. Now they take aim at their frustration through the eyepiece of a spray paint can.

Driving down the pothole-riddled tar road blanketed with a layer of sand is like stepping onto the set of a post-apocalypse film. Rust and stray goats reclaim old barracks and mess halls. The wind whistles through broken windows and rustles into alien pine trees. One can find two R4 assault rifle butts under a layer of dust. The old, disabled, widowed, and orphaned roam the town.

Rural Pomfret has been squeezed hard and residents feel it's deliberate. Water supply is erratic and brown. A mobile clinic visits on Mondays and Tuesdays – sometimes. The municipal offices and the police station have been moved to neighboring towns. There is no government in Pomfret.

Thirty years ago, Pomfret was home to the 32 Battalion – the ultimate mercenary village. Today, legend surrounds the role 32 Battalion played in the border wars like a blood-soaked bandage. Whether the war was useful, and what its purpose was, depends on who you are talking to. Whichever version one listens to, it is caught in the crossfire between the history books and decades of rumor.

In 1984, when the Assassin was sixteen, South Africa was fighting the "Communist threat" in Angola and Namibia. The South African Defence Force "recruited" a group of Angolan fighters, sometimes with force. Armed with heavy artillery like no black South African counterparts had encountered, 32 Battalion was the SADF's most lethal and effective weapon, the best counter-insurgency unit in the world at the time. The first black officers in South Africa came out of that unit. There were 10 of them in 1985. The battalion acted as a buffer between the enemy and other SADF units for many years.

Morgan, for that was the name she'd been given by her adoptive parents, the Terre'Blanches, had grown up on their farm in *Boer* country and had come to believe in all the *Afrikaner* values, most particularly that God had give this wondrous land to the white man and that the *Afrikaner* leadership owed a debt to that God to care for their "little black or brown brothers," the Bantu. Indeed, when he was twenty-two, Morgan's six-years-older brother, Retief, whom she adored with all her heart and soul, had joined the SADF and immediately volunteered for duty in the heart of the Kalahari Desert, not far from where Morgan had grown up.

And grown up she certainly had. Morgan was never a robust-looking Brunhilde, but she possessed considerable beauty which, even then, she knew how to show off to its best advantage. Although she had not aspired at that early date to become a killer, she'd been taught by her brother to be a remarkably good shot. The Pieter Terre'Blanche branch of the family, unlike Uncle Eugène, eschewed political involvement. Pieter's family was a hard-working, tight-knit group, regular churchgoers, and respectable tillers of the soil, and they wanted nothing more than to be left alone and in peace.

The telegram came from the Ministry of the Armed Forces one day at breakfast toward the end of 1984. It said that the Minister was filled with infinite regret to inform Meneer and Mevrou Pieter Terre'Blanche of the death on the South Africa-Botswana border of their son Retief, private soldier in the South African Defence Forces. His personal effects would be returned to the bereaved family at the earliest moment.

Morgan's world disintegrated with the news. Nothing seemed to make sense. The death of her older brother, who had been the bastion of all that was strong and good in her world – a gentle man despite his willingness to fight for what he believed was right – had been shot and killed, for no reason at all except he was defending a way of life that, for her, was as natural as waking up each morning to the sound of the rooster or the endless yammering of wild birds in the Kalahari.

She began to hate. It was the loathsome, dirty, cowardly *kaffirs*, the soulless Bantus, not the ones from Namibia, who populated the 32 Battalion and had been trained by men like Retief to protect *Boer* soil, but the natives of her own country, the Zulus, the Khosa, and the thirty-two other tribes who populated South Africa. The angry ones who would emulate the bastards like Robert Mugabe and his gang, and who would try to steal the government for themselves, just as the Blacks had stolen Southern Rhodesia from its duly constituted and legitimate leadership.

Then Jan came. Quite suddenly, one late summer morning at the end of January 1985, he turned up at the Pieter Terre'Blanche home on a Sunday, when her parents had gone to Bloemfontein for the weekend. The heat of the Kalahari was not oppressive that morning. He looked tan and fit. He asked if he could speak to Miss Morgan Terre'Blanche.

"*Dit is my,*" she responded. "That's me. *Wat wil jy hê, Meneer?*"

He replied that he commanded the platoon in which one Retief Terre'Blanche, private soldier, had been killed, and he bore a letter. She asked him in.

The letter had been written some weeks before Retief died, and he had kept it in his inside pocket during the patrol looking for a band of *kaffirs* who had wiped out a settler family, then fled across the frontier. They had not found the guerillas, but had run into a band of Bantu irregulars – "freedom fighters" they had called themselves. There had been a bitter skirmish at dusk and Retief had taken a bullet through the lungs. He gave the letter to the platoon commander before he died.

Morgan read the letter and cried a little. It said nothing about the last weeks, just chatter about the barracks at Pomfret, the assault courses and the discipline, and how the members of 32 Battalion were "good *swart mense*" who knew their place in society and respected their white superiors. The rest she learned through Jan, the pull-back through the scrub for six kilometers while the irregulars and guerillas engaged in hit-and-run tactics, the repeated calls on the radio for air support, and the eventual arrival of the fighter-bombers with their screaming engines and thundering rockets. And how her brother, who had volunteered for one of the toughest platoons to prove he was a man, had died like one, coughing blood over the legs of a brother soldier, who'd been killed just before Retief had been shot.

Jan treated her with calm understanding. As a man, he was hard as a rock, hardened by his years as a professional soldier. But he was very gentle with the sister of one of his platoon. She liked him for that and accepted his offer to dine in the nearest town of any size. Besides, she feared her parents would return and surprise them. She did not want them to hear how Retief had died, for both of them had managed to numb themselves to the loss in the intervening months and somehow carry on as usual. Over dinner, she swore the platoon commander to silence and he agreed.

But her own curiosity became insatiable. She hungered to know about the border war, what really was happening. Jan started coming around the Pieter Terre'Blanche house, ingratiating himself to Morgan's parents by telling them he'd been in Retief's unit, by regaling them with exciting tales of the border skirmishes, without going into any of the details on how their son had died. Morgan's parents took a liking to the fine young Afrikaner and did nothing to stem what they took to be his budding interest in their younger chid.

In March 1985, Morgan asked whether Jan could teach her the way in which the South African Defence Forces taught the members of 32 Battalion how to shoot to kill those who engaged in civil disturbances. He assented and was gratified to see how much of a crack shot Retief had already taught her to be. Perhaps that was the start of her journey toward becoming a professional assassin. She could never say for certain.

It was from Jan that she first heard of the ANC and their bloody Communist leader. Nelson Mandela was, praise God, now rotting in Pollsmoor Prison after being transferred from Robben Island. There had been more and more talk that the stupidly-named "African National Congress" intended to take over the government of the Republic within the next decade.

In April, Jan took two weeks' leave and went directly to the residence of a friend who was absent in Cape Town. The home was ten kilometers from the Pieter Terre'Blanche homestead. By that time, sixteen-year-old Morgan had built him up in her private thoughts as the symbol of all that was good, clean, strong, and handsome in Afrikaner young manhood. She had kept his picture on her bedside table throughout the day and evening, and pulled up her nightgown and clasped the picture to her belly while she slept.

No sooner she learned of Jan's leave and where he had gone than Morgan arranged to meet him at five each evening, making sure she returned home by nine-thirty that night. Her parents did not know where she went, and it appeared that they weren't the least bit interested in where she went, so long as she spent the night under their roof.

It was in the friend's home that Morgan had happily and vigorously given up her virginity. Even now, all these years later, when she touched her breasts, she could feel Jan's strong, but gentle hands. She could feel his hardness as he entered her, the spasms that wracked her body with unimaginable pleasure as she came and came and came again, often as many as three times in the few hours they spent together each evening. That South Africa should remain white was, for both of them, the combat hardened officer and the adoring teen-age girl – now woman – an article of faith.

Jan never knew about the baby. He returned to his unit at the end of April and a month-and-a-half later a united Bantu front attacked his platoon in his field headquarters eight kilometers north of Pomfret. Early in June, Jan was shot and killed in a skirmish with the attackers.

Morgan, who had expected no letters after Jan returned to active duty, suspected nothing until she was told the news in July. She left home on the pretext of taking a two-month holiday in Bloemfontein, telling her parents that she needed to spread her wings and broaden her horizons. She took a flat in a cheap suburb of the judicial capital of South Africa and tried to commit suicide by closing all the doors and windows in the apartment and turning on an unlit gas burner on the stove. She failed because the dingy flat had too many leaks, but she lost the baby.

By the time she returned, she was slightly pale – her parents thought it was because of the cold winter weather – but otherwise looked fine. On the outside.

On the inside, she had died. She never again used the name Morgan Terre'Blanche. The derogatory term *kaffir*, which many Afrikaners applied to the black Bantu peoples, without differentiating between them, means "soulless one." Morgan Terre'Blanche, who professed such a hatred for the Bantus, had, herself, become a soulless one.

From that day forward, she fulfilled her destiny: she metamorphosed into a trained, merciless professional killer. Her motives were simple: Retief and Jan, who had been indiscriminately, senselessly killed, must be avenged, no matter who the victim was. And if she could make a living from such killing, so much the better.

~ ∫ ~

When the border war officially ended in 1989, the 32 Battalion soldiers couldn't return to Angola – they had fought their own. They couldn't live in South African townships. They had been used by the White government in suppressing anti-apartheid uprisings. The soldiers and their families were given refuge in the army base town of Pomfret. In 1993, the battalion was disbanded. Fighting for the apartheid government made them perpetrators, not victims, in the new South Africa.

By 2000 the army base in Pomfret closed and the officers boarded up their church and bar, but the Angolans remained. The veterans were given pensions. Some of the young and fit were integrated into the newly-formed SANDF, but about a quarter stayed in Pomfret. They had a meager pension allowance, but a set of skills that made them valuable soldiers in war zones worldwide. It wasn't long before Pomfret became a recruiting ground for private security companies.

Things were quiet for a while, until a group of ex-32 Battalion men were arrested in Zimbabwe in 2004, allegedly hired to start a coup in Equatorial Guinea. In 2008, the government ordered police and the military to clear out Pomfret. They declared the old asbestos mine, less than a kilometer from the town, hazardous, and residents were to be moved to RDP homes in Mafikeng.

Wounds became old scars. More than two decades later, the veterans were still not at peace. The 32 Battalion veterans' website lashed out at those who "betrayed us and our families and dishonored our fallen for political exploit."

12

The Assassin was never one to keep loose ends untied. So far she had used the passports and visas of Rudolph Hostetler and Sister Mary Salvatore, as well as the driving licence and insurance papers of Meneer Hostetler, and had absorbed and morphed into their respective identities when she'd been in the Islamic Republic.

Now, in the comfort of her late parents' big old farmhouse, between Bloemfontein and the Botswana border, she carefully checked the original documents from each of her alter egos.

Each of the eight passports had identical information for height and weight: 165 centimeters tall, 55 kilograms. Seven of the eight had been born between April 4, 1968 and October 15 of the same year, three men, four women. One man was much older.

Of the women, Hannelore deWet, the South African farmer had dishwater dark blonde hair and brown eyes; Sister Mary had close-cropped dark hair and brown eyes; the Namibian nurse, Trude Schechter had coarse, straw-blonde hair and blue eyes, and French-Comorian Simone DesMoulins, whose papers listed her as a hotel worker, had medium brown hair and brown eyes. All of them had deliberately neutral coloring, which would allow them to blend in with the landscape.

Of the males, Petrus Jooste, the South African educator, had dark sand-colored hair, which he kept in a short brush-cut, and brown eyes. Hostetler was everyman, with clear eyeglasses to further diminish his individuality. Richard McAdams, was a retired cellist who'd performed with the Pretoria Symphony Orchestra. He kept his iron gray hair cut short and had clear brown eyes. The Comorian, Vito Ligeiro, had emigrated to Comoros from Brazil, where he'd been a martial arts master. His short hair was curly, slightly different from the others.

With a little less than two months to go, the killer began a regimen she'd used successfully for more years than she could remember. Each morning began with an hour of yoga, followed by a ten kilometer run along a path that included uphill rises and downhill descents before returning to the house. After twenty minutes in the wood sauna at the highest heat level she could stand, she immersed herself in a cold water pool for the next quarter hour. By that time, she needed nourishment. Breakfast was Spartan. Afterward she lay on her hard bed and engaged in meditation for the next hour. By the time the sun reached its zenith, her physical exertions and mental exercises for that day completed, she allowed herself the luxury of a couple of hours at her computer, playing mindless games, or simply putting her mind in neutral and listening to YouTube, Pandora, or other sundry programs. The Assassin had no concern that her computer might be traced.

~ ∫ ~

"Colonel, I need a favor." The connection was as clear as though the caller were in the next room. The nonagenarian immediately recognized the voice, although it had been nearly thirty years since the two men had last seen one another.

"How the hell did you manage to find me, you old fart?"

"Way back in the day, when I was Noriega's Number Two and your Ancient Order of Froth-Blowers was trying to muck up the Seychelles, you gave me a very private phone number where I could reach you day or night, and I did the same for you. Of course, you're somewhere between 95 and death, so I wouldn't expect you to remember a little thing like that."

"Ninety-four next birthday, arsehole. And while you're at it, you puppy, you might want to show a little respect for your elders."

"I'll show you as little as I can. You're what, five years my senior?"

"You made it to eighty-eight Jewboy?"

"Uh-huh, Irishman."

The two men had known each other for forty years. Their paths had crossed only infrequently, but they'd developed not only the mutual respect for one another that the very top professionals in any field develop along life's pathway, but also a genuine liking for each other and a trust that one would take care of the other – including the other's "people," if the need arose.

The older of the two, Thomas Michael "Mad Mike" Hoare, an Irishman, had been born in India, spent his early days in Ireland, was educated in England, and served in North Africa as an armor officer during World War II. After completing his training as a chartered accountant, he emigrated to South Africa where he alternately ran safaris and became a soldier-for-hire in various African countries.

His first mercenary action took place in 1961 in Katanga, a province trying to break away from the newly independent Congo. Three years later, Congolese Prime Minister Moïse Tshombe hired "Major" Mike Hoare to lead a military unit called *5 Commando (Congo)*, made up of 300 men, most of whom were from South Africa. The unit's mission was to fight a breakaway rebel group. Later, Hoare and his mercenaries worked in concert with Belgian paratroopers, Cuban exile pilots, and CIA-hired mercenaries who managed to save 1,600 Europeans and missionaries in Stanleyville from the Simba rebels. Hoare was promoted to Lieutenant-Colonel in the ANC and *5 Commando* expanded into a two-battalion force. By the time he "retired," he had become one of the most famous mercenary leaders in the world, the soldier who had swept the Congo clean of "savages," the man who made modern mercenary soldiering briefly, but confusingly, respectable. He'd become the ideal mercenary leader, soft-spoken, quietly confident, cool, collected, charming in manner, boyish in looks, dapper in uniform, every inch the English officer and gentleman.

It was during this period that Hoare acquired the sobriquet "Mad" Mike, when the German Democratic Republic radio in Berlin dubbed him, "The mad bloodhound, Mike Hoare."

Colonel Hoare's last "public" connivance took place in the Seychelles, fourteen years later, in 1978, when "Mad Mike" was fifty-eight years old. Seychelles exiles in South Africa, acting on behalf of the ex-president, contacted Hoare to fight alongside fifty-three other mercenary soldiers made up of South African Special Forces, former Rhodesian soldiers, and ex-Congo mercenaries. Hoare got together a group of white, middle class mercenaries, dubbed them "Ye Ancient Order of Froth-Blowers" after a posh English social club of the 1930s, and took off for the Seychelles, hiding AK-47 assault rifles in his luggage. Unfortunately, the fighting started prematurely when one of Hoare's men accidentally got in the "something to declare" line and the customs officer insisted on searching his bag.

Fighting ensued at the airport and in the middle of this, Air India Flight 224 landed at the airport, damaging a flap as it grazed one of the trucks strewn on the runway. Hoare managed to negotiate a ceasefire before the aircraft and passengers were caught in the crossfire. After several hours, the mercenaries found themselves on board the Boeing aircraft. Always one to take advantage of an adverse situation, Hoare had found fuel for the aircraft. When the aircraft left Seychelles airspace, Hoare's men still had their weapons. Hoare asked the captain if he would allow the door to be opened so they could ditch the weapons over the sea before they returned to South Africa. The captain laughed at Hoare's lack of knowledge about how pressurized aircraft functioned and told him it would not be possible. Four of the mercenary soldiers were left behind and were convicted of treason in the Seychelles.

Ultimately, in 1983, Mike Hoare was found guilty of airplane hijacking and sentenced to 10 years in prison. While still in prison, he began signing up "Honorary Members" in "The Wild Geese." Many thousands of active and former military personnel applied to Colonel Hoare, giving him a huge database of potential mercenary "contract employees." However, no one knows what happened thereafter, for "Mad Mike" Hoare dropped off the face of the earth.

Another Mike, eighty-eight year old Mike Harari, had followed a somewhat different, but not *that* different a road. Harari, an Israeli intelligence officer in the *Mossad*, had been involved in several notable operations.

Harari began his intelligence work facilitating illegal Jewish immigration to Palestine after World War II. By the 1960s, he'd been recruited by the Mossad and ran agents in Europe, eventually advancing to the head of the Operations Branch. It was during this time that he helped build and lead teams in *Operation Wrath of God*, the Israeli response to the Munich Massacre at the 1972 Summer Olympics. In what became known as the Lillehammer Affair, Harari led a team into Norway, where they believed Ali Hassan Salameh, the chief of *Black September* operations, was living. After identifying and assassinating the target, the gunmen learned that they had killed an innocent waiter, who only resembled Salameh. While authorities arrested many of his team, Harari escaped to Israel.

Despite this setback, Harari later scored two major successes for the Mossad. He was instrumental in *Operation Thunderbolt*, which successfully freed Israeli hostages at Entebbe International Airport in July 1976, and in January 1979, Harari led a team that actually managed to kill the real Ali Hassan Salameh in Beirut, by means of a car bomb.

Later on, Mike Harari was reputed to be Noriega's right-hand man, after he had personally trained the Panamanian dictator's elite forces. Still later, more rumors surfaced about his involvement in certain troubles in Malaysia. But regardless of what was said or rumored, at the time of his private telephone call to the ancient "Mad Mike" Hoare, octogenarian Mike Harari was still living in quiet seclusion in a suburb of Tel Aviv.

"What d'you need, Boy?" Hoare asked the Israeli.

"You ever heard of *le bûcheur*?"

"Ezra Caen? Yeah, he's one of the best there is. How old is he now?"

"A little less than half your age, Colonel. He's got something where he might be in way over his head and it's got to be kept so quiet that even with your hearing aids turned all the way up to maximum you'd never be able to hear it."

"I'm listening."

~ ∫ ~

"There's only one person that comes to mind," Hoare said.

"You actually *know* such a person?"

"No one I know *knows* her, not me, not anyone of my acquaintance. She's never been part of the club. Never wanted to be. The ultimate lone she-wolf."

"She is a *she*, then?"

"Yeah. I'm told she was a passably good-looking woman in her day. Might still be, for all I know. You ever hear of Eugène Terre'Blanche?"

"'South Africa for the white man and fuck everybody else.' He's the guy founded the AWB party and when the post-apartheid government took over in '94 he tried to break away and form an independent Afrikaner homeland."

"A real shit-stirrer."

"Didn't he get hacked to death in 2010?"

"He got beaten with pipes and machetes by a couple of Black men, supposedly because they hadn't been paid. Took place at his farm, just outside Ventersdorp, up near the Botswana frontier."

"Near Pomfret, the old mercenary town?" Harari remarked.

"Yeah. Anyway, the rumor – and it's only that – is that she is, or once was, his adopted niece."

"*Once* was? Adopted?"

"She disappeared off the face of the earth more than twenty-five years ago. No one seems to know why. She was only a seventeen or eighteen-year-old kid at the time."

"No name, Colonel?"

"None that I know of. But if she's Terre'Blanche's niece, adopted or otherwise, you might start by looking up any of Eugène's relatives named Terre'Blanche and see if any of them might have adopted a kid way back when ..."

~ ʃ ~

"Marco? Mustafa here." No last names were used. "You got everything I sent?"

"Uh-huh. Do you think the venture is compromised beyond salvation?"

"It may not be, but we've got to warn her immediately."

"Only one way I know. The way we first made contact. It might expose us unnecessarily."

"I don't think we have a choice."

"I'll take care of it."

As the Turk disengaged the line, the intercept, which had been secretly installed in his apartment by the Israeli-Iranian counterterrorists, relayed the conversation to a small, drab office in a working class neighborhood in Tehran.

~ ʃ ~

Within twenty-four hours, a sudden, unexplained fire erupted in Mokhotlong, Lesotho's main post office. Because it was an old wooden structure, no one suspected foul play. As residents remarked, it has just been waiting to happen. Unfortunately, all mail, including a telegram that had been sent from Rome, Italy the evening before, was charred beyond recognition.

13

Count Napolitano knew there was a risk involved, but he had to take it. He'd learned the day after the fire gutted the Mokhotlong post office that all mail and messages intended for that small town had been redirected to the capital, Maseru. Although Maseru was on the opposite side of the country, the distance was a scant 133 kilometers, a little over 80 miles, almost exactly halfway between Mokhotlong and Bloemfontein, South Africa.

It stood to reason that if the Assassin's mail drop was in Lesotho and the hired killer was South African, the best chance of alerting her was by disseminating a message to the two most likely places. Speed and urgency were essential. Within hours he had contacted the Bloemfontein *Courant* and the Lesotho *Times*.

For the next five days a black-bordered ad appeared in the upper left-hand corner of the front page of each of those two newspapers:

"AGRIPPINA. MOTHER HAS DIED. PLEASE CALL NAPOLI. MARCO."

The Assassin drove into Bloemfontein for her weekly shopping trip on the fourth day after the message appeared in the Courant. By sheer happenstance, she noticed the black-bordered advertisement as she went through the checkout counter at the Pick n' Pay Hypermarket on Benade Drive. Curious, she purchased the newspaper to see if there were any further details. There weren't.

The killing machine that Morgan Terre'Blanche had become had not succeeded to the top rung of the ladder in her profession by accident. Her fine-tuned antennae picked up the message, wondering why it hadn't come to her the same way as she'd initially been contacted. She learned later that day that the Mokhotlong Post Office had been razed to the ground.

Back at the farmhouse, she found the contact point for her employers, returned to Bloemfontein, and located a Telkom public phone, from which she anonymously called one of the numbers on her list.

~ ∫ ~

That same day, Ezra Caen boarded El Al Flight 51 departing Ben Gurion Airport at 1:10 in the afternoon. Eight-and-a-half hours later, the nonstop flight landed at OR Tambo International Airport outside Johannesburg.

~ ∫ ~

Hoare's message had been that Terre'Blanche's adopted niece had disappeared more than twenty-five years ago and she was seventeen or eighteen at the time. That meant she'd most likely be in her mid-forties, close to Ezra's own age. And she'd been adopted, which most likely meant that there were records of an adoption in any of the then-functioning adoption agencies. However, the chances of finding official records in the registries of municipalities throughout the apartheid Republic of South Africa that long ago would be slim. It might be better to start with the agencies themselves.

The only parents Ezra Caen ever knew had been completely open with him about the circumstances of his birth and the agency from which they'd adopted him. Cotlands was not only still functioning, it was larger than ever and had spread to five provinces, which meant every community of any size in the Republic. That would be as good a place as anywhere to start his search. The morning following his arrival in Johannesburg, he telephoned Cotlands headquarters and arranged an afternoon appointment with the area director.

~ ∫ ~

"I think it's best we talk in person so that we can provide you with what support we can."

"I told you that I work alone, with *no* interference. My anonymity is the best protection each of us have. But I appreciate you letting me know. You say the Iranians and the Israelis are working together?" She laughed mirthlessly. "Strange bedfellows indeed. I predict they'll have a falling out before – or after – the deed is done," the Assassin said.

"You're absolutely certain they won't be able to trace your identity?"

"I'm not saying they'll never be able to learn who I am. But by that time it will be too late."

"You know, you have the option to withdraw because of the change of circumstances?"

"I appreciate your candor," she said. No names were used. "But this just sets up one more challenge. I did not expect this would be a 'walk in the park' when I accepted the assignment. I'll consider what you said, but my inclination is to rise to the challenge."

"Just in case … is there an address where we can reach you between now and then?"

"As I told you before, if I need to get in touch with you, I'll do so."

"But …"

The line went dead.

In her own way, the Assassin was as proud and headstrong as her intended victim.

~ ∫ ~

"If you don't mind, *Mevrou*, might I look at the registry of births, children Cotlands has saved, and adoptive parents from the period 1965 through 1975?" He'd earlier shown the Matron his credentials and had briefly explained to her the reason for his visit.

"I have no difficulty in letting you see the birth records, Inspector Caen. Frankly, we don't normally reveal the name of the adoptive parents, for reasons of privacy. However, given your position and your *bona fides*, an exception is certainly appropriate in this case."

"You are very kind, Matron."

"What an amazing coincidence that you started your own life here at Cotlands," she continued. "It's *most* unusual – *most* unusual indeed – that one of our alumni returns to the fold. The prodigal son," she chuckled. "When did you say you were born?"

"September 2, 1968."

"Forty-five years ago."

"True."

At that moment an elderly man, somewhere in his mid-seventies, knocked on the director's office door.

"You rang, Matron?"

"Yes, Marius. This is Inspector Caen of the Israeli Security Service. He'd like to review the birth and adoption records for the period 1965 to 1975. As our most senior employee, I thought you'd probably be the best one to help him. Do we still *have* records that old?"

"They're down in archives, Matron. We haven't gotten around to loading them onto the computer retrieval system yet. The farthest back we go in the electronic memory bank is '81."

"Please afford Inspector Caen every courtesy, if you will."

"Yes, Matron. Follow me, Sir."

Two hours later, Ezra had gone through the intake records from 1965 to the middle of 1968. He felt a growing sense of nervousness as he got closer to September 1968. It took all of his patience not to flip immediately to September 2. Minutes later, his hand trembling, he read the entry: "02/09/1968, 0100 hours. Call from Queen Vic. Twins, one girl, one boy. Parents shot and killed in crossfire between police and others. Taken in 02/09/1968." There were no other entries for that period.

Ezra sat in the room stunned. He had never been told he was a twin. Indeed, if this entry was correct and he had a twin sister, he'd never met her or even knew of her existence. The magnitude of what he was reading sent shivers down his spine.

Professional investigators often have a sixth sense of having hit something important. But what Ezra Caen felt at that moment was more than that. It was a strange sense of foreboding. He rose and went into the next room where the man the Matron had referred to as Marius was dozing. Ezra gently shook the man's shoulders.

"Excuse me, Sir, but I'd like to follow a couple of entries I've just uncovered. Would you happen to have the outflow adoption records on two babies that were brought here on September 2, 1968?"

"I'll bring them to your carel. Shouldn't be more than five minutes, Mister Caen."

Ezra returned to where he'd been researching the intake records. The entry preceding his own was two weeks earlier and the entry following his was nearly a month later.

"Here you are, Sir," Marius said, handing him a book marked, "Adoptions – 1968."

Ezra looked at the entry immediately preceding his own admission to Cotlands. The boy that had been born two weeks before him had been adopted by a family named Wertham with a Pretoria address.

Next, he came to his own entry. "Boy, white, born 02/09/1968, adopted 03/11/1968 by Bernard and Helena Caen, 19 Cardiff Road, Kensington, Jo'burg. Name: Ezra Caen."

With trembling fingers, Ezra turned to the next entry. "Boy, white, born 29/09/1968, adopted 10/11/1968 by Helmond and Rosalie Silvestre, 478 Groot Vandevere Way, Pretoria. Name: Helmond Silvestre, Junior."

"There must be a misfiled entry," Caen muttered to himself. He pored through the entire book for 1968. No entry for the girl who'd been born on September 2, 1968 – his unknown twin sister. He rose and went to the attendant's office once again.

"Excuse me, Sir," he began. "There seems to be a missing entry here. Might I ask you about it?"

"Sir?" the other man said.

Caen had brought both books into the attendant's office.

"There's an entry here showing twins, a boy and a girl, born September 2, 1968."

"I remember that one myself," the man said. "I was on duty that night and took the call from a nurse at the Queen Victoria Hospital. ... Let me see ...," he said, scratching his forehead. "Ah, yes, the nurse's name was Monica Broede. There'd been an attack outside the Carlton Hotel ... Bantus and police ... Both parents were killed, but the paramedics were able to save the babies ... fraternal twins, a boy and a girl."

"It doesn't give the details. There's an intake entry for the two infants," Caen said. "But then you go to the adoption book. There's an entry for the little boy, but none for the girl."

The attendant looked carefully at the entry for Ezra Caen, then looked through the rest of the 1968 adoption book. He looked up, clearly confused.

"Could the girl have died, Mister ...?"

"Coetzee, Marius Coetzee ... and no, I have a very clear recollection that she did not die." He looked carefully at the adoption book once again. "Actually, I remember she was adopted a couple of days *before* the boy. Why, look at that!" he suddenly exclaimed.

Coetzee pointed to a tiny sliver of paper between the entry before Ezra's and the detective's own entry. In his haste to get to the description of his own adoption, Caen had only casually glanced at the Wertham boy's adoption and proceeded quickly to his own. He had simply assumed – wrongly as it turned out – that his own entry would come before that of his twin sister, not after.

Now, looking at the sliver, Caen realized that an entry had been cut out, using an X-acto knife. It had been cut so close to the edge of the binding that it could easily have been overlooked when one was flipping from page to page looking for a specific entry.

"Are there any other records – any records at all – that might assist me?" Caen asked, hardly daring to hope that any such document existed.

"Matter of fact, there are," Marius Coetzee said, "but it's completely unofficial. I kept my own private journal during the first two years I worked here, just for myself, of course. It was never a part of the official records and the Matron would have cashiered my arse if she knew I had kept it. Totally illegal, of course, breach of privacy and all that."

"Do you still have the book?"

"That I do, Inspector. If you'd like to follow me home after work, I'd be happy to show it to you. Being that it's your sister and all, I can't see where there'd be anything wrong with that."

~ ∫ ~

Coetzee's apartment was modest, but neatly kept. "I'm a widower, you see, and during our marriage one thing my Frances insisted on was that I keep the place clean. Old habits die hard, but I'm content and it's easy to find things. It'll take me only a few moments to find what I'm looking for."

Less than five minutes later, Marius handed Ezra Caen a book in which all the entries had been handwritten.

Flipping to his own entry, Ezra read the same thing he'd seen in the official registry. One page back his eyes widened as he read the entry:

"Girl, white, born 02/09/1968, adopted 17/10/1968 by Pieter and Hannah Terre'Blanche, Farmstead 18, Ventersdorp, Orange Vrystaat. Name: Morgan Terre'Blanche.

14

On the one hand, it had been a pity to burn down the only house she'd ever called home, even though, since the deaths of Retief and Jan so many years ago, it held bad memories for her. On the other hand, the call she'd received from Count Napolitano underscored that she was now the hunted as well as the hunter and that it would be safest to destroy all vestiges of any trail that might lead to her. And with the insurance money added to her fee for the job, she'd be able to restart and rebuild anywhere in the world.

Like everything else, the Assassin had long ago planned for such an eventuality and had carefully explored every option. Not only was there nothing that could tie her to the house, but nothing that could tie her to the fire. To the sight and sound of any passerby who was willing to drive up a long, unpaved gravel road, the old farmstead had been uninhabited for years. There'd been no electric, gas, or water bills. The Assassin had accomplished this by means of installing several generators over the years. Her Terre'Blanche forebears had long ago dug deep wells throughout the property.

While "Agrippina" had her run of the large residence, no one could ever see a light on or hear a sound emanating from the house once the sun had gone down. Her headquarters occupied the basement of the home – a basement whose only access was either by means of a small trapdoor and stairwell or via a tunnel which she had constructed for entry and exit after her adoptive parents' death. The tunnel emerged more than one hundred meters from the house.

Although insurance companies are invariably suspicious, the only possible suspects would either be employees of the security and maintenance agency that took care of the property on behalf of the Agrippina Trust once each week, or strangers who might be in the neighborhood.

For the past several years, the Assassin had parked her car in an abandoned barn adjacent to the private gravel roadway which led to the public macadam secondary road half a mile to the north. Three days ago, she had moved everything she needed from the house to the barn. She had transferred every file in her computer to two duplicate 3 TB portable hard drives and had then used a sledgehammer to destroy both her laptop and desktop. To ensure that they would not be traced, she drove north toward the Botswana frontier and buried various parts in several depressions which she had dug in the desert

The following day, she had driven into Bloemfontein and rented a public storage locker at Oranjezicht Self Storage in Bainsvlei. When she returned to the homestead for the last time, she made a final survey to ensure that she'd taken everything she needed out of the house and that there was not so much as a photo, a computer connection, or a shred of paper to tie her to any portion of the house that did not burn to the ground. She had systematically emptied out the basement during the past week.

Above ground, the residence's exterior was old wood, dry to the point of rotting, and particularly susceptible to fire in the windy midwinter of the Kalahari. She watched without emotion as the old homestead burned, ensuring that only ashes and charred furniture, plumbing, toilet fixtures, and the like, were left. This was the final act of severing all connection with the country of her birth. She had no intention of returning to South Africa after what she envisioned as her final job was completed. When the last of the smoke had dispersed, the Assassin calmly walked out to the barn, put the key into the ignition of her twenty-year-old Toyota Tacoma, and drove two hundred meters down the gravel road before she emerged, walked back to the barn, and threw a lit match onto the gasoline-soaked rags that surrounded that structure.

She drove her old truck to the end of the gravel road and turned right onto the by-road to the Bloemfontein Highway, five miles away. She felt a momentary tug of discomfort as a late model dark sedan occupied by three men, going in the opposite direction, passed her on her right.

Unaware as two ships passing in the night, the Assassin and Ezra Caen had come within ten feet of one another.

~ ∫ ~

"Henk? Good to see you're still holding it together. I thought you would have followed the rest of the White Afrikaners and gone to Dallas, Texas or Irvine, California by now."

"Or to your neck of the woods, Ezra?" Pretorius remarked.

"That, too. Did Barry Diehl come up with anything on that rumor?" Ezra thought it best, even among friends, not to mention what he'd learned at Cotlands.

"Just more rumor," Henk rejoined. "No name, but the diplomatic guy thought they'd traced her back to Vrystaat. White man's country on the edge of the Kalahari."

"Bloemfontein?" Ezra asked.

"Farther north. Near the Botswana frontier," Pretorius said. "Ventersdorp."

With great effort, Ezra Caen ignored the pounding of his heart. "Isn't that Terre'Blanche country?"

"Uh-huh. Eugène's the most notorious of the lot. He's dead now, of course. Had a younger brother, Pieter, died maybe fifteen years ago. Boer farmer. Actually, the family dated back to the Voortrekkers."

"Like you, Henk?"

"Different line of Pretoriuses," the detective chuckled.

"They ever have any children – the Pieter Terre'Blanches?"

"Not that I know of. 'Course, Eugène was the only one ever raised a ruckus in *Suid Afrika*. Any relatives he might have had were nothing more than footnotes to history."

"Any chance you could find out where Peter Terre'Blanche lived?" Ezra asked casually.

"Pretty close to here, according to rumor. I wouldn't be surprised if it was down one of these gravel side roads." Henk Pretorius did not press the issue, although he knew what Caen was working on.

~ ∫ ~

"You fellows investigating this for any reason?" the constable asked.

"I'm a private detective," Pretorius responded smoothly. "I'm Sarel Tregardt, and this gentleman is Jacob Flint, adjuster for Chartis-AIG South Africa."

"You gentlemen suspect foul play?" the policeman asked.

"Hard to say," Caen replied. "Farmstead 18's been around since long before I was born. Nothing but miles and miles of *miles*, and a big old farmhouse that had been there for generations, according to the nearest neighbor, ten miles down the road. No dry brush or anything else within several hundred yards of the building, and it suddenly goes up in flames three nights ago for no reason we can figure."

"Have you checked with the owner?" the constable asked.

"Not immediately available," Caen said. "The policyholder is something called the Agrippina Trust, which lists its address care of Westpac Bank and Trust, Limited, Avarua, Rarotonga, Cook Islands. The Cook Islands have all kinds of privacy laws, and although we can communicate in real time with Westpac, it may take some time for the message to get to the insured."

"Have you checked the registry in Bloemfontein to determine the record owner of the property?"

"Agrippina Trust," Pretorius confirmed.

"Strange," the constable said. "I seem to remember some time ago – might could be twenty years or so? – Pieter Terre'Blanche owned that homestead. 'Course he died a few year back, so it probably got bought up by that Trust."

"You've been here awhile, Constable?"

"Thirty years, Mister Flint."

"Would you happen to know if the Terre'Blanches had any next of kin?"

"Not living, at least not so anyone would know," the constable replied. "Their boy, Retief, got killed up on the Botswana border a while back. I seem to recall, very vaguely, that they had a young girl living with them, might have been a daughter or a niece or something. She disappeared about the time Retief died and nobody ever heard anything about her after that. Shame, really. That farmstead's been in the family a hundred years or more."

"Thank you for your time, Constable," Caen/Flint said. "You've been very helpful."

~ ∫ ~

During what she perceived as her last two nights in South Africa, the Assassin splurged and stayed at the Mount Nelson Hotel near Company Gardens in the center of Cape Town. She gazed out the window of her luxurious suite, at the jagged spine of mountains, the Twelve Apostles, as they marched south toward the Cape of Good Hope and the meeting of the Atlantic and Indian Oceans. She had arranged to ship all her goods, other than what she could carry and what she had already taken into Tehran, to an area known only to her, at the other end of the world.

After treating herself to a full body massage, facial, manicure, pedicure, and an aromatherapy wrap, the Assassin went into the hotel's guests' business office, where she searched the internet for possible places to which she could retire at the conclusion of her current assignment. It would have to be remote, of course. A place that would be politically secure, private, safe, and warm. Bali was beautiful but overrun with tourists. There were gorgeous beaches in southern Thailand and the Philippines, but again too many people. A loner by nature, she had been spoiled by the sheer isolation of Farmstead 18. Perhaps one day – far in the future – she might even be able to return to the Kalahari.

But enough daydreaming. It was time to immerse herself in the Islamic Republic. Sifting through the information she had learned from Count Napolitano, there were two hunters stalking her, an Iranian named Tabrizi and an Israeli named Ezra Caen. For some reason she felt a chill when she heard the second name. Perhaps she might be able to take out Mr. Tabrizi, in advance of the planned killing. That would even the odds somewhat.

While Ezra had contacted only those people he knew and trusted, he had no doubt that sooner or later there would be leaks. That was the way of the world. Notwithstanding that, occasionally such leaks even worked to the hunter's advantage. Even if he now had a name and an inkling as to *who* the Assassin was – at least at a much earlier age - that would not give him an insight into her *modus operandi*. At the level at which this professional functioned, she would surely not stick to a single set of working methods.

Still, there was now something completely unique in the mix. Ezra Caen was no stranger to the literature about supposed paranormal communications – almost like extrasensory perception - between identical twins – which had been more or less scientifically proved. He well knew that identical twins, who had come from a single egg, shared one-hundred percent of their genetic fingerprint. Even fraternal twins of different sex shared fifty percent of that fingerprint. Which made it possible – even probable – that such siblings shared ways of thinking, ways of reacting, ways of planning, and strategic and tactical mobility.

Ezra Caen was both elated and stunned by what he'd found in Johannesburg and Bloemfontein. The Assassin had a name, a birthdate, coincidentally his own, and tiny slivers of a history, such as it was. The shock was his realization that despite the almost infinite number of identity shifts, the person he was searching for, once all the layers of onion skin were peeled away, was his twin sister.

15

The woman wore a traditional headscarf. Her large brown eyes and dusky skin gave promise that this early-thirties-something woman was both attractive and sensuous, at least as perceived by the male receptionist at the *Vezarat-e Ettela'at va Amniyat-e Keshvar*, the Ministry of Intelligence and National Security, in midtown Tehran.

"Madame?" he inquired.

"Ah, you flatter me, kind sir," she replied. "I am not married. I have come from Moroni to visit my cousin, M'sieu Tabrizi, who is employed in your ministry. I wonder if he is on duty today?"

"Your name?"

"Simone. Simone DesMoulins."

"You are French?"

"French Comorian. You are quite astute, sir."

"Can you describe him, Mademoiselle DesMoulins? We have …" he looked at his desk directory … "fourteen employees named Tabrizi. It is quite a common name, you know."

The Assassin, who had not expected this, said, "Taller than me, thirty-six …"

"First name?"

"Ma – "

"Ah!" he interrupted her. "I know him," he said brightly. "One moment, please."

As she moved to a far corner of the lobby to wait, he pressed a buzzer on his handset. "Mister Tabrizi, Nikahd at reception here. I have a young woman who claims to be your cousin." Then, in a lower voice, "She's really quite attractive."

~ ʃ ~

"So you're not really a cousin?" he said.

"No, a friend of someone who claims to be your cousin. It was very kind of you to take my call. Kinder still that you invited me to lunch."

"Why me?"

"My friend said you knew everyone worth knowing and everything to see in Tehran, and I thought, a woman alone and a foreigner …"

"You certainly chose well," he said. "A bachelor with an afternoon off." He puffed out his chest. "Where would you like to go?"

"I know nothing of this city. Would you be my guide?" she asked demurely.

"But of course." Tabrizi's imagination went into high gear. A foreign woman with a French name, alone and unmarried. An attractive woman, so far as he could tell, although her conservative outfit displayed almost nothing. He'd read more than one forbidden novel about French women, in cheap paperbacks he'd surreptitiously bought in shadowy corners of the capital city where most respectable Persians never went.

~ ∫ ~

Her body was even lovelier than he'd imagined. Hard but with soft, silky skin, and small, uplifting breasts. It had been in incredible stroke of good fortune. He had just started to nod off when he felt a slight pinprick.

He didn't know how long afterward he awoke, but when he did, he found it incredibly hard to breathe. As he tried to raise his head, he felt a wave of nausea. As a burst of panic started to set in, he looked over toward the other side of the bed, where Simone sat, still nude, her lovely breasts clearly visible.

"You may as well relax and enjoy your death, Mister Tabrizi."

"Wha – ?"

"You no doubt felt a slight pinprick after you'd climaxed. Ricin, Mister Tabrizi. It works by getting inside the cells of a person's body and preventing the cells from making the proteins they need. Without the proteins, cells die. And so, Mister Tabrizi, will you. Clever and completely undetectable."

As the man turned a sickly blue-white and started to perspire, she continued, with no more emotion than if she were reading the evening paper, "You of all people should know about that, Mister Tabrizi. I thought you counterintelligence types knew all about that kind of stuff. Surely you remember the Markov incident in '78, when the Bulgarian secret police 'shot' him with an umbrella in London? Of course that may have been before your time."

Tabrizi's wheezing became more pronounced. "But you don't understand … I am not …"

"Trying to talk will only make it worse and hasten the process," she continued. "So you and the Israelis have gotten together and want to know who I am and why I am? Well, Mister Manucher Tabrizi, let me tell you – my name, for your purposes, is Agrippina and I intend to put an end to your Supreme Leader." She laughed, a sharp, humorless bark. "The two of you thought you could stop me. Well, now the odds have been shaved, haven't they? It's down to one-on-one, just the way I like it."

"Bu – but," the man stammered weakly. "I am not Manucher Tabrizi. I am Mansour …"

"Perhaps I might even help the Angel of Death hurry his labors," the Assassin said.

The last thing the man saw was a pair of small, creamy breasts and two arms bearing a pillow. The last thing he felt was the pillow being held firmly between his mouth and nose, cutting off all remaining air.

~ ∫ ~

By next morning, every newspaper and television station in Tehran carried the story, "Manucher Tabrizi, businessman, found dead in hotel room!" The story continued that the victim, whose nude body had been discovered in bed, appeared to have been asphyxiated. The fingerprints which had been taken appeared smudged and inconclusive. Tabrizi's record as a successful manufacturer of men's clothing was detailed at length. There was no known motive for the murder.

~ ∫ ~

"I was so sorry to learn of your death, Manucher," Caen said while both of them were in Tabrizi's office at the Ministry. "Rather a close call, wouldn't you say?"

"It was indeed, Ezra. A matter of a few letters and a couple of seconds at the most. Praise Allah we have – had – fourteen Tabrizis in the Ministry. When I spoke with the receptionist, he recalled that when he asked her Tabrizi's first name, she said the word 'Ma-' before he assumed it was '*Mansour* Tabrizi,' a clerk-typist he knew. Had he known me personally or gone down one more name on the list – *Manucher* instead of *Mansour* ..."

"It was a 'she?'" Caen said. "Did the clerk give you any further information?"

"Looked like an Iranian – headscarf and modest dress. Early thirties, large brown eyes. Sexy. Said she was from Moroni."

"Comoros," Ezra said. "Yes, I will have a glass of Pellegrino water, thank you."

Tabrizi opened a large bottle from a carton on the floor behind him and handed his partner a large tumbler. After filling the glass and taking three large gulps, Caen continued.

"Close enough to the African continent and it was an unstable whore of a country even before Bob Denard."

"The mercenary?"

"The same. Any other information?"

"She told him Tabrizi was her cousin. When he came downstairs they didn't seem to recognize one another."

"Did he say how tall she was?"

"Only that she was shorter than Mansour Tabrizi. He estimated maybe five-four, five-five."

"Anything else?"

"They walked out together and he never came back."

"Car, taxi, anything like that?"

"Not that he could see. Of course, he wasn't looking. Once they'd left the building he took a telephone call and that was the end of that."

"What do you know about Mansour Tabrizi?"

"We didn't travel in the same circles. According to his personnel file, he was thirty-six, a bachelor, and he lived in a one-bedroom apartment two miles south of here. From what I've been told, he worked in the same office at the same cubicle for thirteen years. Quiet. Kept very much to himself according to his co-workers."

"Politics?"

"Apolitical as far as his colleagues were concerned. Never attended rallies, never campaigned for any politicians, never made any comments one way or another about anyone. The closest thing you could find to someone who was completely anonymous,"

"Sort of like our suspect," Ezra murmured. "You say he worked at the same cubicle for thirteen years. When was the last time they upgraded his computer?"

"2010. They're due for an upgrade next year. Toshibas. Good, solid machines. They'd beaten out Hewlett Packard on a bid for the Ministry's needs."

"Is the computer still there?"

"Uh-huh. The murder occurred day before yesterday. Protocol says it stays where it is until four days after an employee has left for any reason. Gives us the opportunity to search every entry to see who might have been communicating with the former employee in case he was planning on giving any secrets away."

~ ʃ ~

Meanwhile, Petrus Jooste, the South African educator, was ensconced in a middle-class hotel off Amir Kabir, reading the local newspaper and watching the continuing saga of Manucher Tabrizi on the television. His antennae were up and alert. Manucher Tabrizi had been his target and the media reported that Manucher Tabrizi had died. But the Assassin was bothered by a small inconsistency. The man the Assassin had killed had said, in his last breaths, that a mistake had been made ... that he was *not* Manucher Tabrizi, but *Mansour* ...

~ ∫ ~

"Turns out Mansour Tabrizi was a naughty boy," Manucher said. "Not only was his computer slaved to the master computer at the top, but if the regime had known he was sending this information out of the country he'd have been hanged without trial. Our suspect seems to have done the job for us."

"Enough information to connect the dots from Prince Majid to our killer and to alert the government to everything we know. But let's not forget, she didn't intend to kill the *other* Tabrizi, my friend. It could have been you," Ezra replied. "Do we have contact points where he sent the information?"

"Svilengrad, Bulgaria, Kyrenia, TRNC, Batumi, Georgia ..."

"Could those be relay points to a different destination?"

"Almost certainly, Ezra. Even though it's not foolproof, an automatic relay never goes through a human being in any of the countries to which the message is originally sent. Although it can be sent anywhere in the world via a smart phone, the easiest way to do this is to send the information to the closest point in a neighboring country."

"Turkey or Greece," Caen said. "Rule out Greece since the Turkish Republic of Northern Cyprus has nothing to do with Greece. Ten percent of the Bulgarian population consists of Turks. You could throw a stone from Edirne and hit Svilengrad," he continued mentioning the two towns on opposite sides of the Turkish-Bulgarian border. Batumi's the closest city to Eastern Turkey and TRNC wants to be a Turkish clone."

"I suggest we masquerade as Mansour Tabrizi and send a message of our own to every place outside Iran where he sent information during the last two months."

"How long will that take?"

"Three, maybe four hours. Let Security know what we're doing, and get emergency approval. I don't think time is that great a factor."

~ ∫ ~

But Manucher Tabrizi and Ezra Caen had underestimated the Assassin. Within an hour after Agrippina had replayed in her mind what Mansour Tabrizi had hinted at, "Petrus Jooste" checked out of his hotel, walked the few blocks to Amir Kabir, where he found an internet café, rented half an hour's worth of time, entered the address he'd been provided by his employers, typed in RED ANGEL when prompted for a password, and carefully worded a very brief message. She signed the message Ink Frutjuxre Cboluve Dianemokvnd, and pressed the "Send" command.

~ ∫ ~

"Damn!" Manucher Tabrizi swore. "Every address to which Mansour sent messages has been shut down or denied us entry."

"Which means the Assassin is on to us. Or that Mansour disclosed more to her than he should have," Caen said.

~ ∫ ~

The four representatives spoke over a secure line.

"She got the wrong Tabrizi," Hsien Yun-Lo said. "Her instincts are every bit as good as she thinks they are. She sent a Red Angel message to us less than an hour before Mansour Tabrizi's computer tried to contact us."

"True," Napolitano responded. "But I have no doubt the Iranian and the Israeli will investigate every internet provider in the country and will eventually decipher the RED ANGEL code, which gives her far fewer options."

"I don't think so," the Turk said. "Did you read how she signed her message?"

"Meaningless garbage," Karroubi snapped. "Probably designed to give the hunters a false name to throw them off the track."

"No, I see your point, Mister Karaca," the Chinese man said. "Please, Mister Karroubi, I don't mean in any way to insult you, but how much experience have you had in dissimulation or cryptography?"

"I am not insulted, Yun-Lo. I've had virtually none."

"On the other hand, Karaca Bey did not get where he is in the commercial world without such industrial spying tools, and I assure you my job was to communicate in the most indirect method possible. I suggest we look at the last thing she wrote very, very carefully and try to come up with whatever message we can. Remember, she impressed us when we met her. She must be much more than a simple mistress of disguise to have survived and succeeded as long as she has."

Less than three hours later Hsien Yun-Lo reconnected with his surviving associates. "Gentlemen, I believe I have the answer. Please, if each of you will look at what she wrote."

The men advised him they each had the message on his monitor.

"Let us start with the proposition that the code RED ANGEL is blown. She knew it would be and she knew *we* knew it would be. So there would have to be an alternate signal for us to communicate. She also undoubtedly concluded that we could not risk what security she might have left by sending her a responsive message, other than she hoped we would know to shut down all the relays, which, of course, we did. Fortunately, Mansour Tabrizi never knew the code to open the master email address. Thus, he was limited to the relays."

"So she intuited we would accept that she had changed the rules of the game by furnishing us with a new master password which she herself dictated." Count Napolitano said. "Extremely clever. Something to be expected from a consummate professional."

"That sounds logical to me," Karaca added. "But Ink Frutjuxre Cboluve Dianemokvnd? I tried to find logical mathematic sequences and couldn't find any."

"Have you ever heard the term 'fuzzy logic?' gentlemen?" Yun-Lo asked.

"Vaguely," Count Napolitano said.

"Meaning not at all," the Iranian said brusquely.

"True," the diplomat responded.

"Gentlemen, fuzzy logic is a form of many-valued or probabilistic logic. It deals with reasoning that is *approximate* rather than fixed and exact. Fuzzy logic variables have a truth value that ranges in degree from zero to one."

"I don't follow you at all," Karroubi said.

"It's not necessary that you do," Yun-Lo replied. "Please simply accept that fuzzy logic has been extended to handle the concept of partial truth, where the truth value may range between completely true and completely false. Fuzzy logic is based on 'degrees of truth' rather than the usual 'true or false.' Natural language, like most other activities in life, and indeed the universe, cannot easily be translated into absolute terms of 0 and 1. Fuzzy logic seems closer to the way our brains work. We aggregate data and form a number of partial truths which we aggregate further into higher truths which, in turn, when certain thresholds are exceeded, cause certain further results such as motor reaction."

"And that's how you found the meaning of Agrippina's gibberish?" Karroubi asked.

"Precisely. Or, to be more fuzzily logical, a higher degree of truth than otherwise. Excerpting the statement 'Ink Frutjuxre Cboluve Dianemokvnd,' I tried various combinations using the letters backwards, forwards, and in several permutations. Ultimately, when none of them worked, I resorted to fuzzy logic and higher probabilities by random deletions. I ended up deleting the letters 'k,' 'r,' 'j,' 'x,' 'C,' 'o,' 'v,' 'n,' 'e,' 'k,' and 'v.' I ask that each of you do the crossouts on your own copy and see what you come up with."

Karaca was the first to respond. "In future Blue Diamond."

"Correct," Yun-Lo said. "The key to the whole puzzle was the color. Her prior code had been RED ANGEL. It would be logical for her to switch to a different color and blue seemed an obvious choice."

"So she is asking us – no, *telling* us – to switch the password from RED ANGEL to BLUE DIAMOND," Karaca said.

"Perhaps true, perhaps not," Yun-Lo said. "But we have nothing to lose if we do as she says, and it may save her life and the project in the process.

16

"Gentlemen, no matter how brilliant our Assassin is, the situation involving the late Mister Tabrizi – the *wrong* late Mister Tabrizi – significantly complicates matters."

Of all the unlikely places to set up a face-to-face meeting, Tirana was as good a choice as any. Still the poorest country in Europe, Albania was rapidly shedding its image of a wild, backward place mired in four-hundred-year-old blood feuds. The Theranda Hotel, located in the very heart of the blloku district, once the private haunt of Enver Hoxha and his cronies during the forty-one years of his dictatorship, and now the playground of Tirana's emerging middle class, was almost impossible to find. If any tourist asked one of these pseudo-sophisticates where the hotel was, he would receive a blank stare in response. All the better for privacy. The group of four had reserved the breakfast room, adjacent to the main building of the hotel, during the hours between 1:00 and 3:00 p.m., when it was completely vacant.

"I suggest," Count Napolitano continued, "that Agrippina may need a diversion to assist her in her efforts."

"That raises its own can of worms," Karaca responded. "First, she specifically told us she did not want our help, our interference, unless she asked for it. She might recoil at such an effort and simply abandon the project. Second, how would we get a message to her in a timely manner, even if she were amenable?"

"I've given that some thought, Mustafa. Assuming we could set up the proper diversion, we would simply advise her, not direct her, and she could use it or ignore it at her own discretion. Obviously we have means of contacting her, albeit indirectly, and there's still a month-and-a-half before the window of maximum opportunity."

"What kind of diversion did you have in mind?" the Iranian asked.

"A good question, Mehdi. The new President proclaims he is a moderate. In contrast to Ahmadinejad, he wants to be seen as opening doors to the lessening of international tensions. Yun-Lo, of any of us you know him best. I believe the two of you worked together on nuclear negotiations some years ago?"

"We did, Marco," the Chinese responded. "Our relationship was quite cordial, even though we were on severely opposite sides of the bargaining table."

The four men spoke at length over what the diversion might be and how they could implement it. At the conclusion, they unanimously agreed that Hsien Yun-Lo's idea was brilliant and that he would be the perfect emissary to "sell" it to all concerned parties.

~ ∫ ~

Elspeth Fraser was seventy-five, a stout widow who'd retired to her home town of Inverness five years after her late husband, Gordon Duff Fraser, O.M., M.B.E., had passed, in the fullness of his years. Duff had been fifteen years her senior. They had met while she was a student at The Queen's College, Glasgow, and he was an associate professor at what was then called Glasgow Polytechnic. They'd loved hiking in the Glencoe Mountains between Loch Lomond and Loch Ness. Even after their two children had come, grown, and gone, she'd continued her lifelong love of Highland Dance. With the exception of their annual trip to the Continent, usually Austria, Switzerland, or Italy, theirs had been a life of quiet satisfaction with one another.

For service to the Crown, Duff had been awarded the Order of Merit and induction as a Member of the Most Excellent Order of the British Empire in 2001, shortly before his retirement from what had become the Glasgow Caledonian University, when Queen's College and Glasgow Polytechnic had merged eight years earlier.

With her husband gone, an ample retirement, and time on her hands, Elspeth Fraser had founded the Inverness Highland Dance Academy (the name Fraser School of Dancing had already been taken) four years ago, and she'd been happily surprised at its financial and artistic success. She'd been even more gratified when two of her students, Kyla Johnstone and Adair Taylor, both sixteen, had qualified for the Scottish Official Highland Dancing Association National competitive championships in Edinburgh last September.

This evening promised to be another packed house presentation. Her performing troupe had been scheduled to appear in the great room on the second floor of the Inverness City Hall. The girls, who ranged in age from 5-year-old Crissa Paterson and her two-years-older sister, Isobel, to 14-year-old seniors, Jamie Drew Muir and Fiona Hughes, were examples of the finest youngsters Scotland had to offer the world. Her grandnephews, Colin Campbell and Brett MacDonald, outstanding bagpipers who complemented one another perfectly, as well as a pair of drummers from the local Highlander Association, had been practicing with the girls all week. Elspeth had not failed to notice that all four young men had eyes for Kyla and Adair, both of whom had consented to provide a special Highland Fling competition demonstration as the closing piece-de-resistance of the show.

Elspeth instructed her girls all afternoon in accordance with her usual pattern. She would not hesitate to hug them and give them all the love they could handle, but she was a stern taskmistress who did not spare the vocal whip when warranted.

"Crissa, you may think because you're the youngest in the troupe you're the most adorable and all eyes will be on you. Let me tell you right now, you get all flouncy about how important you are, and God will knock you on your bum so fast you'll be the one everybody laughs at. And if *He* doesn't knock you on your bum, *I* will, got that?"

"Yes, Mistress Fraser."

"Good. Now, remember, a bow to your partner before you start, and lay the swords down in a perfect cross so you'll know exactly where you'll be when you jump over them. Yes, Isobel?"

"Mistress Fraser, what if I have to pee just before I go on?"

"Do it five minutes before. There's a loo right outside the great room."

"But what if I can't go before I'm on stage? You know how nervous I get once I'm on the stage."

"Isobel Paterson, you'll just have to hold it in and do the best you can. You should be concerned with your dancing, and nothing but your dancing, understand?"

"Yes'm."

"Not 'yes'm,' Isobel, 'Yes, Mistress Fraser."

"Yes, Mistress Fraser."

"Now troupe, I expect all of you will be in full dress, outside City Hall promptly at three-quarters after six. Colin, you and Brett will be on either side and you'll start piping within five minutes after, as soon as a crowd starts to gather. Two busloads of English and American tourists are expected tonight and I expect you will make the whole of Scotland proud of you. Dismissed."

"Thank you, Mistress Fraser," they all said in unison.

~ ∫ ~

Bagpipes are notorious, both for their unique harmony and for the fact that in many instances a single set can be heard over a mile away. With the sound of the pipes multiplied by two, plus two drummers added, there wasn't a living soul between the Ness Bridge and Crown Road and from Post Office Avenue to the bed-and-breakfast houses on Old Edinbrugh Road, who could not hear – and either be stirred or rattled by – the arguably harmonic tones as the pipers launched into the tune originally titled *Baile Inneraora*, the *Town of Inveraray*, until it became known worldwide as *The Campbells are Coming*.

By seven-fifteen, the intersection of Church and High Street was filled with onlookers. Even the American tourists patronizing the McDonald's opposite City Hall had emptied out of the fast-food emporium to hear the pandemonium, and when the Town Clerk invited the entire populace inside, the great room was packed chockablock, standing room only.

The next hour was a highly successful indoor love fest to Scottish Highland dancing. The youngest troupers, sisters Crissa and Isobel Paterson, charmed the audience and every male eye in the chamber followed the beautiful teenaged competition winners as they displayed a combination of vigor, grace, and sensuality.

As the show ended to standing ovation, a distinguished-looking Asian man of middle age, who introduced himself as Hsien Yun-Lo, quietly approached the director.

"Good evening, Mistress Fraser," the man said, bowing politely. "I knew your late husband, Professor Fraser, when he was still teaching. Do you, by some chance, remember one of his students named Hassan Feridon, who was working on a doctorate in the mid-1990s?"

"Vaguely, Mister Yun-Lo. My late husband had so many students over his career, you know."

"I just thought that name might somehow stick out in your memory."

"I'm afraid it does not ring a bell."

"Of course, he's no longer using the name Feridon. He's reverted to his original name, Hassan Rouhani. Does that name seem more familiar to you?"

"I'm sorry. Should it?"

"Only if you follow Iranian politics."

"Mister Yun-Lo, I hate to seem rude, but since my husband's death my interest lies in Highland Dancing and my girls. I've not had the time nor the inclination to dabble in matters outside my own small realm."

"Pity, Mistress Fraser. I was thinking that perhaps your troupe might wish to show on a far larger stage than the Inverness City Hall. It seems your husband's former student, Mister Feridon – Mister Rouhani – was elected the President of Iran last June and I believe I might be able to secure an invitation for you and your troupe to render a very special performance in Iran – one that might open up cooperation between Iran and the International Community."

"I'm listening."

"You might be surprised to learn than the presence of your company might even, it its small way, affect history. ..."

~ ∫ ~

"Mister President, it was so gracious of you to see me. I not only feel deeply honored that you would do so on such short notice, but I must say that your countrymen could not have chosen a better man to normalize relations with 'others.'"

"Yun-Lo, you give me too much credit. You and I both know there's only so much I can do and where the real power resides. I must admit I was fascinated by your suggestion that I might be able to start opening doors without getting involved in the West's never-ending quest to get rid of our nuclear program. Tea?"

"If you'll join me, Mister President."

"Happily."

When the two of them were ensconced in a private room, Hassan Rouhani signaled for Hsien Yun-Lo to expand on his idea.

"Mister President, we've been at the negotiating table before, and we've learned much about one another, personally as well as professionally."

"Agreed, Yun-Lo. Since it's just the two of us in the room, why not dispense with the 'Mister President' formalities?"

"All right, Hassan. Do you prefer Feridon or Rouhani?"

"Quite a memory, Yun-Lo. Why not just plain Hassan?"

"Fine by me. Have you been to Scotland lately?"

"The last time I was there was in ninety-nine when I got my doctorate in law."

"Do you remember a humanities professor named Duff Fraser?"

"If I said 'yes,' I'd be lying. Why do you ask?"

A waiter arrived bearing tea and sweet Iranian pastries. After the man departed, the President poured tea for his guest and they spent a few moments companionably sipping and munching.

"Fraser died a little more than five years ago. His widow retired to her hometown of Inverness and set up a Highland Dancing school."

"Pity he died, although I'd say that for just about anyone. How does that impact Iran?"

"You're the one who said you'd like to open relations with the West."

"Yes?"

"Mahmoud was not, shall we say, the most diplomatic of politicians."

They laughed heartily at that remark.

"And the West is now waiting to see if you, to use their term, 'put your money where your mouth is.'"

"What does this have to do with the widow Fraser and her dancing school, my friend?"

"Hassan, the Supreme Leader keeps pretty much to himself, except for leading the Friday prayers, all through the year. There is, however, one exception where he must – and invariably does – show his face throughout the Islamic Republic."

"The Decade of Fajr, the Victory of the Islamic Revolution. February first through the eleventh," the President said. "The Ayatollah returned to Tehran on February 1 and Pahlavi was deposed at 2:00 p.m. on February 11, Victory Day."

"Correct," the Chinese said. "The biggest crowd of the year turns out …"

"February 11 in Qom, Iran's Holy City."

"For the past thirty-four years it's been an 'in-house' celebration. Non-Muslims need not apply. 'It's *our* party and if you aren't part of us, you don't belong, so please go elsewhere.' And yet, there are a lot of other countries in the world that are not Islamic and some of them don't like feeling the sting of being an outsider."

"Like our American 'friends?'"

"Among others. Yes, I will have some more tea, Hassan. And these pastries are truly delicious."

The President smiled, encouraging his erstwhile negotiating adversary to go on.

"Iran claims it doesn't really give a damn about the U.S. today, but America is always trying to delegitimize the Islamic Republic any way it can. A lot of neutral countries, even Western countries, don't really care much about the political rhetoric between Iran and America. What's always most important – and I'm sure the Grand Ayatollah, who's no dummy, is aware of this, is the *human* connection."

"True."

"Scotland has no bone to pick with anyone. They're part of the U.K., but you lived in Scotland long enough to know that the Scots don't particularly *like* their English cousins – back in '06 they voted to go their own way, at least insofar as internal rule is concerned. Your alma mater, Glasgow Caledonian, was the first one to give Nelson Mandela an honorary degree, and you've got personal connections with Scotland."

"Yes, so …?"

"Hassan, if we can have two ostensibly – but not really – disparate events at the same time in the same town …"

"I get what you're saying. Let's suppose – just suppose, mind you – that the Grand Ayatollah is scheduled to speak to a hundred thousand people in Qom at two o'clock on the eleventh. We announce to the Faithful that Iran wants to show that it accepts everyone of all faiths and that Mrs. Fraser's Scottish dancers will perform at twelve-thirty. We announce that the whole program of festivities will be televised for a worldwide audience …"

"Good, good," the Chinese diplomat said. "But what about their dress? You've seen Highland dancers before. Very short skirts, no head coverings …"

"Winters are very cold in the Scottish Highlands. Adjustments can be made. Long pants can be worn under the kilts. Headdress can be part of the costume. I'm sure we could arrange for some flexibility. I've even got an idea for preserving the Supreme Leader's separation from the heathens," the President said, smiling, a bit wolfishly, Yun-Lo thought. "The dancers and the drummers are there for a strictly prescribed time. The girls then move to the side of the stage. The pipers and drummers signal by increasing their volume that the most important part of the program is about to begin. The Grand Ayatollah comes onto the rostrum and waves at the *people*, not the Scots. Everyone goes crazy while the Scots disappear. The Leader has never formally recognized the foreigners, yet to the world it *appears* as though he has sanctioned the presence of the outsiders, and the Islamic Republic looks like a very human, happy place for all."

"Excellent idea, Mister President!" Yun-Lo exclaimed, clapping his hands together.

"The problem, Yun-Lo, is that we don't currently enjoy diplomatic relations with the United Kingdom. Who could we possibly entrust to approach Mrs. Fraser and her troupe?"

"I do not think that will be a problem, my friend."

~ ∫ ~

"What can I possibly say, Mister Yun-Lo? An all-expense-paid trip to a foreign country? Is this going to be paid for by an enemy state?" Elspeth Fraser asked. While she was overwhelmed by the generosity of the offer, she retained her inherent Scottish caution and suspicion.

"No, no, nothing like that at all, Mistress Fraser. My associates are all citizens of countries friendly to the United Kingdom and the expenditure is both their contribution to peace in the region and, something I'm sure you'll understand, tax deductible."

"But will the school be charged taxes on this income?" she persisted.

"Not at all. This is a privately funded operation. Neither you nor any member of your troupe will see any profit from this venture. And you may rest assured we will clear it to your satisfaction with Her Majesty's Revenue and Customs Authority well in advance of the journey."

"Mister Yun-Lo, I don't for a moment doubt your word, but 'well in advance of the journey' is a relative phrase. It is now December 15. If we assume that we're expected to perform in Iran on February 11, that will give our troupe a little more than a month-and-a-half to arrange for passports, visas, airline tickets, accommodations ..."

"Mistress Fraser, you need not worry. All of these matters are being expedited."

"By now, the magnitude of what was happening and the fact that control was spinning our of her hands overwhelmed her initial reticence. "One last question, Mister Yun-Lo?"

"Certainly."

"I've heard that the Islamic Republic is a dangerous place – "

The Chinese diplomat smiled. "Mistress Fraser, If I were in your shoes I'd have exactly the same suspicions. Let me reassure you that despite what you may have heard from other sources, Iran is a perfectly civilized, safe place. President Rouhani himself has assured me that you will be under the protection of all the resources the State can muster. Shall we arrange to meet with the parents here in, say, three days?"

17

As Count Napolitano had suggested to his colleagues, there was no problem in transmitting the message to "Agrippina" within three days of arrangements having been consummated. Napolitano had no doubt that the Assassin would easily be able to decipher the message, "Diversion arranged 1102," utilizing the European code of putting the day before the month of the planned program.

Agrippina had been both predator and prey in her career, often at the same time, and was quick to surmise that those who were hunting her would be playing the same chess game she was now working on in her own mind. After a follow-up exchange of messages with her employer – "?," "Scottish Highland Dancers" – she had no doubt about the date, time, and nature of the diversion. She calculated – correctly – that the Islamic Republic's security forces would be the first to know everything there was to know about the program and that the hunters had probably been primed even before she received the first message.

Now her own mental chess game began in earnest. *Odd*, she thought. *The ancient Persians originated chess and now it's up to me to beat them at their own game.*

On the one hand, a Scottish Highland Dance Troupe, and more importantly bagpipers and drummers, would create a level of noise that would make the silencer on her rifle irrelevant. The Iranian authorities would obviously orchestrate the largest possible public relations program they could muster: worldwide television and a "volunteer" crowd that would easily triple the thirty thousand which normally turned out for an event of this nature. Cameras and podcasts from every nation on earth, friend or foe, would shoot footage of the event. In such circumstances, security would be an absolute nightmare from beginning to end, and a lone sniper five hundred feet away, firing from three floors up in a random neighborhood building, would be almost impossible to detect. *Almost.*

On the other hand, she had no doubt that those pursuing her were professionals of the highest caliber. She had done her homework well. Ezra Caen? There was no one better in the world at what he did. And she'd killed the wrong Tabrizi through careless happenstance. Manucher Tabrizi, being a *man*, would naturally be out for revenge, she thought. The unknown pieces of the puzzle were how much they knew about *who* she was, what they knew about her previous operations, how the killing would take place, and whether they had developed any leads which would enable them to trace her movements. The largest piece of the puzzle, which was not yet known even to her, was *when* and *where* the assassination would take place.

She assumed they knew who the target was. That much she'd learned in her past communications with her employers. Caen had dealt with mercenaries before – the Israelis had, themselves, fielded one of the best, and she'd wager half her contract price that the detective had been in touch with several of them, perhaps even Mad Mike Hoare.

Many years ago, the Holiday Inn, the quintessential American multinational hotel chain, had used the slogan, "The best surprise is *no* surprise." "No surprise" meant, she was sure, that the hunters would believe that the assassination attempt would take place as close to 2:00 p.m. on February 11 as possible. *Just about* every one of the hunters. But maybe not Ezra Caen.

Earlier, the Assassin had concluded that the most propitious location for the assassination in Qom was the Jamkaran Mosque. The Mosque was heavily guarded, day and night, had a large, adjacent field which could accommodate hordes of the faithful, and, most important for her purposes, was in an area surrounded be tenement blocks and old, in some cases abandoned, factories.

Sixty-eight year-old retiree "Richard McAdams," who'd played cello in the Pretoria Symphony Orchestra and reputedly enjoyed immense popularity as a music teacher in Tshwane – the new name for the old South African capital – espoused a lifelong fondness for *mūsīqī-e aṣīl-e īrānī*, Persian traditional music, and had rented a third floor flat in an old apartment building a month ago. He had told the prospective landlord that he planned on staying in Qom for six months. The flat satisfied his needs: it had a room large enough for listening to and recording Persian music and entertaining visitors from South Africa, a broad window looking out the front of the apartment to the boulevard below, and a den at the side of the apartment with a small window affording him a view of the Jamkaran Mosque. McAdams, who kept his gray hair cut short and who had the faded blue eyes typical of an older man, had paid cash in advance, and had promised both his landlord and his neighbors that he would only teach during midday and afternoon hours – never on Friday, of course – and that any noise emanating from his apartment would cease by seven each night. Indeed, the only time his landlord had ever seen Richard McAdams was the day he had signed the lease and handed the owner not only the complete term's rent, but also a generous security deposit.

Although the flat was furnished, "Richard McAdams" had embellished it with small personal touches: family photos with the tenant and his deceased "wife;" advertising posters for the Pretoria Symphony; several sheets of music; the obligatory cello; a sport coat, some slacks and casual shirts, two pair of shoes, assorted underwear; and some pieces of metal which appeared to be music stands.

From time to time, the melodious sounds of the cello would issue from McAdams' flat. His only student seemed to be a Roman Catholic nun who sometimes left her cello in "Maestro McAdams'" residence, but more frequently carried a large, cumbersome cello case up three flights of stairs to her teacher's studio. "McAdams" himself was hardly ever home. Not one of his neighbors seemed to have any idea what he even looked like.

These precautions were deliberate. In the event any questions were asked, the tenant was legitimate. More important, the Assassin had carefully vetted the apartment to ensure that it left her maximum flexibility, an ideal location for her needs, and the anonymity which, in the end, would prove most useful of all.

If Agrippina elected to use the diversion scenario suggested by Count Napolitano, "McAdams'" apartment would get the call. But the Assassin was not one to jump to immediate conclusions. She would use the next few days to calculate the pros and cons of the Qom scenario. She might even decide to change the venue of the deed, in order to throw the hunters off the scent.

~ ∫ ~

"Damn!" Heyder Moslehi exploded, a rare curse issuing from his lips. "Don't those idiots even suspect how much more difficult this latest move makes our job?" The security group had again assembled in the conference room in the Ministry of Intelligence and National Security headquarters.

"Those idiots?" Ghormani responded mildly. "I believe President Rouhani's simply following the normal politician's instinct of trying to maximize his opportunity to look the best he can to the world. An opportunity for a rather impressive 'photo op,' as they say in the West."

"An opportunity for a monumental screw-up," Saeed Paria said, but his tone was not angry. "Is there any way this can take a favorable bounce for us, Ezra?"

"That depends," the Israeli answered. "Certainly the logistics become much more difficult and involved. If the would-be Assassin intends to do the deed in the most likely manner, a single shot from afar, the tumult surrounding the Ayatollah would certainly reduce the need for quiet, such as a silencer could provide. On the other hand, I suggest that the Assassin would most likely use a silencer in any event, so the equation doesn't change dramatically because of excessive noise. Of course, if the killer wants to try a shot from ground zero, she..." - all eyebrows in the room raised at Caen's conclusion that the Assassin was a female – "can easily get lost in a crowd of a hundred thousand people. So it's *crowd* control rather than killer control which becomes more complex. Has anything come of my suggestion that Khamenei wear a Kevlar outfit or that there be a thin, transparent wall around him?"

"He wouldn't hear of any such thing," Rahman Almotahari, head of the Supreme Leader's bodyguard, said.

"I didn't think he would," Ghormani added.

"I'm certain our Assassin is weighing her options carefully," Caen continued. "There are pluses and minuses to each scenario. She no doubt knows that the greater the crowd, the more confusion it would cause and her getaway would be that much simpler. Conversely, she's got to be aware that well prior to the event we would close and barricade every square meter of space from which she could get a good shot. That means every building, every shack, every lean-to, within a thousand meters of the Supreme Leader. That would effectively cancel the option of a shot from an adjacent building."

"Agreed," Yousef Abbasi remarked, drawing on a Bahman cigarette, a habit he'd gotten into some years ago to help quell nervous agitation. "So where does that lead us?"

Manucher Tabrizi picked up his colleague's thoughts. "The killer is undoubtedly weighing the same options as we are. The choice of Qom has been patently obvious from the first. Now ... perhaps not so obvious. While February 11 is the ideal date – much like nine-eleven would be in the United States, a better choice might be a less *public* holiday. Let's say, for example, that all of us around this table believe February 11 is the most rational, logical choice. If nothing actually happened on the eleventh, or within a week or two after the eleventh, the natural thing the killer might expect to happen is that we drop our guard, become just a hair less vigilant."

"Gentlemen, it seems we are all thinking this out like a chess game," the chairman said. "Am I to trust that our vote would be to plan for the eleventh in Qom, but to keep all options open and keep our vigilance at maximum until ...?"

"I think we're agreed on that," Ghormani said.

"Are we getting any closer to answering the question of who the killer might be?" Ghasem Habib, the senior member of the group asked.

"I think we well may be," Caen remarked, slowly and quietly.

"And?" the Chairman asked.

"Gentlemen," Ezra said, coughing twice and looking everyone directly in the eye before he answered. "I have reason to believe that the Assassin is a person I've never seen and never met." He spent the next two minutes explaining how he arrived at his conclusion before he concluded, "I believe that the Assassin is my twin sister."

18

"First thing, gentlemen," Ezra told his lieutenants, "we comb through every single entry into and exit out of both Imam Khomeini and Mehrabad Airports during the past six months. We look for multiple entries, although, as a practical matter, our target probably used different identities each time she entered or departed the Islamic Republic. While we can't rule out entries into airports other than Tehran, road entries, and even landings by sea, the number of those entries would be so incalculably large that it would be virtually impossible to sift through that much information in the time before we believe the attempt will be made."

"Are we looking for anything else, Mister Caen?" one of the younger men asked.

"Yes, we are, Lieutenant. I have a hunch – and it is nothing more than that – that our target most likely used false fingerprints, plastic casts, when she applied for however many passports she obtained – and that she used the same casts on each of the passports. Although I'm certain she's got more than one set of false fingerprints, it would make it needlessly difficult for her to keep track of which set went with which passport. She may also have calculated that passport control officers are generally in such a hurry to check out incoming passengers and the lines of people are usually so impatient that they don't bother to check such things as fingerprints. Rather, they want to make sure the name and description matches the face and physical appearance of the passport holder."

"So the easiest way would be to use the same set of false casts on each of the passports," Manucher Tabrizi said. "Clever."

"Actually, more practical," Caen said. "What do *you* think the odds are that we'd be hunting through passports for multiple entries?"

"Almost a hundred percent," another lieutenant volunteered.

"And the chances that we'd cross-reference that our girl used the same fingerprints for each trip to Iran?" Caen persisted, pouring himself a glass of Pellegrino water.

The response was unanimous: nil.

"What difference does it make if she used the same fingerprints?" a grizzled older veteran of the force asked. "Once in country, the suspect could switch fingerprints as easily as she changed identities. Who's going to look at someone's fingerprints when they're renting a hotel room or a car, or when they are buying groceries?"

"Absolutely no one," Caen replied. "I believe you're absolutely right, Inspector Mehrab. But our concern shouldn't be with what the suspect does, or, for that matter, whether she stands or squats when she goes to the bathroom. What we want to find out are *names*."

"I see your point," the veteran inspector rejoined. "If we get a certain number of different names – and I'll wager it's a finite number – using the same fingerprints on a passport, then …"

"We at least put that finite number of names on who we look for at hotels, car hire agencies, and the like," Tabrizi said.

"But if the passport control officers don't check the fingerprints, how do we check them?" Lieutenant Gelbahr asked.

"Perspiration, not inspiration, Lieutenant," Caen replied. "Although the customs agents don't physically, or even visually, check the fingerprints, they are required to photocopy every passport of a person entering or leaving the Republic. We, gentlemen, are going to obtain the passport of every person who has come through the gates into or out of our two international airports. And when we've done that, our technicians will employ fingerprint scanners to narrow down comparables."

"Can this be done in the time we have, Mister Caen?" Gelbahr asked.

"Absolutely. I think it's time that someone explained to you how these scanners work. Gentlemen," he said, as he opened the conference room door and a tall man, who could not have been more than thirty-four, entered. "may I introduce you to Doctor Sumit Singh, of CONSO-INDIA. I've used Doctor Singh with great success in my own country. I'd like him to spend a few minutes explaining the current battery of systems available to us, which technologies have taken us light years from the old visual testing."

During the next half-hour, Sumit Singh explained the basics of fingerprint sensors to the assembled group, explaining in laborious detail the differences between optical, ultrasonic, capacitance, and algorithm scanning and analysis techniques. Finally, he said, apologetically, "I see from the way you're staring that I've lost many of you. I am sorry. I don't mean to do that. It is simply that those of us in the field are used to certain technical jargon, just as I am sure you have certain code words in your own profession."

"Doctor Singh," Ezra asked, "assuming we have more than one million images and less than three million, how long would it take an expert using advanced computer technology and any of the systems you mentioned to definitively match up the same fingerprints used on passports in different names with different identities"

"Twenty-four hours minimum, seventy-two hours maximum."

"Very well, Doctor Singh, we have just retained your services. We will have the images to you within five days."

~ ∫ ~

"Gentlemen, we have eight persons whose fingerprints precisely match one another, despite the differences in name, age, and even sex on their passports," Caen crowed triumphantly. He passed around several copies of a single sheet with the following in clear type, and with photos above each name:

Hannelore deWet, South African, farmer, dark blonde hair and brown eyes.

Sister Mary Salvatore, nun, Zimbabwe, close-cropped dark hair and brown eyes.

Trude Schechter, Namibian nurse, straw-blonde hair and blue eyes.

Simone DesMoulins, French-Comorian, hotel worker, brown hair, brown eyes.

Petrus Jooste, South African, educator, sand-colored hair, brown eyes.

Rudolph Hostetler, Namibian, petrochemical buyer, brown hair, brown eyes.

Richard McAdams, sixty-eight, South African, retired, gray hair, blue eyes.

Vito Ligeiro, Brazilian, carrying Comoros passport, martial arts master.

"Gentlemen," Ezra Caen said, "it's time to hit the streets."

~ ∫ ~

During the next week, over a hundred detectives each in Tehran, Tabriz, Mashhad, and Qom, scoured every neighborhood and every hotel. Each of them had in hand several copies of the single page passout Caen had given his lieutenants. To a man, the investigators were scrupulously polite, but they left no doubt in the mind of any of the hoteliers, car rental agencies, gas station attendants, apartment house owners, or anyone else they questioned that this manhunt – or womanhunt – was deadly serious.

From the first day, their investigation began to yield fruit.

A concierge at the three-star Escan Hotel on Somayeh Avenue responded to questioning by a twenty-three year-old wet-behind-the-ears rookie.

"Yes, Officer, according to the hotel records, Rudolph Hostetler stayed here for three nights, October 17, 18 and 19. He checked out the morning of the 20th. I can't be certain, but the picture on that flyer looks something like him. I have a vague recollection of him hiring a taxi on the 19th."

The night manager at the Firouzeh hotel related to a middle-aged veteran of the force, "A Roman Catholic nun stayed here in one of our small single rooms. Let me look it up … ah, yes, her name was Sister Mary Salvatore. I haven't the faintest idea what she looked like but she paid 300,000 rials a night, cash, for room with shower. I'm sorry,

Sergeant, I can't do better that that. Once the head is covered they all look the same."

"That's him, all right," a car-hire agent told a plainclothes office. "Hostetler rented that gray, dinged-up Samand at the back of the lot on November 10. Brought it back three days early. Nothing unusual. Gas tank was full. Rented a Garmin GPS."

"Father O'Flannagan, I hate to bother you, but did a nun named Sister Mary Salvatore meet with you at any time during the past three months?" Not surprisingly, Ezra Caen himself, who was never too much above the fray to walk a beat like any other cop, had decided to interview the resident Priest. It only made sense that a Roman Catholic nun would try to establish even minimal connections with the prelate of the local religious community.

"You're not Iranian, Mister Caen?"

"Actually, no."

"I don't know where you live now, but you still have a trace of South African accent."

"I moved away when I was seven. Is it that obvious?" the detective asked.

"It is. Come into my study, Mister Caen. Let's share a cuppa'."

~ ∫ ~

"Pretty damned serious if Iran hires an Israeli detective," Father O'Flannagan said, smiling conspiratorially.

"More than you might know, Father. Beyond that I can't and won't say anything."

"I understand, and I won't question you farther. I trust this Sister Mary Salvatore is not what she seems. Of course, that's something I knew the day I met her."

Caen's eyebrows arched. "Do you care to expand on that, Father?"

"It's probably nothing important. She said she was from Zimbabwe, the old Southern Rhodesia before they booted out Ian Smith and voted in Mugabe. But I served in RSA and visited Rhodesia enough times to recognize the slight difference in accents. The Sister's accent was clearly South African. Somewhere near Bloemfontein if I had to put my finger on it. But that wasn't particularly unusual. Many people crossed borders during and after the revolution."

"But something bothered you?"

"It did. Here was this supposedly earnest and faithful Roman Catholic nun clutching a missal to her breast – and it was the *Heidelberg Kategismus, Nederduitse Gereformeerde Kerk, Kaapstad, Suid Afrika.* Do you have any idea what that means?"

"I do, Father O'Flannagan. That book is akin to the Bible among members of the Dutch Reformed Church of South Africa. Lutheran. They'd spit on a 'mackerel snapper' as well as look at him."

"Mackerel snapper?" The priest issued a deep belly laugh. "How old *are* you, Mister Caen?"

"I wasn't born in 1850, if that's what you're getting at, but I know the Protestants used it as a slur against the Catholics well into the *nineteen* fifties."

"*Prosit.* Would you like something stronger than tea?"

"You don't happen to have any Pellegrino water, do you, Father?"

~ ∫ ~

"Okay, gentlemen, we've got enough to go to Step Two. I believe the current term is 'going viral.'"

"Starting when?" Tabrizi asked.

"First thing tomorrow morning it'll hit *Donyaye Eqtesad, Entekhab, Etteláat, Jaam-e Jam, Kayhan*, and the *Tehran Times*. Full-page spread, color photos. Tomorrow at five, Channel 1 will headline it as lead story on the five-o'clock news and the rest of the stations will follow. Blogs all over the internet. The widest coverage of any story since the election of Rouhani. Should have some interesting repercussions."

Early the following morning, the Assassin arrived at Imam Khomeini Airport, two hours in advance of the 8:25 a.m. Turkish Airlines flight to Istanbul. The nonstop flight, which very rarely carried a full load, would arrive in Turkey's most cosmopolitan city at 10:20 in the morning. Agrippina did not realize how stifling the atmosphere in Iran had become until a week ago. A couple of days in Istanbul would be a heaven-sent opportunity to recharge her batteries and prepare for the rapidly approaching countdown.

"Hannelore deWet's" dark blonde hair was covered by a conservative headscarf. As she entered the terminal, her eyes were drawn to the bank of morning newspapers. She purchased the *Times* and tucked it under her arm, then stopped at a kiosk to buy a Styrofoam container of tea. The line at the ticket counter was short, no more than fifteen people waiting to buy their tickets to Turkey's largest metropolis. Plenty of time to sit at one of the convenient tables surrounding the kiosk and see what was new in the world before she got into line.

The front page carried the usual political rhetoric and reports about violent revolutions taking place in most of the Middle East. *Alles in ordnung.* She flipped rapidly through the first pages. When she reached page 5, she saw a full-page, full-color ad. As she read it, she felt a huge wave of nausea wash over her.

The words were in monster-size, boldface type:

HAVE YOU SEEN ANY OF THESE PEOPLE?
IRR 25,000,000 – 500,000,000 REWARD FOR
INFORMATION LEADING TO THE ARREST AND
CONVICTION OF ANY OF THE PERSONS BELOW!

The full-page advertisement contained every one of the Assassin's assumed names, the descriptions based on her passports, and eight full-color, sharp, clear photographs, along with a list of crimes of which each of these persons was charged.

The Assassin barely made it to the restroom and closed the nearest cubicle behind her before she threw up.

But she had been in tight positions before. She was a consummate professional and survivor. She would need all of her faculties and coolness of mind to consider her options. After dousing her face and neck with cold water from a sink in the bathroom, she returned to the toilet enclosure, where she remained for ten minutes while she thought through the best way to deal with the new situation.

At the end of that time, she returned to the airport hall, where she purchased a disposable cell phone and a prepaid hour's time. She punched in a number she knew by heart and texted, "BLUE DIAMOND. See p 5, 2day Teh Ts. Need hlp. Gng 2 grnd," and pressed "Send."

JANUARY

19

Money talks. Lots of money shouts. Media, whatever form it takes, thrives on controversy. Conversely, that same controversy tends to cool the ardor of most citizens by confusing and distracting them.

Within twenty-four hours of the publication of the Assassin's eight faces, seriously big money had poured into Iranian media coffers – radio, television, newspapers, blogs, and any other means of transmitting information, or, in this case, *dis*information, which would soften the shock value of Caen's media blitz.

Double-page ads in newspapers or their equivalents in other media carried much the same message: **WHAT'S SO SPECIAL ABOUT THESE EIGHT PERSONS? WHY ONLY EIGHT? WHAT ABOUT THESE FOURTEEN? WHO'S BEHIND THE FRAUDULENT MEGAMILLION RIAL REWARDS?**

The photos of showed fourteen men and women whose pictures had been doctored to make them look far more sinister than the Assassin's eight guises. The crimes attributed to the fourteen new people included murder, child rape, sexual molestation, a litany of the most heinous and vicious crimes know to man – much more serious than those listed for the Assassin in her eight permutations.

Morning and evening newscasters further confused the issue by adding their own comments. A group calling itself the National Coalition to Protect the Islamic Republic organized marches in the four major cities which had been the focus of the first ads. As invariably happens in such scenarios, the vast mass of public raised no great hue and cry, went about the business of life, and eagerly awaited the next scandal. Very few vigilant citizens bothered to apply for the multimillion rial reward.

"No matter," Tabrizi told the daily meeting of Security authority. "What matters is they've seen *our* pictures and they saw them *first*, before they were diluted by whoever's helping the Assassin. Our target has undoubtedly seen them. We now know she has allies with an apparently bottomless large war chest."

~ ∫ ~

As the old year turned the corner and gave way to the new, Agrippina's allies watched the lighted ball drop over Manhattan as the TV camera swept the huge crowd which filled Times Square. The Assassin's employers were enjoying a lavish full English breakfast as guests of the Duke, in his ten-thousand-square-foot "cottage" in the Cotswolds.

"They say English food is positively dreadful," Count Napolitano remarked, "but Scottish kippers proves that the Deity created heaven for taste buds in the British Isles."

"That's your third helping, my friend," Karaca remarked. "You'll be drinking water for the rest of the day and pissing all night."

"Whatever. Thanks to your quick action, we've managed to diffuse and defuse the problem," Napolitano continued. "She'll still need as much help as we can muster."

"Yes, but we can't be seen anywhere near Iran," Karroubi warned, "lest the spotlight of suspicion starts to point to us."

"I disagree," Yun-Lo said. "I'm very much *persona grata* with the new administration. While the Count is gorging on Scottish *kippers*, let's not forget who engineered the Scottish *caper*." He laughed at his own *bon mot*. "But to get much more serious, gentlemen, did it ever occur to you – or to any of our principals – that there might be a paradigm shift with the election of Hassan Rouhani and the newest agreement among the powers that have been choking the Islamic Republic? That time may have erased the necessity of our plan? Or that the murder of Ali Khamenei could conceivably be irrelevant?"

"Surely you don't mean ...?" Karaca stated, voicing a question that had infiltrated each of their minds within the past two days.

"I'm not saying we should do anything to *stop* the attempt," Yun-Lo continued. "I'm merely suggesting that either way it goes could be a win-win situation for our principals."

"But Khamenei won't change," Napolitano protested.

"You think not?" Karaca asked. "People said that about many leaders. Menachem Begin was a terrorist before he became Prime Minister of Israel. Yasser Arafat was demonized by everyone in the Middle East until he became a 'statesman.' Nelson Mandela ... Shall I go through an entire catalogue?"

"Not necessary," Yun-Lo said. "Although the United States with its tunnel vision sees Iran as a pariah nation, Rouhani was democratically elected by real, live voters, and he was not Khamenei's chosen. Whether Khamenei's a Grand Ayatollah or a speaker on a stoop outside a small mosque, he's no dummy and his political instincts have thus far proved infallible. While everyone seems to *think* and *say* he is the Supreme Leader, he portrays himself as a simple teacher."

"So what do we do about our 'wild card' in the Islamic Republic?" Napolitano queried. "We promised her full support …"

"She's told us many times in the past that she didn't need *any* help – she'd contact us if she needed us." This from Karroubi.

"However her recent communication signaled she might not be entirely averse to our aid," Karaca said.

"We might want to consider the consensus of our employers," Yun-Lo said.

At the end of the conference, it was decided that the four agents should continue to support the Assassin, but to hedge their bets … just in case.

~ ∫ ~

"Ah, Mister McAdams, how interesting to see you in town."

"What do you mean, Mister Farrokhzad?" the Assassin asked the landlord, suspiciously.

"Your neighbors have told me they've never once seen you enter or leave the apartment. The only one they've seen is a Roman Catholic nun."

"That's not true," the Assassin replied. "Unquestionably I travel through the country in search of classical Persian music. But that doesn't mean I don't return from time to time. In any event, that's irrelevant. I paid my rent six months in advance. You should be pleased."

"Don't get me wrong, Mister McAdams," the landlord said. "It's just a question of my potentially putting myself at risk."

"Meaning?"

"Exactly who *are* you, Mister McAdams?"

"What do you mean?"

"I think we both know. The nun's name is Sister Mary Salvatore, is it not? And, as has become obvious all over Iran, you have at least six other identities beside. Or at least that's what the newspapers and the television say."

There was a pregnant, meaningful silence before the Assassin responded.

"We are both men of the world, Mister Farrokhzad. If I am correct, your morals are not as important as your greed. How much are we talking about?"

"That depends, Mister McAdams. You need me to confirm to the authorities that I have never seen Richard McAdams, that Mister McAdams never leased a premises from me – an apartment which, by the way, has a small den which affords a very direct view of a place where our beloved Supreme Leader appears every so often …"

"I repeat, how much are we talking about?"

"Fifty thousand …"

"Rials? Swiss francs?"

"*Dollars*. United States currency."

"Those kinds of sums coming into the Islamic Republic would look most suspicious."

"True," Farrokhzad replied. "But I have a nephew in Beverly Hills, California."

"Ah, yes, I believe they call it 'Tehrangeles.'"

"Whatever you want to call it."

"How long do I have to raise the money?"

"Seventy-two hours should be sufficient."

~ ∫ ~

"She needs to show proof that fifty thousand dollars was deposited in his nephew's account at the Citibank branch in Century City."

"Consider it done."

"For real?"

"There'll be an official receipt to prove it."

"What if the man emails the nephew to find out if there really was a deposit?"

"I don't think that will be a problem."

~ ∫ ~

Farrokhzad knocked at the door of the Assassin's apartment two days later.

"Thank you for coming so promptly," McAdams said, pleasantly enough.

"You said you were able to advance the timetable, Mister McAdams. I am pleased."

"As you said, Mister Farrokhzad, there are certain … things … I need to have accomplished. Did you bring the declarations? The 'new' lease?"

"Of course. I trust you have the proof of deposit?"

"Naturally. Shall we seal our new relationship with a small aperitif? Or are you hesitant to touch alcohol?"

The landlord laughed. "I am by no means insulted, Mister McAdams. As we discussed earlier, we are both men of the world."

"Champagne?"

"Why not?"

Shortly after drinking to their new status, the landlord held his hand out to see the deposit slip. The Assassin pretended to be coy about wanting to see the declarations first, then relented. "Ours is a relationship of mutual trust, is it not?"

"As you say."

"I'm sure you'd like to confirm with your nephew that the money really has been deposited?"

"You are prescient, Mister McAdams," Farrokhzad said, extracting a cell phone from his jacket pocket. "Please, would you hand me the deposit slip so I might confirm the date, time, and account number?"

"Of course."

Farrokhzad reached out to take the flimsy piece of paper from the Assassin.

It was the last move he'd ever make.

The Assassin drew back her right arm, extended her right hand with fingers straight and tight together, took calculating aim, and drove her hand like a spear into Farrokhzad's solar plexus. Farrokhzad gave a sharp cry of surprise and pain, dropped his hands, and clutched at the pit of his stomach. Agrippina reared her rigid right hand back, then drove it into Farrokhzad's Adam's apple. Farrokhzad gave another, weaker, strangled cry, and his whole body convulsed. There was but one thing more to do. The Assassin used her stiffened hand like the flat blade of a knife. She swung it sideways, with all of her strength, at the underside of Farrokhzad's nose. Farrokhzad made no further sound and no more movement, except a twitching and quivering from head to foot, and then he lay still.

~ ∫ ~

There remained the means of disposing of the body. The Assassin, who'd purchased the tools do to the job some time earlier, waited until late that night. She started with a well-sharpened, serrated butcher's knife. It took the Assassin three hard punches before she was deep enough to start sawing through the chest cavity.

She took no notice of the visceral substances that spattered over the floor, nor the gases from the prostrate body that forced various liquids and food in a partially digested state onto her hands. When she'd removed most of the organs, she put them into a nearby bucket. These must be disposed of that very night, for the odor emanating from them would be overpowering by morning.

Next, the Assassin took a large axe and a smaller hatchet from her tool kit. With four sharp swings of the axe, she severed the remains of Farrokhzad's head. She found it relatively easy to cut off the arms with the hatchet, and there was little blood. The well-muscled legs, however, presented a problem. She reached for the axe, and brought it through Farrokhzad's thighs. It took several over-the-head swings to do it, for Farrokhzad's thighs were thick with dried gristle and solid bone.

Afterward, Agrippina cut the remains into smaller pieces and stuffed then neatly into garbage bags. Over the next few evenings, she intended to bury the pieces in various dumpsites within and without the city. But for now, she needed to start cleaning the floor and surrounding furniture with rags, mops, and pails of hot, soapy water. By the time she finished, several hours later, every vestige of what had gone on was erased.

The Assassin slept well that night.

~ ∫ ~

The elderly cleaning woman emerged from the bus a block away and shuffled through the streets adjoining the Jamkaran Mosque until she reached McAdams' apartment. Clothed head-to-toe in shapeless, heavy, concealing *hijab* and *rusari* headscarf, she appeared bent over with age, arthritis, and a lifetime of subordination. Her gait was crabbed and her progress was slowed by her need to stop every few moments to catch her breath. How she managed to negotiate the stairs to Mister McAdams' flat baffled most of the neighbors, who looked the other way with shame at the low station that had forced the woman to the dreadfully difficult life she was fated to live.

But B'hiji, for that was the woman's name, somehow managed to climb the stairs each morning carrying a large, cheap plastic bag. She remained in the apartment an hour or two at most, before she descended the stairs slowly and painfully, still carrying her bag, and shuffled her way back to the nearest bus stop. With a shake of the head, she declined the offers of a few of the apartment house's inhabitants to help her carry her bag down the stairs. Despite her station, she maintained a minimal, but ineffable, aura of pride.

"D'you think the foreigner moved?" the woman in Apartment 2 asked her neighbor.

"Hard to tell. Did you ever even see him?"

"Not once. And I haven't seen that nun who was always around for the last two weeks. Do you think maybe they were …?" She giggled like a naughty schoolgirl.

"Not unless she was screwing a ghost or the Holy Spirit, or whatever they call their heathen god."

"Only time I've seen a cleaning woman around since the foreigner moved in."

"Could be Farrokhzad kicked him out and rented it to someone else. That's the only reason I could see someone coming each day to clean the place."

"Cheap bastard, our landlord. He'd chisel down an old lady and pay her a few hundred rials if he thought he could make big money from renting to a new tenant, but fix the plumbing or the heat …?"

"That'll only happen when the Prophet returns. Speaking of which, when was the last time you saw *him*?"

"The Prophet?"

"Farrokhzad."

"Two, three days ago."

"I say the less we see of him the better. Of course he's always here the first of the month to make sure the rent is paid on time, but other than that …"

"How long you think the cleaning lady'll be here?"

"A few days at the most."

"Poor old grandmother."

The two women's gossip would have been far different had they followed the old crone when she left the apartment house. The square abutting the Jamkaran Mosque was the terminal for five different bus lines. Each day when the cleaning woman emerged, she would board a different bus and ride it to the end of the line.

By her last day at the apartment, she had managed to dispose of the contents of each bag with which she had left the flat. The neighbors would have been shocked to learn that the bag she carried when she left the apartment weighed at least twenty kilos – forty-four pounds – more than when she had walked up the stairs. They would have been even more surprised had they seen her carrying the loaded bag for at least a mile after she left the last bus stop. When she found an appropriate locale, usually a desert wadi or such, she would scoop out a shallow depression in the sand, pour out the contents, and cover them over, leaving the ground unchanged in appearance from when she first entered the area.

From time to time, usually late at night, B'hiji would return to McAdams' apartment to make sure no one else had been there. She would remain in the flat until just before dawn, when she'd silently walk through the back streets and alleyways to her temporary abode.

Unknown to B'hiji, her every movement had been followed by one who was so undistinguishable he would have disappeared in any crowd. In his own way, Manucher Tabrizi was much like the Assassin herself.

20

It would have been simple for Yun-Lo to fly from Istanbul's Atatürk International Airport, direct to Tabriz. He would normally have flown business class on the morning Turkish Airlines flight, but he had borne so many such inconveniences in his earlier life that getting up so early to make the 3:20 a.m. departure was no longer his cup of tea. Besides, he was astute enough from his long diplomatic service to know that eyebrows would be raised *somewhere* if he were seen in a place that had absolutely no status as a destination for officials on state business. The last thing he wanted to do was attract attention. Besides, he'd be traveling to Tehran within the month, and his presence would be quite public then.

This trip was to be for a very private meeting, so private, in fact, that he had not disclosed it to his three associates. Yun-Lo felt the forbidden fruit thrill of the journey.

He took the 10:00 a.m. Pegasus flight from Istanbul's Sabiha Gökçen Airport, 23 miles east of Istanbul in the Asiatic suburb of Pendik, to Van, in eastern Turkey. From there, he took a Dolmuş, a shared taxi, to Doğubeyazit, in the shadow of Mount Ararat.

Once in Doğubayazit, Yun-Lo bought some street food to tide him over, then boarded another shared taxi to the Iranian border, a journey over a busy, potholed road which took forty-five minutes. The border road itself was quite congested. Once traffic ground to a halt, the Asian man opted to get out and walk the rest of the way; it was faster than the van. He noticed a large military presence in the area, bunkers, tanks, Jeeps and army personnel

At the first checkpoint, a Turkish border patrol officer looked desultorily at Yun-Lo's ordinary Chinese passport. He'd eschewed the use of his diplomatic passport, since that would only attract unnecessary attention. Then he walked up a two-lane-wide new road to a second station, where a Turkish guard checked to ensure that he had the requisite Iranian entry visa. From there, Hsien walked up another small hill towards the Iranian border. A huge mural of the late Ayatollah Khomeini and a large sign proclaimed, "Welcome to Iran."

A few soldiers inspected his passport before directing him to a ten foot high iron gate. Beyond the gate, at a small glass enclosure to the left, his passport was stamped by a smiling guard, and he entered the Islamic Republic.

Once Hsien Yun-Lo passed through the customs gate, a few ragamuffin kids came up and asked for money. He ignored them, then came to an area where he was accosted by touts, taxi drivers, and peddlers. Yun-Lo headed straight for a local stand where he got into a beat-up gray and yellow taxi to Maku, a city of 42,000 people, fourteen miles inside Iran. The ride cost 2,000 rials and took another half hour.

He glanced at his wrist watch. 4:30. Sunset was another hour-and-a-half away, even in the middle of winter. A shared taxi bearing the elderly cleaning woman would most likely arrive within that time.

~ ∫ ~

The cleaning woman had begun her journey at six the evening before. The cross-country *Mahooly* bus in which, being a woman, she had been required to sit in the rear, had made a stop at four in the morning for a quick breakfast, but she didn't bother to get out, since she had packed her meals for the journey in a small cardboard luggage case. Being old and obviously quite tired, she slept most of the way to Tabriz. Finding a *Domud*, a shared van, to Maku was not difficult, and she arrived at that border town at 5:30 in the afternoon after her 23½-hour journey.

As she alighted stiffly, she adjusted her raiment, then shuffled toward the familiar face who was glancing at his watch.

"Agrippina?"

"Hsien? Your code message was urgent." They spoke English. "Is it safe to speak in the open?"

"I see no reason why not, but you must be hungry."

"Famished."

"Let's adjourn to a local kebap house."

Once there, their conversation was as clipped and circumspect as though they were being watched, which, although they did not know it, they were.

"Cleaned?"

"Yes, but they may be watching."

"Probably. Did he have family?"

"Don't know. Assume so."

"But no one's been there?"

"Not so I'd know. I've had no communication with my neighbors."

"Just as well. You're still okay to do this?"

The woman's eyebrows narrowed. "Why should I not be?"

"You can always back out you know?"

"And give back five million dollars? You must think I'm mad."

"Perhaps an adjustment could be made."

"What do you mean, Yun-Lo?" she asked suspiciously. "Have your people had a change of heart?"

The Asian did not respond directly. "I assure you there's no intent to deprive you of what is justly due. The fact that we tendered your down payment should show our good faith."

"I can assure you I haven't changed my plans ..."

"Despite the, er ... difficulties?"

"It's not the first time I've faced problems. Did you summon me here to test my resolve?"

"Not at all, Agrippina," Yun-Lo said, his palms raised placatingly. "My associates and I simply want to ensure that you have all the support you need. Money, papers, a place to stay ..."

"You've given me enough that I hardly need money," she said. "I appreciated your aid when my security was breached. Papers?"

The Chinese reached into a small briefcase and extracted four additional sets of papers – passports, driver's licenses, photographs, and the like – affording the Assassin four new identities, all of which bore entry visas and stamps indicating that the bearer had entered the Islamic Republic within the past year. Two of the visas were current and the other two had been extended. The Assassin nodded and put them in her luggage case.

When the nondescript waiter brought kebaps, rice, salad, and Iranian flat bread to their table, Hsien had not realized how hungry he was until he bit into the first of his lamb chunks. Agrippina, who'd started eating at the same time as her companion, was hungrily wolfing down her food. As her eyes darted around the small restaurant, she noticed five other people, three at the next table and a pair of single men, each at an adjoining table. One of the men looked vaguely familiar, but not enough to stir any concern. So many Iranians looked alike.

"The problem," she said, "is that the place was perfect for my needs. I've no doubt it's only a matter of time before they discover … and start snooping around the flat. It may be impossible to find similar lodgings. That may necessitate a total change in plans."

"As I said, if you don't feel …"

"Yun-Lo, I committed to an agreement. Whatever else I might be, my word is my bond, and I assume total responsibility for how I go about my task."

"Please, Miss … Agrippina … I never suggested otherwise. What if … I could somehow arrange matters so that you could remain in the flat? As a completely different tenant, of course?"

"Meaning?"

"You know I arranged for the Scots to entertain on the eleventh?"

"Yes."

"The situation at the 'late' Mr. McAdams' flat presents a problem."

"My present identity …"

"Your present identity will have to disappear, soon and completely. I wouldn't bet against the hunters tailing your *persona* to wherever you buried the pieces. I'm equally sure they traced you back to the apartment."

"Do you have any suggestions?"

"I think we should go for a walk." He signaled the waiter for the check. After each of them had made a stop at the half-cleaned, smelly bathrooms and Yun-Lo had paid, they walked out of the restaurant.

"I have a friend, Mahmoud Tabatabai, a crafty old lawyer. He'll approach the law enforcement agencies, and after heartfelt condolences to the Farrokhzad family, accompanied by a check for fifteen percent over the going rate for the apartment house... The title of the place would be turned over to the new buyer."

"You?"

"A Trust which I control."

The Assassin stopped to consider the implications. "How does this affect me?"

"I'll talk with President Rouhani, convince him I need an apartment near the Mosque for at least three weeks before, and maybe a week after, the eleventh, in order to maintain tight controls over the troupe."

"I'm listening."

"I'll tell him I've discovered a vacant flat which would suit my purposes perfectly, within a block of the festivities; I'll tell him that Lawyer Tabatabai was acting as the rental agent and ask if he'd be kind enough to intervene to get me a fair price for the month's rent." He grinned. "I don't think that will be difficult."

"Where do I come in?"

"President Rouhani knows that I travel a great deal and must be on a different continent at any given time. I'll need to have my assistant maintain the apartment in my absence."

The Assassin looked at Yun-Lo oddly. "Putting me under the microscope of every security official in the Islamic Republic?"

"*Au contraire*, my dear. Have you ever heard the term 'submarines?'"

"More riddles?"

"No riddle at all. I'll be more specific. Nazi Germany?"

"I'm not making the connection."

The pair walked into the lobby of a hotel which looked like it had seen much better days – in fact, much better *decades*.

"As of 1945, despite Goebbels' desire to make the German capital *Judenfrei*, there were more than four thousand Jews living in Berlin. Those survivors stayed in one place for two or three months at most, but they continued living under the Nazis' very noses. They called themselves 'U-boats' or 'submarines,' and like submarines, they 'came up for air' only occasionally."

"Why did they stay there?"

"Because despite everything that had happened to the Jews in the preceding twelve years, they still considered themselves German. They took the attitude that no one was going to drive them out of Berlin, not Hitler, not Goebbels, and not the entire Gestapo. They believed they were part of that country. Besides, they really had nowhere else to go except the death camps."

"And you expect me to be your 'submarine,' literally living in the place from where I'll commit the deed for almost an entire month?"

"As my assistant and under my protection."

"And the old cleaning woman?"

"A corpse that looks similar enough and will convince anyone who asks that she died of exposure or some other cause … That will nip the investigation of what happened to Farrokhzad's body in the bud. The only witness will, alas, be deceased. When the investigation is ended, everyone will lose interest, primarily the tenants of the buildings. They'll expect the owner to rent out McAdams' old flat."

"And your assistant?"

"Take a look at the new passports."

Agrippina did, and stopped at the third one. The face was that of a striking blonde in her mid-thirties. Stylish, European, but with a modern headscarf.

"Tariqa Manisa, from Sarajevo, Bosnia-Herzegovina. A perfect Eurasian mix, suave, urbane, and a perfect manager for the enterprises of a wealthy man. And, I might add, absolutely unlike any of the others. Do you speak Farsi?"

"Enough to get by."

"Other languages?"

"Six."

"Excellent! I trust you can 'keep your cool' if any investigators come snooping around?"

"Have you any doubt about that?"

"Ordinarily, no. However, I've recently learned certain, umm, matters which might affect your behavior."

The Assassin stared directly at Yun-Lo. "More riddles?"

"A rather meaningful one, I'm afraid."

"What's that?"

"What do you know about the circumstances of your birth, Agrippina? Or should I say Morgan Terre'Blanche?"

The Assassin blanched. "How …?" she barely whispered.

"My principals have done their homework, too."

"Wh … what?" she said, stumbling for the first time since she'd met the Chinese.

"Are you aware that you were born a twin?"

"I knew that."

"Is that why you cut your entry out of the Cotlands birth records?"

The Assassin said nothing. Her silence shouted the answer.

"You know, then, that you were a girl and your twin was a boy?"

"Yes ... so?"

"What do you know about those hunting you?"

"The Israeli or the one I tried to kill?"

"You've done your homework as well."

"I have. The Iranian's Manucher Tabrizi, supposedly the Islamic Republic's best detective. The Israeli's Ezra Caen, reportedly one of the best in the world."

"Do you know anything more about the Israeli?"

"Other than his reputation, not much."

"Agrippina, my dear, steel yourself – and steel yourself hard. The Israeli hunter, Ezra Caen?"

"Yes?" she breathed in, knowing as if it were preordained, what was coming next.

"Ezra Caen is the twin brother you've never met."

21

"Something is rotten in China," Count Napolitano said softly.

"Isn't the phrase, 'Something is rotten in Denmark,' Marco?" Karroubi asked.

"Doesn't matter how you say it, one of our number has taken to wildcatting, operating on his own without informing the rest of us."

"I thought we had all agreed to hedge our bets by staying on the sidelines," Karaca said. The three men, signally excluding Yun-Lo, were gathered at the same Içaçan Sokak apartment where, some months before, the Turkish businessman had met with the Israeli and Iranian delegations and the marriage of convenience between them had been forged. Karaca stood, stretched to his full five-foot-ten-inch height, cracked his knuckles, went into the small kitchen, and emerged with three tulip cups of apple tea and a tray of *tel kadayif,* shredded wheat tubes doused in honey.

"Marco, you've been the intermediary with whom she's had the most contact. You think he's poaching on your territory?"

"Mustafa, I'm an Italian from the *mezzo giorno*. To us, there's no such thing as a woman who does not present a challenge. Particularly one who's younger than me, independent, and, when she wants to be, quite beautiful."

"Tit for tat, as it were?"

"No one said anything about breasts," the Count rejoined.

"Gentlemen," Karroubi said, sipping his tea and snatching the nearest pastry from the tray. "Regardless of the levity, this presents a serious problem. Despite our association, each of our own employers has a different agenda, and wouldn't hesitate to trump the others if they saw an advantage. They would not have gotten to where they are otherwise. Hsien's relationship with the new president goes back a long way. If Rouhani somehow foils the plot to kill the Ayatollah, the president's stock goes up exponentially. If the president sees Yun-Lo as the source of his success, I need not tell you the influence Hsien and his principal gain."

"He'd throw Agrippina under the bus?"

"Regardless of where the bets are placed, the one nearest the table is the one the croupier sees first. I'm told our Chinese friend has arranged to take over the apartment where the Assassin had been staying and has installed our girl as his personal manager in residence. She's got the perfect location to succeed. On the other hand, if the hunters turn the heat up, she's a virtual prisoner in the flat and a sitting duck when the authorities come a-knocking."

"Win-win for Yun-Lo, and no risk," Marco murmured.

"Maybe, maybe not," Karaca said, stroking his chin.

"How could it be otherwise?"

"The Assassin may be much smarter, more adaptable, and less predictable than any of us suspect. She would not have survived as long as she has in her profession unless she hedged all *her* bets," the Turk replied. He gazed out the window, down toward the city, his view blocked by Ankara's winter pall of coal smoke, then turned back to face his associates.

"Marco, you've been the lifeline to Agrippina up 'til now. If you were in her place, what could you use most?"

"An alternate location from which she could accomplish the deed. One known to nobody but her. Particularly one unknown either to Hsien Yun-Lo or the security forces."

"Not such an easy task," Karroubi remarked sardonically. "With less than a month to go, and with God knows how close the hunters are or what they know, you think they don't know exactly where she is at any given moment?"

"She went to ground once, Mehdi, and didn't get caught."

"Yes, but how do you know she didn't get caught because those who are after her wanted to see if she could lead them to bigger fish? Don't forget, Marco, these are my people. I know how they function."

"You and George Bush," Karaca remarked, gently chiding his associate by alluding to the former American president's gaffe about why the U.S. would easily win the war in Iraq.

"My friends, do any of you know any way – any conceivable way at all – that such a fallback position could be arranged – and quickly?" Napolitano asked. "More important, that we could get word privately, and away from Yun-Lo's prying ears and eyes, to Agrippina?"

"I have someone in mind," Karroubi said. "Someone I trust completely."

"Remember before you go to him – "

"Her."

Karaca's and Napolitano's eyebrows lifted simultaneously.

~ ∫ ~

"By all means, my dear, you should accept this invitation," Yun-Lo remarked. "You've everything to gain and nothing to lose if you're seen hobnobbing with the representatives of Iran's closest allies – Syria, the *Hezbollah* representatives from Lebanon, *Hamas* ..."

"Not to mention the Chinese, the Russians, and the North Koreans," Agrippina replied casually. "Two giants and a Who's Who of the world's outcast nations."

The Assassin had been cooped up in the flat for the past week and felt like a caged animal. Even though Tehran was only a hundred miles – less than an hour-and-a-half drive – from Qom, she needed the heady air of the big city to relieve her of the stifling religiosity of the Holy City.

"Will you be coming?" she asked Yun-Lo.

"I'd love to, but business calls ..."

"Ah, yes, the intrepid world traveler. Maybe I will take you up on it. A couple of nights away can't hurt."

~ ∫ ~

Despite the small number of nations represented and the numerically sparse attendance, the Islamic Republic did its best to put on its happiest face. Champagne flowed, even though alcoholic beverages were anathema outside the hall. Agrippina / Tariqa, dressed in a slinky black sheath gown, sporting an expensive, natural-looking honey blonde wig, and wearing the lightest, most diaphanous headscarf, was more than what Count Napolitano had termed "quite beautiful." She was ravishing.

Moments later, the Assassin felt a chill as she glanced across the room and noticed a bartender some twenty feet away, pouring drinks from behind a bar. Although he was so plain as to be nondescript, and was dressed in slightly rumpled, ill-fitting clothes, she could not avoid noticing that his eyes never stopped shifting from place to place throughout the room. For just the slightest instant, his eyes locked on her. Under ordinary circumstances, she was quite used to the spell she could cast on every man in a room when she was dressed in her "war gear." But this man did not look at her with frank sexual interest. Rather, he looked at her as though he knew her, and could see *inside.* Not inside her clothing. Much deeper than that.

An instant, a snapshot instant, and she knew who he was. More than that, she knew that *he* knew who *she* was. She felt the need to escape the banquet hall immediately, to be anywhere, so long as it was *away.*

As she retreated toward the door, she felt a firm hand on her arm. Startled, she turned quickly and found herself looking at a red-haired woman as striking as she.

"Not to worry, Agrippina," the woman said smoothly. "I was sent by your three other associates."

"Associates?" she said coolly, unwilling to trust anyone.

"Count Napolitano, Karaca Bey, and Mister Karroubi," the redhead continued. "They believe you might not enjoy being Yun-Lo's prisoner."

"How dare you – ?" she started to snap, then closed her mouth in mid-sentence.

"Let's go to the ladies'. More privacy."

Shortly after they had ensconced themselves in adjoining stalls, the Assassin found a five-by-six inch piece of paper, written in English, thrust from under the next cubicle into hers. "Don't talk. You never can tell who's listening. I'll leave first. There'll be a key on the rear lip of the toilet seat, just above the commode." There followed an address and apartment number of a flat in Qom. The Assassin had familiarized herself with the neighborhood where "Richard McAdams" had stayed. The address denoted a building on the opposite side of the Mosque, even closer to its front steps. The note ended, "Your friends have your best interests at heart and want you to succeed. They don't know that the same can be said about Yun-Lo. Watch yourself." It was signed "Hypatia."

Agrippina tore off a small corner of the paper and scribbled, "The bartender at the far end of the room?" and shoved it into the next stall. A few moments later the response came back. "Ezra Caen."

The Assassin flushed the small piece of paper down the toilet, then exited the cubicle where she'd been. The adjoining stall was open and there was no one else in the bathroom. Entering the stall, she saw the promised key, slipped it into her small handbag, and departed the building, not even bothering to return to the banquet hall.

When she returned to Qom, one of the first things Hsien Yun-Lo's dutiful assistant did was to check out the alternative flat to which Hypatia had given her the key. Step-by-step, she measured the distance from the front of the Mosque to the doorstep of the apartment house. Four hundred paces. At an average of two feet per step, eight hundred feet. The alternative apartment was on the second, not the third, floor, so it was closer to where the target would be than "McAdams'"

apartment. A straight shot would be well within her range. Even better for her purposes, the room facing the Mosque was larger, but at the same time less conspicuous than the one in McAdams' flat.

Hypatia had stocked the apartment with food and other staples, from European quality toilet paper to a functioning vacuum cleaner. When Agrippina opened the bedroom closet, she was gratified to see a number of outfits – men's and women's – which, she was certain, would fit her perfectly.

During the following day, the Assassin walked several different routes from the McAdams flat to Hypatia's apartment, carefully timing each route to assure herself of the most expeditious route between the two buildings should the need arise. On the third evening, just after dark, she took her second rifle and appropriate ammunition to her new flat, placed the rifle in a narrow wooden box, and stuffed the box in the closet adjacent to the living room.

~ ∫ ~

There remained the question of the accuracy of her weapons. Time was getting short. With all that had happened over the past month, Agrippina needed to determine if the settings she had cemented between her two rifles and the eyepieces were still accurate. A day's trip south of Qom and some target practice in the desert reassured her that both weapons were perfectly in synch. In order to ensure her own protection, she planted one of the two handguns she had purchased in Tehran in a strategic position in each of the flats.

~ ∫ ~

When Yun-Lo called her at the McAdams apartment, she responded that everything was ready for the arrival of the Highland Dance Troupe.

She did not bother to mention the Hypatia apartment. Whoever considered himself to be her savior, she assumed a neutral position and kept her own counsel. By week's end, each flat was similarly equipped: a rifle with appropriate ammunition, a sidearm, food, clothing, and other indicia of a normal life. With three weeks to go, it was time to hunker down and become a regular part of the street scene.

~ ∫ ~

"I must admit, Mehdi, you've leveled the playing field for all of us once again," Karaca said admiringly.

Each of them had received jpeg photos of "Hypatia's" apartment taken from the street, the Mosque, and every interior angle. The photos traced the distances from each apartment to the dais from which the Ayatollah would be speaking, as well as the distance between the apartment houses themselves.

"Does Yun-Lo suspect anything?" Napolitano asked.

"Only if Hypatia disclosed it to him, which I doubt," Karroubi responded.

"How long have you known her?" Karaca asked.

"Five years," Karroubi said.

"What do you know about her?" from Napolitano.

"Hypatia is, as you've seen from the photo, a striking woman whom men find irresistible. She's a Black Belt in Oriental martial arts, but she's feminine enough to enjoy wearing clothes that show off her shapely body. Hypatia maintains the tightest connections with all the important politicians. Because she's beautiful, intelligent, witty, and, as far as anyone knows, unattached, she's frequently invited to parties held at the highest levels of Iranian society. That's why it was so easy for her to wangle an invitation for our Assassin."

"And her own beliefs?" Karaca asked.

"I couldn't tell you," Karroubi replied. "I wager she plays all sides against one another, but that really doesn't matter. The favor I asked her was well outside the sphere of intra-Persian culture. Since she was paid remarkably well for her efforts, I very much doubt she considered it a favor to me. Like many other women of similar inclination, Hypatia is a well-paid courtesan who stays bought."

~ ∫ ~

"My goodness, Mister Yun-Lo, that airplane is absolutely *huge*," Mistress Fraser gasped. "I'm sure it could hold four times the number of our entire troupe, bagpipes, drums, baggage, and all!"

"It carries 130 people, Mistress Fraser. My principal purchased this MD-87 from Allegiant Air last year."

The troupers were as excited as children with a new toy when they saw the McDonnell-Douglas bird – larger, even, than the Embraer 195 planes that FlyBe flew into Inverness Airport. The air hostess, pilot, and copilot were delightful hosts, showing their charges all over the aircraft, from the cockpit to the loos at the tail. The dancers, drummers, bagpipers, and, of course, Mistress Fraser posed for group pictures with the crew outside the craft.

"How far is it from Inverness to Tehran?" one of the bagpipers asked the captain.

"2,920 miles – a little more than six hours."

"How many stops are there, Sir?" the other piper asked.

"This will be a nonstop flight, Son. With auxiliary tanks our range is 3,427 miles, which gives us an extra hour's worth of fuel if we need it."

Others asked questions about the two jet engines situated near the tail of the aircraft and the controls at the top of the tail. Three of the troupers had flown on a jet plane before, but none had flown farther than Amsterdam or London.

"All right," Mistress Fraser said sternly to her charges. "Time for you young'uns to get home and have a good night's sleep. We leave Inverness at 8:00 tomorrow."

"So we'll arrive in Tehran six hours later, two in the afternoon?" one of the ten-year-olds said, eager to show off her mathematical knowledge.

"Not quite," said the pilot. "Tehran is three-and-a-half hours ahead of Inverness time, so we'll actually be arriving at 5:30 in the evening. Since it's winter, it'll almost be dark by the time we get to the hotel."

Next evening, the members of the troupe, up to and including their director, stared goggle-eyed at the mind-boggling traffic jams, monuments, tall buildings, parks, and high mountain vistas in the Iranian capital, which was *two-hundred thirty-five times* as big as their hometown. Hsien Yun-Lo had booked them into the Parsian Azadi Hotel, in the airy northern suburbs, twenty minutes from the city center. They were transported from Mehrabad International Airport by a chartered "Volvo" bus.

When Mistress Fraser pointed out that this was not a *Volvo* bus at all, but a Magirus Deutz coach, Yun-Lo explained to her, "The name 'Volvo' actually describes the *class* of conveyance. There are two classes of long distance buses in Iran. 'Volvo buses' can be Volvos, Mercedes, Magirus Deutz, or any other kind of bus which is brand new, deluxe class, fully air conditioned, with comfortable padded seats, food service, and every modern convenience. On the other hand, *Mahmooly* buses, which usually cost half the fare of a Volvo bus, and which transport most Iranians, are more than twenty years older and not so fancy."

After two days touring the capital of the Islamic Republic, visiting and having their pictures taken with President Rouhani himself, the Volvo bus whisked them to Qom to start their rehearsals for the big day. It was February 4, one week before their command performance.

FEBRUARY

22

"Any further leads?" Ghasem Habib asked Caen and Tabrizi at the weekly Security Council meeting.

"Nothing," Tabrizi responded. "The cleaning woman disappeared without a trace, as have the Assassin's other known identities."

Ezra Caen sat silently, quaffing a glass of Pellegrino water.

"Nothing from you, Ezra?" Rouhani asked.

"I'm afraid not, Mister President."

"What's the Leader's security like, Rahman?" the president inquired of the Chief of the Ayatollah's bodyguard.

"As good as it's going to get," Almotahari responded. "Which means there's no one-hundred percent foolproof way to protect the Leader."

"How many law enforcement officials and bodyguards?"

"Ten thousand, five hundred."

Ghormani whistled softly. "If there are forty thousand in the square, more than one in every four people will be there to assure the Supreme Leader's safety."

"Yes," Caen said, "but a single shot from a key location, two or three stories above the crowd, and those ten thousand, five hundred won't be worth a single soul." He spoke softly, but his words expressed what everyone else in the room was thinking. The worst case scenario.

"I thought you and Manucher had tagged McAdams' apartment as the most likely place," Chairman Moslehi said.

"True, Mister Minister, but that's now been crossed out. After McAdams disappeared and the landlord was killed – and his remains disposed of by the old cleaning woman, who was probably another of our target's disguises – Mahmoud Tabatabai negotiated the sale of the apartment house to a real estate conglomerate, and our President's friend Hsien Yun-Lo, who's in charge of the Scottish delegation, rented the McAdams flat for the duration," Ezra said. "Either he's there or his business associate is there, and her credentials come up clean as a whistle. She's been minding the store for the past three weeks."

"So we cancel the place most likely," Ghormani intoned.

"Not necessarily, Omid," Tabrizi said. "Although Yun-Lo and the associate seem impeccable, one can never be sure."

"I disagree," President Rouhani said in measured tones. "I've known Hsien Yun-Lo for a dozen years. I'd trust him with – "

"With what, Hassan?" Heyder Moslehi asked mildly. "Your life? Or the Supreme Leader's life?"

"Either or both," the President retorted.

"In the Middle East, who trusts anyone with his life?" Youssef Abbasi asked.

"Are you accusing me of being naive?" Rouhani asked, his demeanor starting to crack under the pressure of the meeting.

"Not at all, Mister President," Abbasi said smoothly. "I simply point out that none of us would have gotten as far as we have in the Islamic Republic if we did not watch our backsides as well as what's in front of us."

"Gentlemen," the Israeli cautioned, "there's no need for us to get upset at one another. We are, after all, on the same team. Earlier, we agreed among ourselves that the McAdams apartment was certainly as good a place as any from which to attempt the Assassination. It may still be. Rahman told us he's got ten thousand, five hundred pairs of eyes in Qom. Detaching one or two pairs of those eyes to simply watch the McAdams flat is neither paranoid nor proof of mistrust. It's simply good business."

~ ∫ ~

The Assassin had not survived as long as she had without finely-honed instincts. Under normal circumstances, she'd have considered the interference of all four of her employers to be so unconscionable that she would have abandoned her assignment. But given the strange direction this matter was taking, she was mildly relieved that she had a modicum of protection, especially in the person of Hypatia, who, so far as she knew, had no last name, but who seemed to be adept at ensuring that what she promised was delivered.

Although Agrippina had always worked alone, and preferred it that way, she admitted, if only to herself, that this situation was entirely different, and not a little threatening. For one thing, there seemed to be a conflict between those who had hired her – not a good sign – although she had no idea what that conflict was. A red flag under any conditions. But far and away the most disturbing specter was that the man who apparently was in charge of the hunt shared many of the same genes with her, most likely thought in the same ways she did, and seemed to be able to intuit what her every next move would be.

It would not have been too late for Agrippina to abandon the assignment and escape not only with her life, but with five million U.S. dollars. Indeed, Hsien Yun-Lo had suggested as much to her. A normal, rational human being, even a trained professional killer like she was, would, at the very least, have weighed the options.

But – and she could not have known this – she and her twin brother were made very much of the same stuff. Once she had committed to a position, she would not back down. Similarly, Ezra had remained with Galit, even after her numerous affairs, even after Meir's death. No matter how much of a trash heap their marriage was, at the end it was Galit who had walked out on Ezra, not the other way around. The Assassin had researched everything that was publicly known about Ezra in excruciating detail. He was *the plodder* – dogged, stubbornly persevering, tenacious, and obstinate.

Morgan Terre'Blanche / Agrippina / the Assassin was similarly "hard-wired." She simply could not back away from the assignment no matter if her chances of succeeding and getting out alive were less than one in twenty.

Beyond that one character flaw, if it could be called a defect, her skills as the consummate killing machine were beyond reproach. After studying all of the alternatives, she had concluded several days ago that the best opportunity to succeed really *was* the one that she – and probably her employers as well as those who were hunting her – had also determined was the most likely scenario: the killing would take place on the afternoon of February 11, Islamic Victory Day, on the steps of the Jamkaran Mosque in Qom, the Holiest City in the Islamic Republic of Iran, the one place in Iran where the Supreme Leader was certain to appear.

The Scottish bagpipe, drum, and dance troupe was bound to increase the crowd. The government's announcement that the event would be televised worldwide was most likely to incite the spectators to further ardor. And the combination of everything happening at one time in Qom was certain to increase the crowd's frenzy to a point that crowd control and security would be virtually impossible, even if there was one law enforcement official for every man, woman, and child in the audience. To coin a modern Western phrase, what was brewing was "the perfect storm."

~ ∫ ~

"I dun wat u asked," Hypatia texted Karroubi. "Enyting els?"
"Nting, t.u.," Karroubi texted back.

~ ∫ ~

"You're on your own," Hsien Yun-Lo said. "If for some reason you need to contact me ...?"
"I won't."
"I trust when I return you'll be gone. Good luck."

~ ∫ ~

"Are all the hotels as lovely as this one?" Elspeth Fraser asked Yun-Lo as they entered the Qom International Hotel on Helal Almar Street, two minutes' walk from the Fatima-al-Massumeh Shrine.

"This is the best one in the city. Although the Shrine is one of Qom's major attractions, your group will actually be performing in the Great Square outside the Jamkaran Mosque, which is a bit farther away."

"Will we be rehearsing there?"

"I'm afraid not, Mistress Fraser. Because of the need for security, the rehearsals will take place some distance outside the city. However, the Iranian government has erected duplicate wooden stages, one at your rehearsal venue and one which will be moved into the Square the morning of the actual performance. Each is cut to precisely the size and dimensions you gave me, so your troupe will have no problem at all."

"What about the sound system?"

"Since all the speakers will be directed outward, your troupe will hear the same sounds they hear in Inverness. It will, however, be quite magnified when it reaches the audience's ears."

"Might we at least visit the Mosque?"

"I'm sorry, but that's not possible. The Mosque is strictly reserved for males of the Muslim faith. Not even I am allowed admission. We will, however, go to the Great Square this evening. I promise you that when the young men and women of the troupe see the Mosque and the Square all lit up, it will be a sight they'll remember for the rest of their lives."

~ ∫ ~

That evening, February 8, the weather was clear and crisp. The thermometer registered an unseasonably warm 42 degrees Fahrenheit, and although it had rained most of the day, the moon and stars gave the Great Square a cloak of magic that enthralled the Scottish young people and their chaperone.

Several hundred people strolled the Great Square, each thinking his or her own thoughts. Ezra Caen and Manucher Tabrizi occupied a dark alcove, their eyes sweeping over the crowd, looking for one face in particular. Had they known that their target was in the same Square, less than a thousand feet away, wearing a face covering and headscarf, her own eyes darting back and forth over the same crowd, searching for them, they might have been surprised, but most likely not.

Hsien Yun-Lo, herding his Scottish ensemble around the center of the vast open space, might have seen all three of them, but if he did, he gave no hint that he had. A fifth figure, completely unnoticed by any of them, sat at a café somewhat off the square, calmly sipping tea and enjoying the peaceful quiet than ensued, in spite of the deceptively large number of people in the immediate vicinity.

It was the calm before the storm.

~ ∫ ~

During the two days next preceding the eleventh, Qom was searched as it never had been before. Every hotel from the smartest and most expensive to the sleaziest roach motel was visited and the guest list checked. Every pension, rooming house, hostel, and homeless shelter was searched. Restaurants, what few night clubs there were in the holy city, cabarets, and cafes were haunted by plainclothesmen, who showed the single sheet bearing eight photographs to waiters, concierges, janitors, and maids. More than ninety men and women who bore even a passing resemblance to the faces in the photos were taken in for questioning, later to be released with routine apologies, even these only because they were foreigners and had to be more courteously treated than indigents.

Hundreds in the streets, in taxis, and on buses were stopped and their papers examined. Late night strollers were accosted a number of times in the space of a mile. Besides the ten thousand, five hundred men in the employ of the security forces, an additional ten thousand informers, part-time employees, reporters, and even stringers, were on the lookout. Those making a living off the tourist industry by day or night were briefed to keep their eyes open.

Plainclothes and uniformed detectives checked out every residence, apartment, and storefront within a thousand yard radius of the speaker's platform. When they reached the McAdams apartment at two-thirty in the afternoon on February 10, Hsien Yun-Lo greeted them courteously and showed them through the entire flat before he presented the letter from President Rouhani attesting that he was in charge of presenting the Scottish Highland Dance Troupe the following day and requesting that all officials in Qom extend him the greatest courtesy. The officers looked no farther and respectfully bade him a good day.

For some reason, the one place in the area which the investigators did not check was the alternative apartment which had been arranged as a temporary residence for Mehdi Karroubi, a high-ranking Iranian Opposition leader, who'd been afforded special dispensation by the Rouhani government to attend the following day's festivities, and who was expected to arrive on the morning of the eleventh.

~ ∫ ~

On a gray, cloud-covered February 10, preparations began in earnest.

Television crews set up shop in a special raised, glass-enclosed booth provided for them by the government. The Iranian Ministry of Information had arranged for three secure trunk lines that provided electricity, sound, and light-enhancing apparatus which fed into each news service's facilities.

Below the booth, construction workers set up bleachers sufficient to seat thirty thousand of the Faithful, as well as a sophisticated sound system that would ensure loud, clear sound to everyone in the audience. A man dressed in a plain grey suit, whose voice emulated that of the Supreme Leader, tested the battery of microphones on the raised dais to make certain that they caught and transmitted his every word and inflection.

A nondescript middle-aged man with salt-and-pepper gray hair and a bushy moustache, who wore an open-necked shirt and carried a clipboard in his left hand, wandered through the Square, pacing off distances from the speaker's rostrum to the stage, thence to several other points radiating from the platform from which the exalted Leader would speak. At each point, he made notations on a piece of paper held in place by the clipboard. The Assassin wanted to be certain all distances and angles were accurately reconfirmed. After her measurements were complete, she went for a long walk to the al-Massumeh Shrine, then out into the countryside. The Assassin was gone from her flat from one in the afternoon until shortly after six that evening, when she returned.

Almost no one took notice of her.

Almost.

Three people did. Ezra Caen, Manucher Tabrizi, and one other.

~ ∫ ~

That evening, the Scottish troupe, which had rehearsed nearly the entire day twenty miles outside the city, returned to their hotel completely exhausted. After an early dinner, Mistress Elspeth Fraser checked every single room assigned to her charges and made certain each of the young people was in bed by eight o'clock that evening.

~ ∫ ~

Although the Assassin retired before ten and took a 50 milligram dose of diphenhydramine hydrochloride to help her relax, she had disturbing, and recurring dreams throughout the night. Dreams of her adoptive brother Retief, her long-dead lover, Jan, and the vaguely familiar face of the bartender at the party where she had met Hypatia.

At four-thirty on the morning of February 11, the Assassin rose, dressed in black pants and turtleneck sweater, and tiptoed down the stairs in stockinged feet. As soon as she had opened the front door and stepped out onto the stoop, she put on a pair of black sneakers and proceeded the short distance across town to Hypatia's apartment. She intended to wait there until noon, when Yun-Lo had told her he'd be leaving to help set up the Scottish Highland Dance Troupe.

23

When Ezra saw Heyder Moslehi at 8:30 on the morning of February 11, the Minister of Intelligence and National Security looked haggard and strained. He gestured the Israeli to a chair opposite the desk he'd requisitioned in Qom's Security Headquarters building. Moslehi seated himself in the hard wooden swivel chair, from which he could spin round from the window with its unobstructed view of the Great Mosque. This time, he did not look out the window.

"We can't find the Assassin," he said briefly. "Vanished off the face of the earth."

"We kept our eyes on McAdams' apartment from yesterday morning until five in the afternoon. Yun-Lo was in and out several times. We saw lights come on and go off shortly before ten, but no one came into or out of the apartment."

The Minister sighed. "Is there anything more you might know about this person?"

"No more than I've already told you, Mister Minister. The fact that she's my twin sister is very helpful theoretically, but that knowledge crashes and burns when you realize I have no idea what she looks like in her different identities. What are today's plans?"

The Minister grabbed at his stomach and winced in apparent pain. After a loud belch, he excused himself. "I'm sorry, Mister Caen, that's not like me at all. Nerves, you know."

"The plans?" Caen continued.

"The Supreme Leader won't change a thing. I spoke to him last night. He was not pleased. So today's events remain the same as announced earlier. This morning he will spend time in private meditation inside the Mosque. At eleven, he will take lunch and a small nap. He will be awakened shortly after one. He'll watch the Scottish Dance Troupe from a concealed space where he cannot be seen. He will emerge onto the rostrum in front of the Jamkaran Mosque at precisely two o'clock and he will lead prayer and speak to the Faithful for two hours, more or less."

"Wonderful," Caen remarked sourly. "A huge window of opportunity for the Assassin. What ever happened to the notion that if you can't say what you have to say in less than fifteen minutes, no one will pay any attention to what comes after?"

"This is Iran, Mister Caen. The Grand Ayatollah Khamenei is the Supreme Leader. No one would dare *not* listen, particularly when his neighbor will look left and right from time to time to make sure he *is* listening."

"What about crowd control, Minister?"

"Ten thousand, five hundred uniformed. Ten thousand more in the audience. Steel barriers were put up yesterday afternoon. We'll redouble the search of every suspicious house and flat. Before and during the speech there will be watchers with guns on every nearby rooftop surveying the opposite roofs and windows. Nobody gets through barriers except officials and those taking part in the ceremonies.

"The Jamkaran Mosque, inside and out, will be infiltrated by policemen, up on the roof and among the minarets. All imams will be searched for concealed weapons. The police and plainclothesmen are having special lapel badges issued, even as we speak, in case the Assassin attempts to masquerade as a security man. Things are tighter than a gnat's arse, Mister Caen."

"And the protection for the Supreme Leader?"

"You already know of the bodyguard surrounding him?"

"The 'gorillas?'"

"And you know he's forbidden protective plastic anywhere from his midsection to the top of his head."

"A security nightmare."

"Ezra," the Minister sighed again, "there's nothing more we can do. He refuses to wear *Kevlar*. We've built a bulletproof clear ceiling above his head, but the chances of someone firing straight down at a ninety degree angle are rather slim, wouldn't you say?"

Caen reached for a large bottle of Pellegrino water, then thought the better of it. "Minister, might I excuse myself for a moment? If I'm going to refresh myself I'll have to clear room in my body to do so."

When Ezra returned from the bathroom, Minister Moslehi continued.

"Everyone who comes within two hundred meters of the Ayatollah will be frisked. No exceptions. All press and diplomatic passes are going to be suddenly changed at noon today in case the Assassin tries to slip in as one of them. Anyone with a package or a lengthy-looking object will be hustled away as soon as seen. Anything more you can think of?"

Ezra Caen thought for a moment, twisting his hands on the desk, looking like a schoolboy trying to explain himself to the headmaster. He found the Iranian counterterrorist methods a bit arcane, but then he considered his own experience: a cop on the beat who had spent his life catching criminals by keeping his eyes open a bit wider than anyone else. At length, he spoke, his words measured. "I don't think she will risk getting killed. She's a mercenary who kills for money. She wants to get away and spend her money. I would assume that with a target this large, she will have a *lot* of money should she succeed. More than she could ever hope to spend in a lifetime. I'm certain she has worked out her plan in advance, during her numerous reconnaissance trips to the Islamic Republic. If she had any doubts, either about the success of the operation or of her chances of getting away, she would have turned back before now.

"So she must have something up her sleeve. She could work out for herself that on one day of the year, Islamic Victory Day, Grand Ayatollah Ali Khamenei's pride would insure that he wouldn't stay indoors, no matter what the personal danger to himself. The Assassin has probably worked out that the security arrangements, particularly after her presence had been discovered, would be as intensive as you have described, Mister Minister. And yet, she didn't turn back."

Caen rose once again and paced up and down the room. "She didn't turn back and she won't turn back. Why? First, because she is constitutionally incapable of yielding to defeat." *In that way, she is much like me,* he thought to himself. "Second, because she thinks she can do it and get away. Therefore, she must have hit upon an idea that no one else has ever thought of. I can think of two options: a bomb triggered by remote control or a rifle. With all the security in place, it's more likely than not that a bomb would have been discovered by now, and that would ruin everything. So my conclusion is that it would be a gun."

"But she can't get a gun near the Ayatollah," the Minister said. "Nobody can get near him except a few, and they are being searched. How can the Assassin get a gun inside the circle of crowd barriers?"

Caen stopped pacing and faced the Minister. He shrugged. "I don't know. But she thinks she can, and she's not failed yet. She's had some bad luck and she's had some good luck, just like us. Despite our attempts to track her down, despite all the modern techniques we've used, despite our promising a veritable fortune for information leading to her arrest and conviction, she's here. With a gun, in hiding, almost certainly with yet another face and passport. One thing is for certain, Mister Minister. Wherever she is, she must emerge today. When she does, she must be spotted for what she is. And that comes down to one thing, and only one thing: keeping our eyes open.

"There's nothing more I can suggest. So I may just wander around the square and see if I can spot her. It's the only thing left to do."

Heyder Moslehi had hoped for some flash of inspiration, some brilliant revelation from the detective who had been described to him as the best counterterrorist in the world. And all this vaunted genius could come up with was to keep his eyes open. The Minister rose. "Of course, Mister Caen," he said, "Please do just that."

~ ∫ ~

"Are the gorillas in place?"

"Affirmative, Mister Minister."

The "gorillas" were the four bodyguards who most closely flanked the Grand Ayatollah at his every public appearance. They looked so much alike that no one could differentiate one from the other. Indeed, their names were not known to any but a select few in the top echelons in National Security. Their job was to stand, two behind each of the

Grand Ayatollah's elbows and two on either side of the Great Man.

The term "gorilla" marked a close approximation not only of their looks but also of the way they moved. There was a practical reason for their almost grotesque appearance. Each man was an expert in all forms of combat. Each had heavily muscled arms, chest, shoulders, and legs. When their muscles were tensed, their chests and shoulders forced their arms out from the sides so that their hands swung well away from their bodies. Each man carried his favorite automatic weapon under his left armpit, emphasizing the gorilla-like stance. They walked with their hands half-open, ready to sweep the gun out from its shoulder holster, and start firing at the first hint of trouble.

Each gorilla was prepared to die or kill for the safety of the Grand Ayatollah.

A small, wizened *Imam* stepped onto the platform to lead the early prayers of the truly Faithful. The worshipers were heavily infiltrated by plainclothes police, who did not kneel nor close their eyes, but who prayed as fervently as the rest: *"Please dear Allah, author of life and death, do not let anything happen on my watch."*

Several bystanders, even though they were two hundred meters from the door of the Mosque, were hustled away when they reached inside their jackets. One had been scratching his armpit. Another had been reaching for his binoculars.

~ ∫ ~

Shaham Sohrab was miserable. He was hot, his shirt was sticking to his back, and some bystander had tripped, accidentally spilling hot tea on his shirtfront, scalding his stomach, which had probably blistered by now. The submachine carbine had gotten heavier as the morning progressed, and its strap was chafing his shoulder through the soaking material. As he glanced at his wristwatch, he saw it was 12:15 – close enough to the start of the performance of those foreign dancers that he knew he was going to miss lunch. On top of everything else, he was thirsty. Maybe not always, but certainly at this moment, he regretted joining the police service.

Of course it hadn't been that way at the start. He'd been laid off as redundant from his job as a hod carrier in the oilfields adjoining the Gulf of Hormuz. The Human Resources Officer had suggested that a strong young man like Shaham should consider a job as a police officer in the Islamic Republic. He could go anywhere – Qom, Isfahan, Tabriz, Tehran – the opportunities were limitless.

When Shaham had spoken with the recruiting officer in Isfahan, he had looked at a poster in the outer office with the words, "The hardest job you'll ever love," and a picture of a beaming young man in a sharply creased, immaculately tailored police uniform, who seemed to be telling the world that he had a job with a future and he was on the cutting edge, protecting the civilized people of the world from the lawless savages.

No one had mentioned that life in the barracks was Spartan in the extreme. Nor had anyone talked about the drills, the night exercises, the hours of waiting on street corners in bitter cold or blazing heat for the great, heroic arrest that never took place. People's papers were always in order, their missions always mundane and harmless. It was enough to drive anyone mad.

He knew he was efficient, obedient, and complaisant, qualities which resulted in his sergeant in Isfahan recommending Shaham for temporary detached duty, which at least afforded him an occasional different view of the world, maybe even an occasional woman. Now he'd been sent to Qom, the Holy City. He had thought it would be a bit of a holiday from the small towns – tiny dots on the desert landscape, really – to which he'd been sent for a week here, a month there, when someone went on holiday, or, more likely, when someone cracked up and quit the local constabulary.

Not a hope, not with Sergeant Reza Javed in charge of the squad. Just more boredom. "See that crowd barrier, Sohrab? Stand by it, watch it, see that it doesn't move, and don't let anyone through it unless they're authorized, understand? You've got a responsible job, Sohrab."

Responsible? What a crock. Rumors is what this was all about. Rumors and more rumors. They never came to anything.

Sohrab turned around and looked back up the road leading to the Mosque. The crowd barrier he was guarding was one of a chain stretched across the Great Square from one building to another, two hundred fifty meters away from a group of tenement buildings on the other side of the Square.

An hour-and-a-half to go until the Great Man spoke. Then another two hours of intense boredom and lethargy during the hottest part of the afternoon, when he'd feel both logy *and* empty. Allah, would it never end?

Along the line of barriers, he estimated that more than fifty thousand had assembled in the midday heat. What fantastic patience, he thought. Or were they more like fatalistic dumb sheep? He could not imagine waiting in this heat for hours just to see a talking head three hundred meters away and know that the face that was old, grizzled, and bearded like so many others was, in fact, the Supreme Leader, who commanded the forces of life and death to come and go with just a word or a nod of the head.

There were about two hundred scattered along his particular barrier when he saw the woman. A foreigner with striking dark hair and a figure that caused him a completely unexpected momentary erection.

Tight black sweater, tight black pants, her hair covered with the most minimal headscarf the law allowed. She had a canned soft drink in her hand. Every now and again, she'd sip from it.

Turning toward Shaham, she caught his eye.

"You look like you could use something cool, Officer," she said in perfect, unaccented Farsi. Reaching into her backpack, she extracted an aluminum can of Zam Zam Cola. "I hope you won't consider this a bribe, Mister Policeman, but you look hot, bushed, and bored."

Sohrab reached out appreciatively, hardly daring to believe his good fortune.

"Your name?" he said, trying to sound strong and official. His voice came out a croak, strained as it was by thirst.

"Simone DesMoulins," she said without hesitation. "Would you like to see my identity card? My passport?"

"Please."

She whipped them out and he glanced cursorily at the photograph, concentrating more on her address in Qom – an address only a couple of minutes away, on Fahroudiyeh Street.

"Perhaps later this evening …" he murmured.

"I'd like that," she said, her voice filled with promise.

"Will you be at …?" he read the address out loud, "15/5 Fahroudiyeh Street?"

"Yes, Officer. It's on the third floor. What is your name, by the way?"

"Sohrab, Madame … Miss …"

"It's Miss, Officer."

"I am Shaham Sohrab."

"Perhaps our paths will cross sooner than we think. Now that you've seen my papers, may I please cross the Square and go to my apartment?

I understand foreign women are not particularly welcome during the ceremonies when the Ayatollah is speaking to the Faithful."

"But of course," the policeman said, blushing.

The woman was gone in the swish of her body, leaving a musky perfume scent behind her.

The Assassin, returned from her cross-town foray just as the Scottish dancers were lining up onstage. She entered the McAdams flat, crossed to the small alcove with the window looking out to the Mosque, and made final estimates and measurements as her eyes darted back and forth. Across the road, on the rooftops of apartment blocks in every direction, she could see snipers in Security Service uniforms moving into position. She had returned to the flat just in time.

Agrippina unclipped the window lock and swung both halves of the frame quietly inward until they came back against the inside of the adjoining walls. Then she stepped well back. A square shaft of light fell through the window onto the carpet. The rest of the room appeared darker. If she stayed away from that shaft of light, the watchers on the adjoining rooftops would see nothing.

Stepping to the side of the window, keeping to the shadows created by the withdrawn curtains, the Assassin found she could look downwards and sideways to the rostrum from which the Ayatollah would speak, a hundred thirty-five meters away. Eight feet back from the window and well to one side, she set up a small dining table, which she had brought in from the kitchenette. She removed the tablecloth and a decorative brass vase, and replaced them with a pair of cushions from an armchair in the studio. These would form her firing nest.

No need to change her outfit. It was dark and, but for her figure, it would not unduly attract attention. Just to make sure, however, she removed the padded bra she had been wearing, which rendered her appearance far less provocative. Moving to the bedroom, she painstakingly began the final assembly of the rifle.

She caressed the shining percussion caps of her shells, the silencer, the telescopic sight, the breech and barrel of the weapon. She slid the two steel rods which, when fitted together, would become the frame of the rifle's stock. Lovingly and meticulously, she assembled the rifle – breech and barrel, upper and lower component of the stock, shoulder guard, silencer, and trigger. Finally, she slid on the telescopic sight and clipped it fast.

Sitting on a chair behind the table, leaning forward with the gun barrel resting on top of the upper cushion, she squinted through the telescope. The sunlit square beyond the windows and forty feet down leapt into focus. The head of one of the men who was still marking out the standing positions for the "gorillas" passed across the line of sight. She tracked the target with the gun. The head appeared large and clear, as large as the Persian melon had looked when she had tested the gunsight in the desert south of Tehran.

Satisfied at last, the Assassin lined the five cartridges on the edge of the table in a straight row. She slid back the rifle's bolt and eased the first shell into the breech. One should be enough, but she had four spares. She pushed the bolt forward until it closed on the base of the cartridge, gave a half twist, and locked it. Finally she laid the rifle carefully among the cushions. She leaned back to wait for another hour.

24

Ezra Caen's thirst rivaled that of Shaham Sohrab. His mouth was dry and his tongue stuck to the roof of it. It was not simply the heat. He was sure something was going to happen that afternoon, and he still had not the remotest clue as to how or when.

Over lunch with some of the men from the Committee, he had felt the mood change from tenseness and frustration to almost manic hope. There was less than an hour to go. Everywhere he looked, the holes had been closed, the area sealed up.

As expected, the Scottish pipers and drummers excited the entire crowd. Seventy thousand pairs of hands clapped in rhythm to the pounding drums. Although the sound of the bagpipes was strange and distinctly foreign, Ezra could not deny that it was hypnotic. And the revealing legs of the dancers ... he had not seen such *nakedness* since Israel.

Ezra Caen prowled nervously, disconsolately around the edge of the crowd, far away from the dais. Each policeman and guard he spoke to on the barriers had the same message. No one had passed through since the barriers had gone up an hour ago.

The main roads were blocked, the side roads were blocked, the alleys were blocked. The rooftops were watched and guarded. Every available building was crawling with security men. Inside the perimeter, every building had been scoured from basement to attic. Many of the flats were empty, since their occupants had chosen to absent themselves from the crushing crowds of the Decade of Fajr.

Caen slipped through the side streets, showing his police pass to take a shortcut, and emerged on that part of the Square nearest Fahroudiyeh Street. It was the same story: the road was blocked off two hundred meters from the Square, the crowds massed behind the barriers, the streets empty except for patrolling Security men. He started asking again.

He glanced at his watch. 1:40. Twenty minutes until the Great Man would emerge onto the dais.

"Seen anyone pass? Anyone at all?"

"No, sir. Not this way."

"All right, carry on."

As it closed in on 2:00 p.m., the crowd behind the barrier a few yards ahead of him, started to push forward, hoping to gain a place just a little bit closer to the Ayatollah.

Caen looked up at the rooftops. The watchers on the roof ignored the spectacle below them. Their eyes never stopped flickering across the rooftops and windows across the road from where they crouched on the parapets, watching for any slight movement at a window.

He reached the western side of the Square. A young policeman stood with his feet planted squarely in the gap where the last steel barrier abutted the wall. He flashed his card at the man, who stiffened. "Anybody pass this way?"

"No, Sir."

"How long have you been here?"

"Since ten-thirty, Sir, just before they closed off the street."

"Nobody been through that gap?"

"No, sir. Well ..." The young man blushed crimson. "Well, only a very beautiful young woman ... a foreigner ... Her identity papers showed she lives at 15 Fahroudiyeh Street, Apartment 5. Not to worry, though, Sir. I checked her papers thoroughly. She even gave me a can of Zam Zam Cola."

"A beautiful young woman, you say?"

"That's affirmative."

"Did she give you a name?"

"Of course, along with her identity card and her passport. It was a French name, I think. Simone something-or-other."

"Simone DesMoulins?"

"Yes, that's it!" the young policeman cried.

His hand trembling, Ezra Caen reached into his rear pocket and extracted a sheet of paper, the same paper on which eight photographs and passports had appeared since his idea to publish those photographs three weeks ago.

"Do you recognize any of these people?"

Shaham Sohrab looked at the pictures, then involuntarily stiffened.

"That's her all right, Simone DesMoulins. Where ...?"

But he had no chance to say anything more. Ezra Caen was running down the street, faster than the young policeman thought the older, smaller man could possibly run, yelling at the top of his lungs for Officer Sohrab to follow him.

~ ∫ ~

The Grand Ayatollah Ali Khamenei, the undisputed Supreme Leader of the Islamic Republic of Iran stood just inside the front doorway of the Jamkaran Mosque, waiting patiently for the moment, a few seconds later, when he would emerge into the sunlight and onto the dais.

~ ∫ ~

The Assassin raised her rifle and squinted down toward the rostrum. She picked the 'gorilla' nearest to him, the one who would stand at the Supreme Leader's left elbow.

~ ∫ ~

"This one?"

Caen stopped panting and gestured toward a doorway.

"I think so, sir. Yes, this is it. The number 15 is to the right of the door."

The older detective ran down the hallway. Sohrab followed him at a distance. He didn't see the figure who came in the front door after him until the man nearly collided with him.

"Excuse me. I must get back to my flat immediately to make sure everything's in order for the State Dinner."

"And you are?" Sohrab snapped.

The man, an Asian, took out a red-covered diplomatic passport. "Hsien Yun-Lo. I'm staying on the third floor, apartment five."

"But … That is … I mean …"

"Is there some problem, Officer?"

"No … uh … yes …"

"You seem confused."

"Well … uh … there is a woman whose address …"

"Of course, my assistant. She's been staying here for three weeks. Tariqa has been of inestimable assistance to me."

"Tariqa? No, the woman's identification card said Simone DesMoulins …"

"You must be mistaken," Yun-Lo said smoothly. Meanwhile he was thinking, *Why in hell did she decide to use a poisoned identity card? She must have a plan in mind."*

"A detective just went up to that apartment. Little fellow, older. Seemed to be very much in charge."

Caen, Yun-Lo thought. *If he's on to her and she panics, my hide could be hung out to dry.* While he stood there, he calmly deliberated his own options. *She's our employee and we should protect her. But charity begins at home.*

He waited an instant longer, than said, "Officer, you stay down here and make sure the building is secure. I'll go upstairs and deal with this. I'm sure there's a logical explanation."

He left the young policeman standing there indecisively, a puzzled look on his face.

~ʃ~

The Supreme Leader quietly made his entrance at the precise time he was scheduled. He raised his arms in a wide "V," acknowledging the adulation of the huge crowd

Three floors up and a hundred and thirty-five meters away, the Assassin held the rifle very steady and squinted down the telescopic sight. She could see the features quite clearly, the brow shaded by bushy eyebrows, the piercing eyes, the hooked nose. She saw the raised arms come down. The crossed wires of the sight were directly on the exposed temple. Softly, gently, she squeezed the trigger. ...

A split second later, the Assassin was staring down onto the rostrum as if she could not believe her eyes. Before the bullet had passed out of the end of the barrel, the Supreme Leader had snapped his head forward without warning.

Immediately thousands of voices in unison barked, "*Afiat Bahsheh*! - May it be for your health!" as the Ayatollah recovered from his mighty sneeze.

It was later established from forensic evidence that the bullet had passed a fraction of an inch behind the moving head. Whether the Supreme Leader heard the whipcrack traveling down the flight path of the bullet was never determined.

The slug tore into a stone door immediately behind the Ayatollah. While it could easily have torn through bone and flesh and muscle, disintegrating the bodily structure of a human being, this was not the case with a solid granite door which was two feet thick. The Leader, after using a handkerchief to wipe his nose, straightened up and moved sedately back to the podium to begin leading the Faithful in prayer.

Behind her gun, the Assassin swore softly. She had never missed a stationary target from less than a hundred fifty yards in her life. Then she calmed down. There was still time. The Ayatollah would go on for at least the next two hours. She tore open the breech of the rifle, ejecting the spent cartridge, which fell harmlessly on the carpet. Taking a second shell off the table, she pushed it home and closed the breech.

~ ∫ ~

Ezra Caen was panting as he reached the third floor. There were two doors, one leading toward each apartment. As he looked from one door to the other, Hsien Yun-Lo reached the landing. Caen hesitated in front of the two doors. Then he heard a low, but distinct, *phut* from behind one of them. He raised his sidearm and pointed it at the door.

In response to the BLAM! of his gunshot, the door buckled and swung inwards. Caen and the Asian entered the room almost simultaneously.

The Assassin rose from her seat behind the table. Swinging in one smooth motion at a half-crouch, she fired from the hip, growling "You sonofabitch, you betrayed me. *Me*? When you *hired* me, you fucking Chinaman!" The single bullet made no sound. The slug from the rifle tore into Yun-Lo's chest, struck the sternum, and exploded. Yun-Lo felt a tearing and ripping, and great, sudden stabs of pain. Then even they were gone. The light faded. A piece of carpet came up and smacked him on the cheek, except it was his cheek that was lying on the carpet. The loss of feeling swept up through his thighs and belly, then his chest and neck. The last thing Yun-Lo remembered was a salty taste in his mouth, like he'd had the day he was nine and his parents had taken him to the South China Sea. Then it was all dark.

Ezra Caen stared into the Assassin's eyes. The tension he had felt moments earlier had vanished. His heart did not seem to be pumping anymore.

"Morgan," he said simply.

"Ezra," she responded. She fumbled with the gun, tearing open the breech. Caen saw the metallic glint as the cartridge case dropped to the floor. The Assassin swept something off the table and stuffed it into the breech, her eyes still staring at the twin brother she'd never met.

She's going to shoot, Caen thought. With superhuman effort, he looked her calmly in the eye and said, "So it's down to you and me, Morgan. I suppose you're eager to kill me."

"Wouldn't you do the same to me?"

"Not really." He was surprised at how casual their conversation was, given the magnitude of what was happening. "You managed to elude us all. You really *are* that good."

"Thank you. But you managed to find me. I'm told it's what you do better than anyone else."

There was a moment's pause. Then the Assassin spoke. "I was hired to do a job and paid very well to do it. My job was to kill the Supreme Leader of Iran, not an Israeli detective. And why should I kill my own brother?"

They stared at each other, each trying to mask their feelings. Finally she spoke. "A glass of Pellegrino water? That's what you like best, isn't it?"

"Thank you. I suppose you'd like a glass of Malbec?"

"You've been advised of my tastes as well."

As strange as it felt, they toasted one another and drank.

"I suppose I'm to be your prisoner?" she finally asked.

"That's my assignment, just as you have yours."

With studied calm, she extracted a sidearm from inside her blouse. His eyes widened when he saw the small handgun. Before he had an opportunity to do anything, she fired the trigger twice, hitting him once in the ankle, shattering it, and once in the opposite calf.

As he fell to the ground in crippling pain, Ezra Caen's eyes asked the simple question, *Why?*

"I said I wouldn't kill you and I won't," she said quietly. "But I have a job to finish and I don't need you standing in my way. Don't worry, there'll be someone who'll come to assist you by and by. I'm sure they'll patch you up just fine."

With that, the Assassin departed.

No sooner she'd gone, Caen radioed Security Headquarters, explained what had happened, gave his position, and summoned help.

~ ∫ ~

The Assassin skirted the area of the Square outside the Jamkaran Mosque, glancing only briefly at what was going on there. The Ayatollah Khamenei continued to exhort the multitudes, his voice dipping from an almost *sotto voce* tone before rising to a commanding, authoritarian *fortissimo*. On and on and on.

She took a longer route than she would normally have taken to Hypatia's apartment, making sure to keep to the almost empty alleys and backstreets three blocks behind the Great Mosque. The Assassin was in no hurry. With her pursuer disabled and the security forces concentrated on the opposite side of the city, she felt unthreatened, almost lightheaded.

Agrippina was momentarily furious as she thought back to the Asian who had so obviously betrayed her. But he was now only a meaningless footnote to her history. Dead beyond dead, and let the buzzards and carrion-eaters graze on his remains.

~ ∫ ~

Caen's last conscious sensation was Manucher Tabrizi's familiar, welcome voice. "I'm coming, Ezra. We'll take care of everything, don't you worry." And Ezra passed out.

~ ∫ ~

In Hypatia's apartment, the Assassin took her second rifle out of the closet and assembled it with the same scrupulous care as she'd done with the first one. She arranged the nest in a much larger room, with a comfortable chair and broad view of the Ayatollah.

The Great Man's hands and arms raised and lowered as he stirred his follower to a paroxysm of religious ecstasy. An easier target this time, even if the Ayatollah sneezed or made any sudden movement.

The Assassin sighted down the barrel again. Only a hundred and twenty yards. Much closer than from the McAdams flat. She glanced at her wristwatch. Three-ten. He seemed to be droning on, far below the ultimate crescendo. If he continued at this pace, it would be another fifty minutes or more. In that time the Assassin would have had time to escape and be halfway to Isfahan. But no time to think of such things. It was back to business as usual. Coolly professional, the Assassin lined up her shot.

Almost tenderly, the Assassin fondled the stock for a brief moment before her right index finger embraced the trigger. She pulled it slowly, smoothly, gently …

At the moment the gun went off, there was an explosion from the other side of the room that was so loud it could be heard in the square. Later press inquiries were met with the explanation that it had been a faulty muffler that had fallen off an oil truck.

Half a magazine full of nine millimeter bullets hit Agrippina in the chest, picked her up, half turned her in the air, and slammed her body into an untidy heap in the far corner of the room, near the sofa. As she fell, a heavy floor lamp crashed down upon her, unnecessarily breaking her neck.

She gasped as her eyes fluttered in what she knew were her death throes. Her last words were spoken in a tone of utter shock and surprise. "Hypatia? You?"

She breathed her last and expired.

Hypatia calmly walked over to the dead body and pulled down the Assassin's eyelids.

~ ∫ ~

In the Square, seventy thousand voices roared and a hundred television cameras whirred as the Supreme Leader concluded his speech, one hour and thirty-five minutes after he'd started.

"We ask Allah the Exalted to help us. We ask the immaculate souls of our martyrs and the immaculate soul of our magnanimous Imam to help us. By Allah's favor, you and I will benefit from the prayers of the Imam of the Age, May our Souls be sacrificed for his sake. Greetings be upon you and Allah's mercy and blessings."

~ ∫ ~

The following day the body of a woman was buried in an unmarked grave in a suburban cemetery in Qom. The death certificate showed the body to be that of an unnamed foreigner, killed on February 11 in unknown circumstances. Present was a Roman Catholic priest, a registrar, two gravediggers, a small, middle-aged man in a wheelchair, and a strikingly attractive auburn-haired woman, who stood with her hands on the rails of the wheelchair. The ceremony was desultory, as if the participants could not wait to get on with the business of living. When it was over, the woman pushed the wheelchair up to the cheap coffin. The middle-aged man gently laid a single rose onto it. Then the woman pushed the wheelchair back to a waiting black Samand sedan. Without a word, two men lifted the middle-aged man into the back seat. The woman walked around to the other side of the car, and got into the rear seat beside the man. The driver turned on the ignition, and the car slowly edged toward the exit. After looking both ways, the driver turned left onto the highway and the Samand headed north toward Tehran.

EPILOGUE –
ONE YEAR LATER

The beach at Tel Aviv is regularly ranked as one of the ten best in the world. Israel's largest city, unlike the Holy City of Jerusalem, is a brash combination of Miami on the Mediterranean and the luster and bluster of Los Angeles.

Hadassah hospital had not only totally repaired his ankle and calves, but during the past year he'd taken to a regimen of a healthy diet, and lengthy swims every day, both in the Mediterranean and in the pool at the local gym. He felt – and looked – better than he had in years. As he emerged from the sea, he walked gingerly on the hot sand 'til he reached a pair of towels fifteen yards from the water.

The luscious woman with him raised herself on her arms, so he could see not only the beauty of her face, but the stunning declivity between her breasts. At forty-four, she could easily be mistaken for a woman fifteen years younger. Her bronze-tan skin was soft, firm, and youthfully exciting. He thought back to when they'd awakened earlier that morning and engaged in slow, delicious lovemaking before coming to the beach. Galit was a dim and distant memory.

"How did you choose the name Hypatia, anyway?" Ezra asked.

"It was as good a name as any," the woman answered. "Look it up on Wikipedia."

"I already have," he said, lying on his stomach beside her. "How long were you in Iran?"

"Ten years."

"Deep cover the whole time?"

"Mmm-hmm."

"So how did you find out …?"

"I got around. Remember Valerie Plame?"

"The American CIA agent? Uh-huh."

"Men being men, they like to have arm-candy or eye-candy so they can impress other men with their 'conquests.' I'm not too modest to admit I fit the bill – except I was the 'ice goddess.' I never had to 'put out.'"

"So now you're back in *Eretz Israel*. The spy who came in from the cold."

"Thank you, Mr. LeCarre, but thank God I didn't end up like that fellow. And," she said, pinching him on his buttocks, "I didn't end up so badly at the end of my run. Nor did you, my friend. A job at the very top, a great pension, and, God willing, many more years of a healthy life."

"I'd like them to be with you, Rachel," he said, using her real name.

"That sounds awfully good to me, too."

"So where do we go from here?"

"We enjoy each day as it comes. Maybe the loving will get more wonderful as time goes on, maybe not. Let's just see, shall we?"

"I'd like to grow old on the same pillow as you, Darling."

"As I said, I'm not averse to that, Mister Caen. Who knows? Maybe some day some writer will say, "And they lived happily ever after.""

"Maybe so."

And they did.

THE END